The Man Who Met Moses

The Man Who Met Moses

A Mystical Novel

By
JUDITH MERENFELD-MOSCU

RESOURCE *Publications* · Eugene, Oregon

THE MAN WHO MET MOSES
A Mystical Novel

Resource Publications
An Imprint of Wipf and Stock Publishers
199 W. 8th Ave., Suite 3
Eugene, OR 97401

www.wipfandstock.com

PAPERBACK ISBN: 979-8-3852-6048-5
HARDCOVER ISBN: 979-8-3852-6049-2
EBOOK ISBN: 979-8-3852-6050-8

VERSION NUMBER 121725

To my husband, Marian, whose steadfast presence
has been my anchor.

To my children, Sami and Karina, for inspiring me
to strive for my best.

To my parents, Rubén and Lia, who paved the path I walk
with love and wisdom.

And to God, the source of it all.

Contents

Acknowledgments

To Maura Poston, editor and friend, whose keen eye and wise counsel strengthened both my writing and this book.

To Mark Malatesta, who provided valuable tools and direction through the intricate path of publishing.

To Isaac Benzaquen, biblical scholar and kabbalist, who through the years has helped me deepen my understanding and love of Torah study.

List of Characters

Jochebed: Moses' biological mother, of Levitical descent.

Joseph: Son of the patriarch Jacob. Sold into slavery by his brothers, rose to become the grand vizier of Egypt. Before dying, he asked that his bones be taken out of Egypt to be buried in Canaan, a request Moses later fulfilled.

Joshua: Moses' successor. He took command over the Israelite tribes after Moses' death and led the conquest of Canaan.

Keturah: Concubine of the patriarch Abraham. After the death of Sarah, Abraham married her, and together they had six sons.

Kohath: Second son of Levi. Father of Aaron, Miriam, and Moses. His descendants were in charge of the ark and the holy vessels in the Tabernacle.

Libni: Descendant of Gershon. Worked alongside Ithamar in the Tabernacle.

Levi: The third son of Jacob and Leah, founder of the Israelite tribe that bears his name, the Levites, from whom the priestly line (Kohanim) descends. Through his son Kohath, he is the grandfather of Aaron and Moses.

Mahli: Descendant of Merari. Worked alongside Ithamar in the Tabernacle.

Merari: Third son of Levi. His descendants were responsible for the planks, pillars, sockets, bars, pegs, and ropes that formed the framework of the Tabernacle.

Miriam: Sister of Moses and Aaron. A prophetess who accompanied the Hebrews in their journey through the desert. She died during the wilderness migration.

Moses: The leader of Israel's liberation from Egypt and the mediator between YHWH and the people He delivered God's law to the Hebrews and oversaw the establishment of the covenant between them. Born a Levite in 1526 BC, he was raised in Pharaoh's court and was legally adopted by the young princess Hatshepsut. At forty he fled to Midian to escape death (1486 BC) and at eighty he encountered YHWH in the desert and returned to Egypt to lead the massive Exodus of the Hebrew slaves (1446 BC).

Neferure: Daughter of Tuthmose II and Queen Hatshepsut, born in 1473 BC. Designated by her mother as God's wife of Amun, she died at the age of sixteen.

Phinehas: Grandson of Aaron, son of Eleazar and grand priest of YHWH.

Senenmut: Queen's Hatshepsut trusted confidant and advisor. He was the architect of many of her monuments and of her burial place.

Tuthmose I: Son of Amenhotep I. He ordered the killing of all newborn male children of the Hebrews. With his Great Royal Wife, Ahmose, he fathered a daughter, Hatshepsut.

Tuthmose II: Son of Tuthmose I by a lesser wife. Married his half-sister Hatshepsut to legitimize his claim to the throne. Together they had a daughter, Neferure.

Tuthmose III: Son of Thutmose II by a secondary wife. He served as coregent of Egypt with his stepmother Hatshepsut and assumed full leadership after her death. Moses was forced to flee Egypt during his reign (1486 BC).

Webensenu: Eldest son of Amenhotep II and Queen Tiaa. He died during the tenth plague that struck Egypt.

Zipporah: Wife of Moses and daughter of Jethro, priest of Midian. A discerning woman, she journeyed with Moses and bore him two sons: Gershom and Eliezer.

Pharaohs of the Eighteenth Dynasty—Regnal Years:

Thutmose I (ca. 1529–1516 BC)

Thutmose II (ca. 1516–1506 BC)

Queen Hatshepsut (ca. 1504–1484 BC)

Thutmose III (ca. 1506–1452 BC)

Amenhotep II (ca. 1455–1418 BC)

Fictional Characters

Abital: A descendant of the tribe of Benjamin, wife of Zakai wife and mother of Shemaiah. A hardworking woman, she raised her son in the tradition of the Levites, priests of YHWH.

Aviel: Son of Shemaiah and Dinah.

Athope: Headmaster priest of the temple of the god Khonsû. He mentored Kadmiel in the arts of the scribes and in the lector priesthood of Egypt.

Ama Shuah: See Shuah.

Aqhat: A Canaanite from the city of Akka and a servant in Abital's household.

Auserra: Father of Kadmiel and a lector priest of the god Amun.

Daliah: Daughter of Hanan and Elah and Zakai's third sister.

Dinah: Daughter of Ohad, wife of Shemaiah and mother of Zehava and Aviel.

Eglon: Son of Kadmiel and brother of Hanan. He died in the rebellious uprising led by Korach.

Epher: A Midianite hermit who aided Shemaiah on his journey through the desert.

Hanan: Son of Kadmiel and husband of Elah, with whom he had three children: Zakai, Naamah, and Daliah. Born in 1479 BC he left Egypt in the Exodus at age thirty-three and later died in the uprising lead by Korach.

Hedvah: Female relative and wife of Kadmiel. Mother of Hanan and Hevel.

Horemheb: Egyptian scribe and friend of Kadmiel.

Joash: Son of Ohad and brother-in-law of Shemaiah.

Kadmiel: Son of Orpah, a Hebrew handmade of Hatshepsut, and Auserra, a lector priest of Amun. Father of Hanan and great-grandfather of Shemaiah, he was born in 1514 BC. Kadmiel met Moses in the Royal Palace in 1492 BC, and was sixty-eight years old at the time of the Exodus. Trained as a scribe and as a lector priest of the god Khonsû, he died at age 108, just before entering Canaan.

Keret: Originally a Midianite and a member of the Shosu, a group regarded as outlaws. He was a shepherd known to Aqhat, the Canaanite who served Shemaiah.

Korach: Leader of the rebellion against Moses and Aaron (1422 BC), supported by Levites and other tribal leaders.

Menna: Egyptian scribe and friend of Kadmiel.

Moriyah: Daughter of Ohad and sister-in-law of Shemaiah.

Naamah: Daughter of Hanan and Elah. Zakai's second sister.

Ohad: Head of the tribe of Reuben and father-in-law of Shemaiah.

Orpah: Of Levite descent and a Hebrew handmaiden of Hatshepsut. She was the mother of Kadmiel.

Shemaiah, Shemaiahu: Born in the desert in 1416 BC and ten years old when the Hebrews conquered Canaan (1406 BC). Of Levite descent, he lost his father Zakai, at the age of twelve. At nineteen he began a pilgrimage to recover his father's lost shofar. He learned the art of the scribes and of storytelling from his great-grandfather Kadmiel as well as from his father.

Shuah: Zipporah's younger sister, born in 1488 BC. She was a seeress and guided Shemaiah on his journey to find Moses.

Yassib: From the city of Ugarit, he was a servant in the household of Abital.

Zakai: Father of Shemaiah, son of Hanan, and grandson of Kadmiel, all of Levite descent. Born in the desert in 1443 BC, and died in Canaan in 1404 BC. He was twenty-seven when Shemaiah was born.

Zehava: Daughter of Shemaiah and Dinah.

PROLOGUE

Moses Prepares to Die—1406 BC

And Moses was a hundred and twenty years old at the time of his death,
his eyes had not grown dim, and his vital strength had not fled.

—*DEUTERONOMY 34:7*

"I AM MOSES," THE old man whispered as he contemplated the inevitable. "Soon, I will be but a mere ripple in the waters of eternity."

Clad in a striped robe and holding the rod of God in his right hand, he took a few more steps up the mountain. He stopped for a short time to take a long look around. Before him stretched an immense expanse of arid land, land as dry as the feeling in his heart now that he knew his life was ending. Careening thoughts mirrored an inner discord. He thought mournfully, *If only I could bargain for more time. If only I could finish my mission and help deliver the people all the way to the promised land.* But he knew better; there was no one with whom to negotiate.

A booming voice cut sharply through the rabble that filled his mind. "Enough," the voice roared. "It is a condition in the long path of spiritual ascent that you accept what you receive and are happy with what you have harvested. Go up to the top. Look to the west, the north, the south, and the east, for you shall not cross the Jordan River."

Moses complied. As if hoping to gather in the dear ones he had loved enough to guide through the desert for forty long years, he gazed hungrily in every direction.

Obstinate but hardworking, these people, the Israelites, were yet to complete their journey. Their time of deliverance had not come. Moses knew that his acolyte, Joshua, would guide them the rest of the way. And yet he felt unsettled. Having spent so much time with this mixed multitude of humanity had shown him how far they still had to go in their spiritual evolution. They were to understand that despite their diversity, they were brothers and sisters with a common purpose, that war and strife were never the answers to life.

Realizing that there was little daylight remaining, Moses resumed his trek. He had to hurry to reach the top of Mount Nebo before nightfall to get a glimpse of the land that God had promised Abraham. His eyes followed the mountain path to the top, and a sudden shiver cascaded down his spine. Until now, he had lived in the predicament of being neither a man nor an angel. Soon, a path not yet trodden by any other human being, one meant for only himself, would open before him.

And then, he hoped, maybe someday someone else would follow in his footsteps . . .

CHAPTER 1

Following the Path of Moses—1385 BC

THE NIGHT HAD NOT fallen, and yet the path, hidden by the deepening twilight, was barely visible. Shemaiah was tired. Even so, hoping to seize every bit of remaining light, he continued to explore the mountain. This was Mount Nebo, the last place where Moses had been seen.

Shemaiah had been taught that Moses disobeyed God's command at the water wells of Meribah. He was told that God had decreed that Moses would not enter the promised land along with his people. Though Shemaiah's body and mind wanted to rest, he found the strength to go farther. At last, he saw a huge boulder. On one side of the boulder was an overhang of bushes that camouflaged the opening of a small cave. It was an opening high and deep enough for a man to creep inside. This would be a good place to shelter for the night. Shemaiah took a long drink of water from his canteen but was too tired to eat. He spread his blanket on the ground, placed his staff and knife beside him, lay down, and fell asleep.

✳✳✳

The next morning he woke in a daze, unable to remember where he was. He sat upright. His head felt congested. Leaning with his elbows over his knees, he supported his head and let his gaze explore the surroundings. *Oh, yes.* Now he knew where he was. He had left his family and his town—but why? Was he out of his mind? What was he doing here? Was this a sound decision? Who was he to have undertaken this lonely, uncertain pilgrimage in the hope of finding Moses?

"You must be crazy!" he said aloud.

More than twenty years had passed since Moses left the people of Israel. Some people believed he had died, but Shemaiah suspected that he had not, and this uncertainty had pushed him forward into his adventure. There were so many questions he wanted to ask Moses! Questions about life, yes, but most of them were about God.

Still in a foggy stupor, he remembered last night's dream. In it he heard the voice of his mother, Abital, softly calling his name. She seemed weary and in need of rest, as if she had just arrived somewhere following a long journey. With a pang, Shemaiah realized that it had been long since he last saw her, this mother with whom he had been incredibly close since his father's death. In the dream Shemaiah sat beside her, holding her hand, while his father, Zakai, leaned forward as if to greet her, welcoming her to his side. A little white bird fluttered around his parents, and they both seemed happy.

As he recalled the dream, a white flake of a bird's feather appeared from nowhere and found its way onto his lap. Shemaiah was certain that dreams were emissaries from the beyond, so he saw the feather as a sign that this dream had come with a message. Maybe his mother had died and her soul had joined her husband in the other world. Shemaiah's mind was racing, his heart was heavy, and a feeling of darkness overpowered his spirit.

A memory from his younger years came to him. He remembered the day many years ago when he had left his mother's home in Shiloh to wander the wilderness in search of the family's most precious belonging: Zakai's shofar, which had been lost during the conquest of Canaan.

That day, Abital's voice had sounded coarse and heavy with dread as she warned, "Take good care of yourself. I wouldn't be able to survive if something terrible happened to you."

All his life, Shemaiah's mother had worked tirelessly to assure his sustenance. She had also encouraged him to be hardworking and to become proficient in the duties of a Levite, the honorable rank he inherited from his father. He remembered her joy on the day he and Dinah were married, so pleased was she that Shemaiah had chosen well in accordance with this rank. And hadn't Abital traveled from afar to attend their wedding? She had danced, feeling fulfilled because she believed her son had a good life before him.

Tears came to his eyes. He cried not out of sadness, but out of gratitude for the qualities of strength and endurance Abital had instilled in him. These were tears of appreciation for this noble woman. A fresh thought, coming from nowhere, flitted across his mind, as if its deliverance had been commissioned: *The time that the person leaves the world is determined. No one can advance or delay this date.* This thought brought him comfort.

Shemaiah remained sheltered inside the cave for three days. He had only enough food and water to last barely a day, but the protection of a close, dark space was more important to him than food or anything else. He needed the containment of a motherly womb. Much had happened to him in a short span of time, more than what many human beings could endure. After having searched for his father's shofar, he had again turned his back on the security of home and the support of his community, but this time he would wander in the desert on a path not yet walked by any other human being.

He did not yet know that he was following a path that none other than Moses himself had forged.

CHAPTER 2

Memories of Abital—1385 BC

FOR THREE DAYS, MEMORIES of Abital intruded Shemaiah's mind, and as the pain gave way, he understood that it had been his mother's strength of character that prompted the journey. So, too, would it sustain him along this challenging journey.

Going back in time, Shemaiah remembered the day he had entered their home and found his mother sobbing. Tears streamed down a face that was contorted with anguish and pain. He had never seen her in such distress.

"Mother," he asked, alarmed. "What has happened?"

"I cannot find your father's shofar."

Words came in a torrent. The previous night, in the middle of her sleep, she had heard a voice asking, "Where is the shofar?" She recognized the voice as Zakai's. She jumped out of her bed and started searching for the horn. But her husband's treasured ceremonial horn was nowhere to be found.

She turned sad eyes to her son. "Who knows when or where it was lost? Maybe it was a long time ago, during the tortuous years that followed the capture of Jericho—maybe there, where your father died and was buried. Then you and I entered into the promised land. So much packing and unpacking, packing and unpacking went on . . . so many things to be watchful over." Abital spoke so frantically that Shemaiah feared she might be losing her mind. "The last time I saw the instrument was the day your father covered it with a woven bag that he hung over his shoulder. This was the preparation he made to join Joshua in the mission of conquering the promised land." She fell silent, as if spent, or lost in thought, then walked away, as if needing to be alone.

Later that night, Shemaiah heard muffled moans coming from behind a pillar in a corner of the room and he realized that she hadn't stopped crying since he had left her side.

Shemaiah had never seen the horn, but while his father was alive, he told his son the marvelous story behind the shofar. It was Gabriel, the angel of God, who had handed the shofar to Zakai's own father, Hanan. Zakai described in detail that it had happened early in the morning. Hanan approached a great stone that rose in the midst of an immense expanse of otherwise unbroken desert. To the Israelites, the stone was like a faithful sentinel. It was a landmark that offered positioning and direction and, at times, protection from the strong gusts of winds that threatened to blow travelers off their course.

"On that particular day," Zakai told Shemaiah, "the desert started out pleasantly serene. However, it was warming up quickly, water was scarce, and the flock had to be protected. Hanan's workday would end sooner than usual." Zakai painted with his words a picture of that seminal day. He described his father as slim and delicate, with features that revealed he was a descendant of a house with privileges amongst the people of Israel: the priestly house of Levi. In his mind's eye, Shemaiah watched Hanan bend to untie his leather sandals, then stand upright again to remove the hood that covered his light brown hair. Three months had passed since the day of a massive exodus from Egypt. At Moses' command, the Israelites had left in haste to build an encampment at the foot of a large stony mountain in the Sinai Desert. They traveled through vast and torrid lands, unsure of their final destination. The initial days were harsh and the challenges were many. Shepherds like Hanan had a hard time finding pastures in which to feed their flock.

Zakai went on to describe the deafening loud noise that rose from the ground when Pharaoh's army approached the fleeing crowd in angry pursuit. Moses had promised his people that they would be protected by a divine agency, and so they were. Hanan saw with his own eyes the miracles that saved the Israelites. He watched the waters of the sea as they opened up before them and witnessed how they formed a wall to their right and to their left,[1] thereby allowing the Israelites to cross over into safety. Once he and the others had reached the other side, Hanan turned and witnessed the Egyptian soldiers and their horses perish by drowning as the seawater returned.

Then, only a few days later, other miracles happened. The Israelites had nothing to eat or drink but they survived because of the food God sent

---

1. See Exodus 14:22.

them from the heavens above and the fresh water that came gushing from a rock. Hanan had no doubt that these miracles were signs that he could trust the God whom they were following. The God Moses had taught them to call "YHWH."[2] However, among the complex mixture of people that left Egypt, there were some who did not share Hanan's unwavering belief in the Hebrew God. That precise morning when Hanan left the encampment with his flock, he heard people grumbling and muttering amongst themselves. The people were worried because almost forty days had passed since Moses had left the campsite to go up into Mount Sinai. Nearly forty days and still he had not returned! Hanan overheard one man talking to another.

"Do you truly believe he will meet with his God?" sneered the man with more than a hint of defiant mockery in his voice. Hanan didn't want to get involved in that discussion and so he merely continued along his path. After all, there was nothing he could do to appease or persuade the unbelievers, and besides, there was sheepherding work to be done.

The drama and tension quickly faded away as he was seated under the shadow cast by the huge stone. He pulled a flute from the leather bag that hung from a strap across his chest. He leaned with his back against the rock, lifted the flute to his lips, began to play, and got lost in the music.

＊＊＊

The day wore on. After some time, Hanan glimpsed with surprise at the figure of a man approaching him. It was someone he had never seen before. The stranger wore a long robe of very light color, almost white. He seemed old. The stranger came toward him steadily and with gentle and fluid movements as if he were floating just above the ground. There was a radiance about him. His skin glowed, and his golden hair shone in the sunlight. The thought came to Hanan that this was an angel.

Hanan had heard stories told by the elders in the camp. Stories about the Ivrim, his Hebrew ancestors, who followed Jacob through the desert into the land of Egypt. These adventurous nomadic herdsmen believed that there was something mysterious about the desert. *The desert is a gateway to other worlds, and this stranger before me must be an angel*, he concluded. In fact, his forefathers Abraham, Isaac, and Jacob had been visited by divine messengers when they crossed the desert. Now it was also happening to him, and he felt excitement tinged with fear.

---

2. Yahweh, the God of the Israelites. The name was revealed to Moses as four Hebrew consonants, called the "Tetragrammaton."

As the figure came closer, Hanan could see that he was holding a ram's horn in his hand. The angel stopped in front of Hanan; he brought the horn to his mouth and blew into it. A deep, warm, wailing, plaintive cry was set free. It was the most beautiful sound Hanan had ever heard. The song of the horn filled the air so profoundly that Hanan felt an internal shift. It was as if something inside was being rearranged. Changed. Expanded. By the time the ethereal note had sailed away into the farthest reaches of the desert, Hanan was a different man.

He was dimly aware of a wish as it moved through the river of his mind.

As if his wish had been heard, the angel handed the horn to Hanan and vanished.

Hanan understood that he had been given a gift that was now his responsibility to protect. He was unsure why this had happened, but it was as if his heart had opened up in preparation for something unknown. Something yet to come.

✳✳✳

Shemaiah finally stopped musing. His late grandfather Hanan had experienced a precious solitary moment—an encounter with a celestial being. It was an experience that deeply inspired his father, Zakai, and guided him throughout his life. Shemaiah realized that losing the shofar made Abital feel like she was also losing Zakai again.

Reviving the past, he remembered coming out of his room to find Abital huddled on a bale of hay. She looked like an injured baby lamb. Her sorrow thickened the air; so much pain she exuded! Softly he lowered himself to the floor beside her, avoiding her eyes because he could not confront the raw pain reflected in them. He put his arms around her and made her a vow that he would find the lost shofar. A deep sorrow grew inside his chest. He hoped that the promise he just made to his mother would be something he could keep, but how was he to know for sure? A thought flitted through his mind that perhaps Eliha, the well-meaning Levite who had brought Zakai's dead body to the house, would know something about the shofar. Maybe he had kept the horn? Or perhaps he knew of someone who did?

"Mother," he said, "I will speak to Eliha tomorrow," and she nodded.

Early the next morning Shemaiah walked hurriedly toward the center of the town, where the Levites met and prepared for their daily chores. Eliha was there. He recognized Shemaiah as the son of Zakai and greeted him warmly. As the two men spoke, Eliha's expression turned somber. He had not realized that he may have left the shofar behind, nor did he want to be the cause of the enormous grief its disappearance was causing the family.

Shemaiah returned home dragging his feet. He had come to a decision. His eyes radiated resolve and determination as if he had matured many years in a mere minute. He had decided to return to where his father had died to search for the missing shofar. "I will search everywhere," he said aloud. "Behind every rock and inside every cave until I find it." As he often did, he needed to sit alone to meditate and pray upon this decision. He needed to be assured of YHWH's blessing upon this plan.

Shemaiah entered the small shrine on the roof of the house. Most Israelites had a sanctuary known as a bet-elohim in their homes. This was where they came to pray to YHWH and several lesser deities known as the teraphim. Abital kept an Asherah, a wooden pole, on their family shrine, hoping that befriending the goddess would bring abundance to her house. Shemaiah felt deeply conflicted by all of this, but avoided discussing it with his mother. At nineteen years of age, he was still too young to have a say in the matter.

The sons of Levi—and he was one—had been given the reward of foretelling the will of God[3] and partaking in the art of lower prophecy.[4] So, sitting on the rooftop floor, Shemaiah went deep within himself and prayed. He held the question in his heart, then remained still while waiting for an answer.

A message formed in his mind.

Aware that the heart and the mind must always be in alignment, Shemaiah pondered its meaning. By the time he rose from meditation, he was sure that searching for the lost shofar was right. He was confident that YHWH would be by his side in this quest. It would take some days or maybe a week; it was difficult to tell. But he would do it.

That night Shemaiah spoke to Abital about his plans, and she helped him prepare for the journey. He would take a woolen blanket to cover himself up in the cold nights in the desert. They packed a small bag with bread and figs. He filled a goatskin canteen with water. Finally, he carefully placed a short, sharp knife in the straps of his sandals. This was the sign that he might be gone for some time. When he was finished with his preparations, she gave him her blessing.

When the sun rose Shemaiah headed into the desert. He did not realize this then, but he was leaving more than just his home. He was leaving behind his childhood. He was embarking on a journey not yet fully revealed.

---

3. Deuteronomy 33:8.
4. Moses Maimonides, *Guide for the Perplexed*, chap. 36–45.

A journey that would force upon him tasks and trials which were his alone. It was a journey of discovery that would take him through new gates of perception and into the development of consciousness, for himself and for others.

CHAPTER 3

Life in Canaan—1403 BC

AFTER ZAKAI'S DEATH, ABITAL and her only child, Shemaiah, settled in the city of Geba in the land of Benjamin, the land that Moses assigned to her ancestors. Shemaiah was fifteen years old, soon to be sixteen. Being a Levite, the expectation was that at twenty-five he would move from there, live among his tribe, and tend the holy abode of YHWH.[1] Abital shook her head at the thought. Times were difficult and she feared being left alone. *It is still too soon to be concerned about that,* she tried to convince herself. Zakai had left a plot of land and some livestock; these were enough resources for the family to survive, and Shemaiah was a good companion who willingly shared the burdens of the household with his mother.

Abital's appearance could be misguiding. She was slight, but not weak or fragile. In fact, she was capable of very hard work. Her skin was deeply tanned as a result of the long hours spent working under the desert sun. The hardships of life had indeed forged a toughened, resolute character. After Zakai's death, Abital showed unusual determination and strength. She risked selling part of the land to buy ovine livestock. She then focused on the herding of the flock, taking care of the wool of the sheep, which would be carefully shaved, patiently cleaned, and prepared as yarn to be sold in the marketplace.

Abital had no qualms about slaying with her own hands a cow if needed to feed her and her son, nor did she shirk from the unsavory task of sorting the clean from the unclean parts of its carcass. She did this with the utmost care, keeping in mind Moses' admonition that this was the will of YHWH. Moses had taught that a flesh torn by the beasts was unclean and should not be eaten; he also taught that a calf should not be cooked in its

---

1. See Numbers 8:23–24.

mother's milk. Abital was careful to observe these essential guidelines. She was anxious to avoid incurring the wrath of God which might then fall on her or her family for generations to come.

Smart and crafty, Abital employed two foreigners to help her in the household and do the more demanding physical labor with the animals and in the fields. Aqhat was a Canaanite from the city of Akka; Yassib was a foreigner from the remote town of Ugarit. Both were respectful of the young widow and her fatherless son. They tended to the small family field, sowing the seeds and harvesting barley and flax; they shepherded and milked the flock every day.

Aqhat and Yassib had also suffered significant losses in their lives. Many battles had rampaged Canaan and its neighboring areas. Most members of their families had been killed or taken as prisoners, then sold as slaves in the armed conflicts that erupted in the region. Large groups of Semitic-speaking people, fierce savages, had also invaded the lands, searching for pastures to graze their herds. The Amorites came from the east, and the Hittites came from the north. But the strongest and fiercest of all were the Hyksos, also called Amu. These were the most ruthless of rulers and they were highly trained and organized.

Aqhat believed that the Hyksos raided the fields preceded by their gods, gods of the storm and war, which made them unleash tremendous power. One day, sitting next to Abital in the kitchen while savoring her meat stew, he described a Hyksos raid in vivid detail.

"The Hyksos came riding on enormous monsters of war, a sight too overpowering to behold. Their brave horses puffed hot air through their noses; they were tall and strong animals! They pulled whole battalions of soldiers that looked fearless as they stood erect and proud upon their rolling thrones. The Hyksos were ushered by the storm gods all along the path. They were covered with a cloud of protective dust every step of the way. Under their gods' protection, they reached the south until one day, they conquered Egypt. Even defeating the Egyptian gods!"

These were some of the beliefs that Aqhat held as truth. Yet, amidst the struggle that had enveloped their lives, both Aqhat and Yassib had been lucky to be taken in by a household where they were treated respectfully and were appreciated, and this brought forth the best efforts each had to offer. YHWH had ordered, "Do not mistreat or oppress a foreigner, for you were foreigners in Egypt,"[2] and Abital was mindful of this mandate. True to her character, she was both wise and generous in managing her household and her son, and this treatment was extended to her servants. It had become

2. See Exodus 22:21.

customary that if the servants showed loyalty and stayed long enough within the family they would be granted an allowance of goods and maybe money. Abital promised Aqhat and Yassib that they would enjoy such a blessing. But as much as she appreciated their help, she also feared that, in the absence of a father, these foreign men could influence her son, perhaps winning him away from her and her people. This fear she kept to herself.

***

The Jezreel Valley was a flourishing center of commerce located at a crossroads with easy access from the north, the coast, and the south. The Canaanite kings had signed alliances between them to protect their cities from invasions. In an attempt to avoid confrontations, the Israelites stayed in unoccupied, infertile areas. Joshua, however, negotiated pastures for his people and this, he believed, would guarantee a peaceful coexistence.

The Israelites were a tribal society. They maintained a simple life, working the fields and breeding their cattle. Each tribe grouped its members through extended family ties, be it biological or forged through marriage or adoption. Although patriarchal, in each family unit, both parents held the responsibility for maintaining law and order.[3] If matters could not be resolved within the family, the village elders were in charge of carrying out justice.[4]

To the Israelites, the people of Canaan were an alien multitude who observed unfamiliar practices and customs in their towns. They were merchants and traders and they were ruled by kings who owned the land. The Canaanite cities were prosperous and sophisticated, surrounded by orchards, vineyards, grain fields, and pasture land. They produced wine, dried fruits, grain, and milk products, and had factories where wool and flax were woven and dyed. Bartering and commerce constituted an active part of everyday life.

The tribes of Israel spread alongside the Canaanite cities. They honored mainly YHWH, but neither did they exclude the other gods of the region. Some of them practiced rituals common to the people of the land and a product of the mutual influence that had accrued over the years.

***

3. See Deuteronomy 21:19–21.
4. See Deuteronomy 21:19.

As Abital had feared, the Canaanite cities did become an attractive bait for youngsters like Shemaiah, lads who were raised in the scarcity and barrenness of a life lived in the desert. In strong contrast, Canaanite women wore dazzling adornments of silver, copper, and gold. Wealthy families lived in magnificent villas built around central courts overflowing with flowers and gurgling water fountains. All of these luxuries were tended by servants and slaves.

The Israelites began to engage in the worship of Yam, the god of the sea, and Mot, the god of death, who were believed to bring the dead back to life. Primarily, however, they worshiped Asherah, the mother goddess and queen of heaven. Asherah was the consort of Baal, the supreme god. She was a goddess of fertility, sexuality, and war. Her priests and worshipers would often indulge in excessive drinking and sexual rites that, although prohibited by YHWH, had proven irresistible to many young men.

Abital remembered clearly the days not long ago when the Moabites and the Midianites tempted the Israelites into worshiping Baal Peor, and YHWH responded with a plague. She worried that her son would fell prey to such practices. Nonetheless, Shemaiah remained blissfully unaware of his mother's concerns. He would follow Yassib early in the mornings to help him with the flock. Like his father Zakai, he liked being in the countryside with its pastoral activity. Tending to the flock gave him time to muse. Being in nature encouraged contemplation and allowed him time to practice his writing.

✳✳✳

Sometime later, Abital finally moved away from Geba to the encampment of the Levites in Shiloh, a town located in the hill country of Ephraim. Here, Abital believed, Shemaiah would be better shielded from extraneous influences. He would more likely be able to remain true to his Levite heritage.

Shiloh was a ring-shaped town. The houses were built in a closed circle and were surrounded for protection by a long wall. The town nestled amidst an open land, where dwellers kept two or three bulls to fertilize the cows and a few donkeys for transportation. Abital moved into a two-story pillared house constructed of limestone and wood. The house bordered on one side with a large number of homes—crosswise, with a fenced courtyard that kept the livestock safe. She and Shemaiah kept cows, rams and sheep, goose and hens, and an occasional rooster.

Abital felt uprooted and lonely in Shiloh, but chose to remain in the place where it seemed more likely her son could fulfill his destiny in the service of YHWH. She always took special care to convey his ancestral lineage to Shemaiah. To this end, she hired an older Levite with whom Shemaiah would spend time learning the chores of the priests and practicing the elaborate rituals of caring for the Ark of the Covenant.

CHAPTER 4

The Priestly Rank—1416 BC

THROUGH BIRTH, SHEMAIAH INHERITED the priestly rank of a Levite from his father Zakai. His parents took special care to provide him all he should know about his ancestral lineage, and Zakai liked to tell and retell the stories about their family past. When the sun set he would sit on large cushions that Abital placed on the floor and talk. "Sit here by my side, Shemaiah," he urged. "Have I ever told you about our ancestor Levi, the son of Jacob?"

Zakai felt animated as he told the stories of how Levi had lived to be 137 years old, the longest of all of the sons of Jacob. "Levi lived to see his great-grandsons, Moses and Aaron. He also lived to watch how his descendants were brought into servitude. At first, they worked in their Egyptian masters' fields and stables and in mines and quarries, and in Egyptian homes where they served as cooks, maids, and nannies. They were sometimes paid a wage, but mostly they were given only food and shelter as compensation. In time, however, the Hebrews were brought down into the depths of cruel slavery. Forced to build enormous construction projects designed to exalt the names of Egyptian kings."

Shemaiah remained silent, then turned his head to gaze at his father and said with a hint of disapproval in his voice, "I heard that Levi was chastised by his father for his continuous outbursts of anger."[1]

"Yes, so it was. But nevertheless, four generations later, Moses blessed the tribe of Levi, for they were righteous people, of loyal nature, ready to rally to his side to avenge God's honor.[2] In time, the Levites were able to

1. See Genesis 49:5–7.
2. See Deuteronomy 33:8–11.

channel their strong character and put it to the service of God. This is why God instructed Moses, 'The Levites are to be given wholly to Me.'"[3]

In these conversations, Shemaiah learned that Kadmiel, his great-grandfather, had been significantly honored by serving Moses as a scribe. Hanan, his grandfather, was given the honor of guarding the body of Joseph, their ancestor and vizier of the land of the Pharaohs, when it was taken out from Egypt. And Shemaiah's father, Zakai, now was privileged to serve under Joshua, Moses' lieutenant.

Listening as his father recounted his ancestry, Shemaiah felt proud of his Levite lineage and of his membership in a long and honorable line of scribes. Zakai kept a great number of old parchments carefully folded inside large wooden chests, and Shemaiah devoted long hours to reading these stories of the past. Even as a child Shemaiah was able to retain every little nuance, every detail, in all that he read. He came to believe that the vigor of a nation is reflected in the stories told by its people, and so he devoted time to put their stories into writing. He told his mother, "The role of a scribe is to record the stories so that they will remain engraved in the collective memory for generations to come." It was Shemaiah's deepest desire that one day he would do the scribal work for an influential leader of his people. Far was he from knowing that his dream would come to be true. Just as his great-grandfather Kadmiel had done, he too would someday record the teachings of Moses. The significant difference was that when Shemaiah would be taking down his words, he would do so sitting at the feet of the Prophet in the hereafter.

As for Abital, all throughout her life she felt such immense respect for Kadmiel, it was no surprise that she loved to recount stories about him to her son. "Kadmiel would spend time each night teaching Zakai the art of priesthood and of writing, and sometimes invited me to join them as he told the stories of our past. We would sit on large cushions and drink a cup of warm goat milk sweetened with honey." She continued, but her words came more slowly. It was as if she were still savoring the taste of warm milk in her mouth. "Kadmiel described the days after God's epiphany at Mount Sinai. It happened on the third day of the third month, after the people had left Egypt.[4] The air felt denser, he said, as if charged by a strange vibration—very difficult to describe. God's momentous revelation was so real it felt as if it could happen again, in any instant."

Shemaiah felt a vibration crawl up his skin and down his spine. He closed his eyes, as if seeking to relive that wondrous moment of revelation.

---

3. See Numbers 8:16–18.
4. See Exodus 19 and 20.

"These were the days in Sinai, when the gates of heaven opened completely. The transparency between heaven and earth was absolute and it would remain like this for an indefinite amount of time. On those days your grandfather Hanan saw an angel that moved toward him very smoothly, as if floating on air. And without a word, the angel handed him a horn. On these days Moses came to speak with Kadmiel and a group of seventy leaders and officials known as the elders; he sought to engage their help in the handling of the encampment. Moses conveyed God's commands, saying, 'These are the words of the Lord to you. You will stand by my side and share the burden of the people; I will not carry it alone. You, the elders, will take some of the power of the Spirit of God that is in me, and it will be in you.'"[5]

Utterly absorbed in the memory of that moment, almost as if it had happened also to her, Abital fell silent for a few moments. Then she roused herself and continued the story.

"Moses told the elders that God promised to send an angel ahead of them as a guide into the promised land. Moses warned them to listen to the angel, and to not rebel against his guidance, for God's name was in him.[6] And Kadmiel told me with great excitement that he realized it would not be just one angel, but many who would come their way. A host of angels would guard them and lift them up in their hands.[7] This was God's promise to the people."

✳✳✳

Abital's enormous appreciation for Kadmiel was more than justified. She told Shemaiah of an event for which she would always be grateful to him. It was a time when, in a moment of great desperation, Kadmiel helped turn her life around.

"One cold night in the desert, the old man seemed melancholic. Zakai started to play the flute, as he often did, hoping this would lift his grandfather's spirit. Kadmiel listened in silence for some time and then, looking at his grandson, he said, 'Dear son, soon it will be an anniversary of the day of my birth. I'll be one hundred and two years old. And I'm prepared to go.' Zakai stopped playing. With both concern and curiosity born of innocence, he asked, 'Where are you going?'

"'I am going to meet with my ancestors. Soon it will be my time. I need to prepare, but you must prepare as well.'

"Kadmiel's words trailed off into silence. After some time he continued.

5. See Numbers 11:16–17.

6. See Exodus 23:20–21.

7. See Psalm 91:12.

"'Your task in this world is still incomplete. You, my child, need to marry.'

"Zakai's body shrank, as if his very physicality was recoiling from Kadmiel's words. Why did he need to get married? Life was good just the way it was. He liked the company of his flock more than he liked being with people.

"'How old are you, my son?'

"'I'm twenty-six years old, grandfather. I'm too old to get married.'

"But Kadmiel did not back off. He already had figured an arrangement.

"'Listen, Zakai. Your late father's brother, Eglon, had a son who died young. His wife was left with no child.'

"According to the customs of the people, a woman whose husband died before she could conceive should not marry outside the family.[8] She was to marry the husband's brother or, in his absence, another close relative. This was a way that would ensure the line of succession.

"'Her name is Abital. She is a good woman and will be a good woman for you,' the old man concluded."

Abital's eyes glistened as she looked at her son. "And so this is how I came to be married to your father," she explained. "And in time you were born! We named you 'Shemaiah' because God had listened to our prayers."

Two days after their son was born, Zakai visited Kadmiel. He wanted to share his happiness with his grandfather and thank him for nudging him into this marriage. The newborn child had moved him in ways he never expected would happen. In fact, he now felt his life had more value because there was a fragile being depending on him. He pushed aside the heavy curtain at the entrance, stepped inside the tent, and saw in an instant that Kadmiel's chest was heaving. Zakai ran to the bedside. He raised his grandfather's torso so that he could blow into his face in an effort to help get some air into his lungs.

"Grandfather," he pleaded. "Grandfather, please!"

But he got no answer. Still holding on to his grandfather, Zakai fell to his knees. Kadmiel's labored breathing intensified until, to Zakai's shock, he took one deep, gasping inhalation. Zakai grabbed his grandfather's hands, but felt nothing so much as the crazy pounding of his own heart in his chest. Was his grandfather dead?

But then, after what seemed a very long time, Kadmiel started breathing again. Zakai exhaled with relief. He pulled a wooden bench over to the bedside. Kadmiel's eyes were half-open. He seemed to want to say

---

8. See Deuteronomy 25:5.

something, but his voice was so feeble it was barely audible. Zakai put his ear close to his mouth.

"We have been graced!" Kadmiel exclaimed.

Although Zakai did not understand what these words meant he felt immense relief that his grandfather seemed to be regaining his strength.

"I'm thankful to God for the life I have lived. But more than anything, I'm thankful for having lived long enough to know and experience in this world such a being as Moses. Because of his example I have no fear of death." A smile curved on Kadmiel's face. He took a shallow breath. "From Moses, I learned to listen within for God's voice. I learned that this is how I would be guided by God. Moses showed me that we have capacity for discernment. We have the capacity to choose our thoughts and actions rather than merely react. We have the ability to recognize and anticipate what lies ahead. That, my son, is one level of the prophetic gift. We must remain attentive to perceive when it happens, and above all, we must be grateful."

Kadmiel looked to Zakai for validation and Zakai nodded.

"But remember: Moses is not a man like us. He has reached a level of prophecy that surpasses human attainment. A level of interaction with the beyond that approaches the angelic. He penetrates all veils and surpasses all barriers. He has no physical limitations that may hinder him. There are no perceptual nor mental imperfections that obstruct him.

"Moses has control over his sensory and imaginative faculties. He is not overwhelmed with confusion, or fear, nor any other obscure emotions that may hinder him in any manner. He governs his drives, his instincts, and his human desires, and he is free to function with the purest intellect."[9] With enormous effort, Kadmiel lifted a hand to emphasize an essential point. "We humans struggle with *all sorts* of dark thoughts and conflicting emotions. Beware my son, and be cautious! They are like a plague! Jealousy and envy in particular are dangerous. These are toxic human emotions that cloud your vision and obscure your judgment. It happened to Moses' brother and sister, Aaron and Miriam;[10] don't let it happen to you."

Kadmiel closed his eyes. His breathing became smooth and even, unlike how it had been before. Zakai decided that he would stay close and watch over his grandfather while he slept. It didn't take too long for Kadmiel to wake up. He cleared his throat, then continued saying what he felt compelled to convey to his grandson. To posterity.

"Moses loves his people, and wants the Spirit of God to live in all of them."

9. Blumenfeld, "Maimonides #7."

10. See Numbers 12.

He looked at Zakai as he added for emphasis, "And that is how it is. The Spirit of God lives freely in every one of us. In every person alive. There are prophets among us, and when God reveals Himself to them, He does so in visions. He speaks to them in dreams. But this is not true of Moses. Moses is above all. With him, God speaks face-to-face, clearly, not in riddles. He alone sees the form of the Lord."[11]

Zakai noticed his grandfather's face growing pale. He seemed to be at peace. But suddenly, as if he were about to collapse, Kadmiel took a series of ragged, rasping breaths through his open mouth. His body twitched and then he simply ceased breathing. He was dead.

That night, the elders came to the tent to cleanse and prepare the body for the burial. Feeling painfully insecure, Zakai watched in profound silence. The moment he had feared had in fact arrived, and he was on his own. But all of a sudden, he heard a deep voice speaking to his ear. This voice, he would always recognize. This was the voice of Kadmiel, and it was delivering the last of his directives to his grandson.

"And so it is. Life must go on."

Zakai felt the release that was intended in this, his grandfather's permission to move on and his encouragement not to plunge into sorrow. And he was ready to obey. He could do this out of love for his grandfather.

Kadmiel the scribe was buried in Kadesh-Barnea. Not long after, however, the Israelite encampment moved up north toward the edge of the land of Edom, and Kadmiel's remains were left behind where they had been buried. On the same day of Kadmiel's passing, Aaron the high priest ascended Mount Hor at God's bidding to die there. It all happened on the first day of the fifth month, on the fortieth year after the Israelites came out of Egypt. Kadmiel was 102 years old and Aaron was 123 years old[12] on the day they died.

✳✳✳

While sitting next to her son, Abital looked into Shemaiah's eyes and told him, "Dear son, Kadmiel, Hanan, and Zakai are not with us anymore, but their shofar confirms a message of deliverance. We must treasure the horn and keep it with care, for it was meant to serve a purpose."

"What is the purpose?"

"Too early to know."

---

11. See Numbers 12:6–8.
12. See Numbers 33:37–39.

CHAPTER 5

Gilgal Rephaim
The Lost Shofar—1403 BC

SHEMAIAH WALKED MANY DAYS, heading toward Gilgal Rephaim, the site where the Israelite fighters camped before entering the land at Jericho. This was the area where his father had died and was buried. Perhaps the shofar would be inside the grave near the casket or hidden within the bushes or underneath a rock. How he wished that he would be able to find it!

His feet hurt, but his mind spun impatiently, pushing him to continue moving forward. The scorching sun made the way seem longer than anything he could have imagined. When the sky began to darken, Shemaiah knew enough to look for a safe spot in which to take shelter. He found one between two large boulders where he would be protected from the winds and from animals. Mindful of his meager store of rations, he ate a frugal meal of bread and figs. Using his knife, he cleared the ground between the rocks, lay down, and covered himself with his woolen blanket. Maybe he would be lucky enough to sleep through the night in peace.

But, alone under the starry firmament, Shemaiah felt insecure. He hoped that YHWH would be his shield,[1] as He had promised his ancestor Abraham He would be. Trying to avoid thinking too much, Shemaiah started counting the stars. God said that Abraham's descendants would be as numerous as the stars in the sky and promised a land where they would be able to thrive. Shemaiah had lived through this; he had seen this happen! The thought of this ancestral promise was reassuring. He believed that YHWH would help him too.

---

1. See Genesis 15:1.

A wolf howled in the distance, and a chill of fear ran through Shemaiah's spine. Wandering in the wilderness had made him acutely aware of his human vulnerability. Instinctively, he reached for his knife, but then, shaking his head, as if to dismiss his disturbing thoughts, he let it go. Instead, he called to mind his father.

Seven years had passed since Zakai died, and yet Shemaiah remembered him clearly. He longed for his company, his invaluable advice, and more moments of shared laughter. He would never forget the day Zakai had gone running after a baby lamb that had strayed from the flock. Zakai held the lamb in his arms and scolded the animal as he would a child, asking the lamb where she was going without her mother. Then, laughing, as if he had received an answer, Zakai admonished the lamb for doing stupid things. Later that day, as Shemaiah and his father headed home, Zakai circled back to the incident as a teaching moment. "You should never wander away from home if you do not know the way back," he counseled.

Tonight, Shemaiah wondered whether his father would see any wisdom in his son's adventure. Looked at from one point of view, Shemaiah had done the opposite of what his father had instructed. He had left home and walked into the desert not knowing when or how would he be able to return home. But then there was another way of looking at his quest. As a dutiful, loving son, he had made a promise to his mother. Wasn't this what his father would have wanted? Firm resolve swelled in his heart. He *must* bring the shofar back! That ram's horn was all that was left from his father. And with this determined thought, Shemaiah fell asleep.

He was awakened by the warmth of the sun on his skin. After folding the woolen blanket, he nibbled some figs and bread and swallowed a sip of water from the canteen. Gazing toward where the sun was rising, he noticed some structures to the left. Reasoning that this was the Israelite compound at Gilgal Rephaim, he began walking in that direction. He reached the settlement and was shocked at what had become of it. The place was barren, with no sign of a human presence anywhere. In front of him stood an impressive arrangement of enormous stones in shades of gray and golden brown. They were laid in three concentric circles surrounding a big platform in the middle.

This must be where the Tabernacle was positioned, he thought. He approached the center of the compound. His body was covered with goose bumps. Overcome with emotion, Shemaiah fell to the ground.

"This place is sacred!" he mumbled in reverent recognition.

Then he sat very still, unsure what to do next, until he realized that this was the place where the search for the lost shofar should begin. With an effort, he stood. He spotted a long wooden stick to the side of one of the boulders and fetched it. It would help him explore the terrain.

Shemaiah proceeded slowly. He looked under every bush and searched behind every stone. He used the stick to push aside wild, unruly shrubbery. At the end of the day when the sun had set, he still had not found any sign of the shofar. Neither had he discovered any other human artifacts. Seven years had passed since the siege of Jericho, and nothing remained to provide any clue of what had happened. Suddenly Shemaiah understood that he had not prepared enough for what he now realized would be a very, very long journey. Feeling both sad and discouraged, he decided he must retrace his steps back to Shiloh.

That night, in a dream, Shemaiah saw his father walking toward him. Zakai's face seemed serene. Speaking softly, Zakai instructed, "Listen to the sound." And a sound, deep and long, came at that very moment. Shemaiah knew that sound. It was one he had heard before. It was the sound of a shofar.

Zakai whispered, "The sound that you hear is the plea of the soul in its longing for God. It is my soul calling for the heavens to open and let me into the Temple." Leaving no room for doubt, he added, "Look no more, Shemaiah. The shofar is nowhere to be found because it is very much a part of my soul; it has never left my side—as is also true of you, my son! Listen to the sound within and seek God's face. Seek His goodness in the land of the living."[2]

The scene in the dream changed rapidly, and Shemaiah became even more alert. He did not want to miss anything. A man, taller and more prominent, was now standing beside his father. Bright golden light shone in an aura around the figure. The halo of light pulsated outward so that its radiance also enveloped Zakai.

Awed, Shemaiah whispered, "Gabriel. That is Gabriel with my father."

The scene changed again, as usually happens in dreams, and now Zakai was holding the shofar in his hands. Shemaiah turned his gaze from his father to Gabriel. In the hands of the angel were two precious blue sapphires, each of them shining with fulgurant golden undertones.

Gabriel stretched his hands forward. "Take these stones, my son," he communicated wordlessly. "Guard them carefully. These are two fragments of the tablets of law that fell to the ground the day that Moses broke them. They are fragments of the very first tablets inscribed by the finger of God.[3]

---

2. See Psalm 27.
3. See Exodus 31:18.

These two pieces are missing in the ark that sits in Shiloh. Moses is waiting. He knows that you will bring them to him."

Shemaiah watched as the bright golden light surrounding the angel extended toward him until he, too, was enveloped in a cocoon of light. The two stones floated toward him. They merged into his body through a gap that opened in his forehead right between his eyes. Shemaiah felt a painful pressure between his eyebrows. Instinctively, he shut his eyes tightly as the pressure intensified. Then, suddenly, he felt an explosive release and the pain vanished.

The dream ended. He opened his eyes. His father and the angel Gabriel had disappeared. Like the elusive shofar, they were nowhere to be found. Shemaiah's mind was keenly alert and active, but, curiously, his body remained unresponsive. He was temporarily paralyzed. As he lay on the ground, his mind opened up to a new understanding. It became clear to him that the shofar had never gone astray. It had entered into a parallel sphere of reality, and there it remained, concealed.

In his dream, he had interacted with disembodied spiritual entities whose purpose was to transmit essential information.[4] And so it was meant to be. Dreams are sacred tools, vehicles for that which has remained hidden in the beyond, but now is ready to come forth and be revealed. Dreams are an instrument of prophecy,[5] as was this powerful dream of his.

The disappearance of the shofar was a purposeful strategy that had prompted Shemaiah to make a dramatic change in his life. It had forced him out of his comfort zone, where he had been resting in an unchallenging, secure environment. The alternatives had been laid out for him to choose: either remain passive or get up and move. Shemaiah had chosen to move.

The dream changed the quest. What started as a search to find the shofar morphed into a new mission. A new personal destiny. He understood now that his actual quest was no other than to find and connect with Moses! This new task would allow for psychological growth as well as spiritual development. In the course of one night, Shemaiah's mind and heart became attuned with the Universal Mind that remained obscured behind the veil. His challenge was to undertake a wholly different journey.

Shemaiah felt ready to assume the challenge and accept the invitation. He was open to whatever it entailed. He was prepared to search for Moses so that he could hand over the stones entrusted to his care by Gabriel. Again, he heard that note of longing that seemed to come out of nowhere, and the sound of the lovely shofar seemed to sanction the truth of the message in his

4. Luzzato, *Derech Hashem* 3:1:6.
5. Talmud Brachot 57b.

dream. Then, still lying on the floor and unable to move, Shemaiah heard a choir of voices singing praises to God.

"*YHWH, YHWH*," they sang. "*Benevolent, compassionate, and gracious, slow to anger and abundant in lovingkindness and truth.*"[6]

This was the instant that he knew, as if having been hit by lightning, that his entire life had changed direction.

"I am ready," he affirmed, and got to his feet. He felt a strange combination of both excitement and fear. He had a keen awareness of being the carrier and protector of the sapphire stones, and although he felt the weight of an enormous responsibility, he felt ready to fulfill it. With his whole heart he was willing to set out for Moses, the Prophet.

But where was Moses to be found?

He didn't know.

Nobody knew.

And so, Shemaiah headed back to Shiloh to regroup. The search for the shofar was over and a new search needed to be undertaken. A supernal being had given him a different task, a task that was larger than life, a task with implications that he did not fully grasp. Was he too young to undertake this quest? Little did he know that life in the spirit world is timeless, and so, there were no timelines to the new task he had been assigned. Years would have to pass to allow him to prepare and become a suitable tool for an encounter with Moses. He must first become a refined instrument before he could deliver the stones that held essential information not yet known in the world.

---

6. See Exodus 34:6.

CHAPTER 6

Kadmiel the Scribe—ca. 1500 BC

KADMIEL, SHEMAIAH'S GREAT-GRANDFATHER, HAD been born in Egypt. His mother, Orpah, was a daughter of the house of Levi and one of Queen Hatshepsut's favorite handmaids. His father, Auserra, was a lector priest and scribe in the Temple of the Great God Amun-Ra, the sun god. It is said that Auserra was so exceptional that the god Thoth himself instructed him and made him unusually skillful in the noble office of the scribes.

People spoke very highly of Auserra. They said he could understand all the hard passages in the writings as effortlessly as the ease with which the River Nile flows. Auserra was trusted to utter spells as well as recite influential hymns to the gods during official ceremonies. The number of auspicious deeds and prophecies attributed to him were abundant. It was expected that through his mediation, the gods would bless Egypt with goodness.

Kadmiel, then, being the son of Auserra, was taken to the Royal Palace to be educated at the Kap, the Royal Nursery, starting at the age of four. There he was taught the ancient traditions of Egypt. He learned reading, writing, mathematics, and was trained in the physical and military arts.

One night, at eight years of age, Kadmiel overheard a conversation between two older pupils of the school discussing what path to follow in life. One was admonishing the other in sharp tones of urgency and apprehension. "I have been told that you have abandoned writing and that you reel about in pleasures. I have been told that you give your attention to work in the army. That you have turned your back on hieroglyphs. I have come to tell you, my friend, about the condition of the soldier, that much-afflicted one. I have come to tell you that he is confined in the camp, a searing beating is given to his body, an open wound inflicted on his eyebrows. He is laid down, and he is beaten like papyrus and struck with torments. Now I say to you: turn back from those who assert that the soldier's life is more pleasant than that of the scribe. Turn back!"[1]

Even at that tender age, when Kadmiel heard this, he made up his mind that he would forsake the high honors and riches that might be derived from war. He would become a scribe like his father. As he saw it, this was the best profession of all. It was an art that filled its practitioners with joy. From then on, Kadmiel held to his vision of who he would be and what he would do with his life.

And so Kadmiel learned the hieroglyphic and hieratic scripts, which were complicated scripts incorporating many different signs that required intense study and memorization. But he enjoyed the way they triggered his imagination and ushered inspired ideas into his mind. He learned how to prepare the sheets of papyrus and then write on them with reed brushes dipped in ink. All this required both patience and dexterity, and he spent long hours practicing the characters that he then copied with painstaking artfulness onto the papyrus.

Like Auserra, Kadmiel also wanted to learn about the movement of the stars in the sky. It was a mystery that captivated his soul and his mind. To him, the sky was a giant canvas on which the moods, actions, and warnings of the gods were written, and he wanted to learn how to read these signs.

Auserra's prominence also gained nine-year-old Kadmiel admittance to the Temple of Khonsû. In his father's eyes, the boy was mature enough to take on the responsibilities of the priesthood, which he conveyed to his son as they walked together early one morning toward the gates of the temple. Kadmiel felt the clamoring of both pride and fright in his heart. The god Khonsû, known also as the god of the moon, was a mysterious deity and, together with the great god Thoth, these two governed the mysteries of time. Already at the gate, Auserra placed his hand on his son's shoulder, and in a grave voice, reminded him of something he already knew: "Only those found fitting can be greeted and accepted into the temple."

Kadmiel looked at his father and nodded. The position was much coveted, and he wished to honor his father by proving suitable for the task. The temple was a magnificent structure. Its central entry was flanked by two enormous quadrangular towers engraved with images that glorified the gods as well as scenes that revealed visions of the afterlife. Kadmiel looked around him with delight. The air felt fresh. When they went inside, the rooms were clean. Soft light filtered into every corner and highlighted the crevices that gave character to the walls. Above a tall arch was chiseled, "He

---

1. Manuscript written during the reign of Pharaoh Seti II of Dynasty 19 (ca. 1210 BC); see Simpson, *Literature of Ancient Egypt*, 346–47.

who enters the temple must be pure," and Kadmiel felt himself to be ready for this.

A young boy approached and asked them to remove the sandals from their feet, which he collected from them. An older man appeared and motioned for them to follow, and he led them to an adjacent hall where they were greeted by the headmaster priest, Athope.

Athope was a robust man with dark skin and a shaved head. His dark eyes sparkled with serenity, or maybe joy. His torso was naked and gleaming, the skin having been shaved and then polished with oils. The white linen skirt of the priesthood was wrapped around his thighs. He wore a broad, shiny bronze band around his neck and wide bronze bracelets on his arms and ankles. Like the lesser priests who were working in the room just beyond, Athope was barefooted.

In fact, all of the priests of Khonsû lived within the walls of the temple so that they could more diligently practice the rituals of hygiene and prayer that pleased the gods. The common conviction was that an agitated mind and impure heart were obstacles to spiritual growth, thus every new priest, having survived a rigorous selection process, was subjected to strict, exacting, in-house training in the disciplines of calming the mind and the mastery of passions.

Kadmiel, the son of righteous Auserra, would be under the direct counsel and tutelage of Athope. He himself would guide Kadmiel through the hardships of initiation. Three young priests were assigned to take him to an exclusive precinct in the back of the temple, where they prepared him for what was to come.

First, all of his hair was shaved from both his head and body. Then, water was sprinkled all over in an ablution ceremony intended to cleanse and renew him. Every crevice and fold, even the most intimate, was washed with scrupulous attention. His nails were trimmed and cleaned beneath. Fragrant oils were smeared all over his body. Three priests approached Kadmiel in silence. They gave him some white crystals which he was instructed to chew; this made him gag and choke. This, too, was part of the cleansing ritual because even his mouth and teeth must be bathed. Incense was now lit, and a priest carrying the incense walked in a circle around him so that he was enveloped in its smoke. The fragrance would further purify him, and would chase away any demons that may have dared to try to stay attached. The smell was so dense and concentrated it caused him to feel lightheaded.

A white linen kilt was tied around his waist. From this moment on he was to wear only this, the garb of the priesthood. In the early stages of the priesthood, other decorative accessories were forbidden. Kadmiel was instructed that he must repeat these cleansing rituals twice daily. He was to purify himself in this manner once in the daytime and once at night. The thought pleased him because he felt greatly enriched by this initiation ritual.

Five years later, when Kadmiel came of age, he had grown to be quite striking in appearance. He was tall, unlike the majority of his peers, and he was handsome. His olive skin was clear and smooth. His dark eyes, big and round, blazed with eagerness and kindness. He had earned a reputation for brilliance, agility, and meticulous precision in his work. He had all the makings of a fine priest.

One day, two senior priests of grave countenance and somber intentions approached him. Athope was at their side. They announced that a ceremony of the highest importance was to be performed, then led him to a secluded room in the temple to be undressed. One of the men restrained his arms while another kneeled before him.

Kadmiel had absorbed the lesson of obedience even in the face of fear, and so he stood, silent and tall, as Athope delivered an inscrutable order to the priest who kneeled before him. Athope said, "Sever indeed, thoroughly."

The priest bowed his head and responded, "Yes, Master. I will proceed carefully."

Athope looked to the other priest standing behind Kadmiel. "Hold him fast. Do not let him faint and fall."

The restrainer responded, "I will do as you say."[2]

The moment felt odd, surreal.

Kadmiel watched as a hand pressed a stone blade against the foreskin of his maleness, and then he fainted. When he came to, he saw Athope looking down at him with concern.

"Circumcision is the summit of bodily purification. It is demanded by the gods," he said. Placing his hand on Kadmiel's arm, he added, "Tomorrow, you'll be fine." And then he left.

Kadmiel felt alone and unsure of where this process of ordination was taking him, but he also realized that there was no other choice but to endure. With sadness, but without shedding a single tear, at last he fell into a long, deep slumber.

✳✳✳

As the rigors of training continued, Kadmiel was made to repeat daily the principles of virtuous living that he learned from Athope. They were principles by which the soul of the deceased would be judged when reaching

---

2. Free descriptive version of the oldest extant depiction of the act of circumcision from ancient Egypt in Kanawati and Hassan, *The Teti Cemetery at Saqqara*.

the Hall of the Two Truths during his passage to the underworld. Kadmiel complied with all he was instructed to do. He learned the names of the gods to which he was to pay homage, as well as the names of the evils, forty-two in all, that were to be avoided.

He chanted: "Oh, Wide-Strider who came forth from Heliopolis, I have not done wrong. Fire-Embracer who came forth from Kheraha, I have not robbed. Nosey, who came forth from Hermopolis, I have not stolen. Swallower-of-Shades, who came forth from Kernet, I have not slain people. Terrible-of-Face who came forth from Rosetjau, I have not destroyed the food offerings. Double-Lion, who came forth from the sky, I have not reduced measures. He-Whose-Eyes-Are-in-Flames, who comes forth from Asyut, I have not stolen the god's property. Burning-One who came forth backward, I have not told lies. Breaker-of-Bones who came forth from Memphis, I was not sullen. He-of-the-Cavern who came forth from the west, I have not fornicated with the fornicator. He-Whose-Face-Is-Behind-Him, who came forth from his hole, I have not caused anyone to weep. . . ."[3]

Kadmiel memorized every word and repeated their names every day, wanting to remember their meaning on the day of his final priestly investiture. He wondered when this would be. The end seemed far away.

Life in the temple was demanding. The temple liturgy had to be executed rigorously, every hour of the day and of the night. In the very early hours of the dawn, Athope broke the seal that locked the entrance of the holy of holies, where only he was allowed to enter. Upon his request, four priests joined him to help with the practices. The priests worked diligently to accomplish the daily chores that had been assigned to them. They lit torches, burned incense, chanted prayers, and kept the gold statue of the god cleaned and polished, using the same cleansing rituals that the priests performed on themselves. Each day the god was dressed in fresh clothing and adorned with radiant jewels. Offerings of food and drink were placed near him so that he could eat. Singers offered hymns of praise to the god, and the chanting continued until the end of the day when the god was returned to its chamber inside the holy of holies. Only then could the priests leave the shrine, walking backward as a sign of respect and sweeping their footprints from the ground as they retreated. When the room was emptied, the high priest sealed the sacred area for the night.

The priests ate the principal meal of the day at this time. Their meals were made from the offerings of food that had been brought to the temple by generous pilgrims. After everyone had eaten his share, they turned their

---

3. *Book of the Dead* ("Negative Confession," Papyrus of Ani), in Faulkner, *Ancient Egyptian Book of the Dead*, 20–34.

attentions to completing the cleaning of the temple. If the god was pleased with their work, he showered blessings upon the people and their families.

Kadmiel studied the secret teachings of Ancient Egypt—the knowledge that made Egypt great. He learned to measure the days and times. He was taught that one year lasted about 365 days, with twelve months in one year, thirty days long each, and that one day was partitioned into twenty-four hours. The new day started at sunrise and was divided into twelve hours, and the night into another twelve. He learned that in the summer, the hours of the day were longer than the hours of the night. But during the winter, this was reversed. The priests would carefully measure the days and the nights and the seasons of the year in a solar calendar. They knew that Egypt's prosperity and welfare depended on the yearly flooding of the Nile River. Time was rigorously measured to ensure proper treatment of the fields and the crops.

However, Kadmiel noticed that the ordinary people ruled their lives by the cycles of the moon. This made perfect sense to him, as they could easily follow the luminary with a naked eye. Every night as he lay on his bed, he reviewed what he had studied, engraving it in his memory.

One day, Athope took Kadmiel to one of the back rooms in the temple. There, he kept some tools that were used to observe and measure the movement of the stars.

"The Goddess of the Sky, Nut, stretches her body in a perfect arch over the earth. From her body the sun, the moon, and the stars are hung and kept in place," he explained. Then he showed him the merkhet, a narrow, straight wooden bar with a hole in one end from which a plumb line was suspended. The instrument allowed knowing the positioning of the stars at night. "The merkhet should be aligned with the North Star, encircling the North Pole. That star is called Indestructible because it never rises nor sets down. The priests rely on the North Star to trace the direction and the positioning of every imaginable event." Taking a long stick, Athope drew a thick line on the ground, following the signs of a second merkhet. "This line is the north-south axis," he said, "and the death chamber of the king is built to be perfectly aligned with this line. In that way, his soul will always be able to find the way to heaven and therefore will live forever."

Athope took Kadmiel to the courtyard, where a sundial showed the hours of the day. "During the day, the sun journeys the sky, leaving markings on the sundial that show the hours of the day." Adding a note of caution, he said, "The nights are different, as numerous stars speak to us in the dark, telling the hour. But we should follow the Indestructible and never lose sight of it, so as never to make mistakes when estimating time or get lost when traveling."

Athope didn't seem to tire of explaining the advances in knowledge in which he had played his own part. They covered all areas of human endeavor, including the construction of massive monuments. "With their instruments, architects have managed to give proper orientation to some of Egypt's greatest monuments." He spoke of the magnificent Pyramid of Giza, an impressive construction filled with astronomical information. He spoke about Senenmut, Queen Hatshepsut's chief advisor. "Senenmut is an intelligent man and ingenious architect who has built all of the Queen's majestic buildings." His voice was filled with excitement. "The gods talk to Senenmut in his sleep, showing him all that will come. He has been able to draw a most detailed plan of the location of every star in the sky!"

As he taught, Athope liked to sit on the ground next to his pupil. They spent long hours of the night gazing fixedly into the darkness of the sky. The master explained all that he knew of the essential knowledge that secured the perpetuity of life in Egypt. "The lector priests paint the stars in the ceilings of the mortuary temples. They want to make sure that the soul of the departed king will know the time and the place where he was buried. In this way, the king will never get lost, agonizing in the beyond. The king, like the stars, is destined to be eternal."

Kadmiel was proud of having learned to read and write. He was proud of being a scribe. Whenever his teacher allowed him some free time, he would go into the temple and sit in a corner just to watch as the lector priests consulted the skies and predicted what was to come. He registered in a scroll of papyrus all that he heard and then offered it to Athope for his ratification. Kadmiel's goal was to become a lector priest, and he knew there was much more he must learn. He became preoccupied with purifying his body and training his mind. He wanted to be worthy of eternal life. Written on the walls of the temple was an admonition that he took to heart: "Never go about revealing the rituals you see, in all their mystery, in the temples. Lest your soul may be punished and go astray."[4] So, too, was he careful to keep to himself what he had been taught. The priests, having been meticulously chosen and trained, were very conscientious and respectful of the gods. It had been assured to them that a life guided by the principles they had learned would be eternal, and Kadmiel adopted that belief.

✳✳✳

---

4. Inscription in the Temple of Edfu, West Bank of the Nile, Upper Egypt, in Chassinat, *Le Temple d'Edfou*, 361 (line 3).

There came a time when Kadmiel thought he must have learned everything there was to know, but one day, Athope called him to his side. He whispered confidentially, "From now on, on the first hour after the sunset, when there is still some light in the sky, I will devote that time to teach you what I have left for last. These are the most secret writings in all of Egypt: *The Treatise of the Hidden Chamber*."

This treatise was a sacred text of instructions meant as a guide for the initiate into the mysteries of the path the soul takes as it enters the beyond. It showed how to bypass sentries that guarded the way. It revealed many dangers the soul would encounter. The text disclosed that at the end of the journey the deceased would meet with Osiris, after which it would live forever.

In this last of the great lessons, Athope took special care to teach his beloved pupil all the things that a high-ranking priest knew. "After the deceased's soul has seen and known the mysterious visions and beings that are in the beyond, it is transfigured into an akh-spirit. It has become one of the spirits that survived death and now mingle with the gods. This spirit, even after death, will have an influence on the things of the world. Never forget this: the akh-spirit can enter and leave the netherworld as he pleases, and, even more, he can always speak to the living. It can connect the world of day and the world of night. This has been proven to be true, a million times."

Athope now inquired whether Kadmiel remembered the forty-two names of the gods that are to be called when entering the netherworld. He also examined Kadmiel on the names of the evils and monsters to be avoided. These things were important because this knowledge could help the deceased person survive if his soul was confronted by evil.

"It will help your soul in the time of your passage from the world of the living," the master concluded softly. Hearing something new in his tone, Kadmiel looked at him with concern. Athope seemed very tired. "Now let us take some time to rest." And they parted ways.

The next day, Athope confided to Kadmiel that he would soon depart from the world.

In the following days, Athope spoke at length with his pupil about the riches to be found in the world to come. "You are one of the fortunate ones, son," he said. "The knowing you have acquired has come directly to us from the gods themselves. It will greatly benefit a person while he is on earth as well as in the moment he is ready to depart. It is a true remedy for the ills of life."

As the hours passed, Kadmiel watched his master languish. One night, lying on his bed and barely breathing, he murmured, "I feel Him coming," then closed his eyes. Kadmiel sat in silence by Athope's side waiting for Osiris, ruler of the cycles of life and death, to extend his hand and take him away. He loved his master and would always be thankful for all he had shared with him. When he finally passed away, a number of priests entered the room and, for what seemed a long time, worked diligently cleansing Athope's body. He would be mummified, as was every member of the nobility and high officials after they died.

CHAPTER 7

Shemaiah's Life Has a New Direction
Shuah the Seeress—1398 BC

FIVE YEARS HAD PASSED and Abital and Shemaiah had become established in Shiloh with new friends and new routines. The hardships of the past were left behind, and not a shadow of fear lingered over them. Diligent as she was, Abital liked to spend her free time rearranging even the most minute corners of the rooms of her house.

On that seemingly fatidic day when Abital opened the wooden chests in which Zakai had placed the large cache of scrolls he had written and realized that Zakai's shofar had been lost, Shemaiah left on a journey to Gilgal Rephaim. It was a desperate quest to try and find it. This event marked the beginning of a new chapter in Shemaiah's life. In Gilgal Rephaim, where his father lay in the grave, a task had been delivered to him from the beyond. He was to bring two sapphire stones to Moses. But how?

Shemaiah's life had taken a new direction. A supernal being had instructed him to find Moses, and, bizarre as this command might be, he felt ready to undertake the challenge.

Day was dawning over Shiloh. Shemaiah woke to the familiar crow of the roosters. He was unable to remain in bed once the noises from the village could be heard. He got up quickly from his bed—a thin folded woolen quilt—rolled it tight, and set it in the corner until night returned and he needed it again. He had returned from Gilgal Rephaim only a few hours before. He did not know if his mother would be satisfied, as he did not bring the lost shofar, but only an uncanny message from his father. He walked to the patio where he guessed he would find Abital kneading dough.

The vision of his father and the angel Gabriel stood fresh in his mind, infusing his life with a new sense of purpose. He had not found the lost shofar, which never left his father's side, and thus, a door had been closed. But then another door had been opened when Gabriel assigned him a new task, one that had implications he did not fully understand. Even so, he was willing to embark on this epic journey. He needed to prepare, but how?

Abital sat by the stove listening to her son as he recounted what happened in Gilgal Rephaim. It was a magical place, he told her, a place where the ark of the covenant stood during the times that the Israelites crossed the Jordan River and conquered Canaan.

"The sound of the music still lingers in my ears," Shemaiah exclaimed. "It was so majestic! I wish you could hear it, Mother! The angelic voices blessed mighty God in a way that made me feel His power." Shemaiah fell quiet. His eyes became unfocused, as if looking into the beyond.

Abital waited respectfully until his voice came to him again.

"Father told me that the shofar is with him," Shemaiah continued. "I saw it as he held it in his hand. I heard its sound, deep and long. Father says that you, Mother, should worry no more."

Hearing this, Abital burst into tears. Shemaiah sat patiently as she poured out her grief. Nothing could bring Zakai back to her. Watching this sturdy woman cry, Shemaiah realized how fragile she had become. At that moment, he decided to stay home by her side, at least for some time, and allow her to recover.

But the task assigned by the angel nudged him within. It was something he had never experienced before. He tried to numb himself by engaging with his daily routines and caring for the flock. The search for Moses would have to wait. But during the nights, alone in his bed, a vague, free-floating anxiety prevented him from getting restful sleep.

Months went by. Shemaiah became irritable. His face darkened and his mood became somber.

"You don't feel well," Abital said out of concern, but Shemaiah didn't answer. He did not want to worry her by talking about his imminent departure. Even more, he was uncertain where to begin his journey, what direction he should take. How would he ever find Moses? The Prophet died more than a decade ago!

As the memories of a supernal encounter in Gilgal Rephaim lessened in strength, his mind filled with uncertainties. What if evil forces had been playing with his mind? What if what he was envisioning was simply figments of an overburdened imagination? What if the two sapphire stones never existed in the first place?

Shemaiah plunged into an even darker mood. *I should seek help and ask the high priest*, he thought. But then, *No!* He argued with himself. Not even the Urim and Tumim, those wondrous oracular stones that were cast by the high priest when seeking direction from God, would be able to help him decide what to do. Nothing, it seemed, could help him find a way out of the dark space where he was now submerged. Feeling estranged from everything, he said to himself in despair, *I'd rather be blind, mute, and deaf.*

Shemaiah stopped working at the Tabernacle, and he spoke to no one but Aqhat the laborer because he was a simple man who asked no questions. Shepherding the flock became Shemaiah's sole activity as well as his only involvement with the things of the world.

One day, as they sat under the protective shadow of a protruding boulder, Aqhat expressed his concern. He had seen Shemaiah languish, and he grieved for him. "Master," he said, "I don't know if I'm allowed to say this. You, a Levite, are consecrated to God and are more knowledgeable than I am. But I have watched how you have set yourself apart from people, how you have distanced yourself from life." Aqhat's voice trembled, "Please, I beg of you: talk to a dear woman that I know. I am sure that she will help you clear the way."

Thinking that he had nothing to lose, Shemaiah nodded.

The next day, in the early hours of the morning, Aqhat came to Shemaiah's house, leading two donkeys saddled for their journey. When Shemaiah's expression showed a measure of surprise at the two donkeys, Aqhat hurried to explain, "It will be a two-day journey, Master." But Shemaiah did not respond. His eyes immediately retreated to that remote place where he seemed to live these days.

Aqhat did not let Shemaiah's emotional distance discourage him. He knew firsthand the face of desperation and pain, for he, too, had experienced something of what Shemaiah was going through. This is why he knew that Shuah the seeress would be able to help.

And so, they journeyed together until at last they reached a beautiful area filled with lush vegetation. Shemaiah roused himself enough to ask, "Where are we?"

Aqhat explained that they were at an oasis, the location of which lay between Jericho and Heshbon. This oasis was also the dwelling place of an unusual man named Keret. "Keret is a Shasu," Aqhat explained, "and Shuah the seeress is his mother."

Shemaiah's face contracted. The Shasu were Midianites, wandering herdsmen known to be troublesome bandits.

"Don't worry," Aqhat said, "Keret is a friend, and he honors YHWH."

The two men dismounted and secured the donkeys. Aqhat led the way to a tent, and there they stood at the entrance, waiting for a signal from Keret. A big hairy man with a long, unruly beard approached. He wore a black tunic with long sleeves and a leather girdle tied around his waist, sure signs of seniority. With a sweeping gesture of one hand, he indicated that they should enter the tent. Aqhat put his hand on Shemaiah's back to nudge him forward, while Aqhat's feet remained planted, and Shemaiah understood that he was to go inside by himself.

Inside, he saw a woman seated at the far end of the tent. She was very old. Her face was so deeply creased with wrinkles, her eyes seemed lost underneath the flesh. She sat so still and silent, Shemaiah wondered if she was even alive. Keret, who had trailed him into the tent, now signaled that he should take a seat upon the floor at a prudent distance from the woman. Shemaiah lowered himself to the ground and sat with folded legs.

Following a long, sibilant exhalation, and looking at Shemaiah, Keret spoke. "My mother"—and then he paused, choosing his next words with care—"the gods would do well to keep her for many more years, she is so strong and clever. She never ceases to amaze me. A few days ago, she announced that a young man would come to our village, asking to see her. And now here you are." He then addressed his mother, saying, "Ama-Shuah, here stands the young man you predicted would come visit. We are both here by your side." He looked at Shemaiah and explained, "Shuah is blind. Neither does she hear well. But I can tell that she wants to feel your presence, so move a little closer."

Shemaiah scooted forward. With a crooked forefinger, Shuah let him know that she wished him to come even closer. Her head tilted upward and her nostrils flared. Shemaiah realized that she wished to inhale his scent.

A long, awkward silence followed.

In order to safeguard the propriety of the encounter, Keret remained seated between the two of them and, since Shuah's words were sometimes barely audible, he remained present to ensure that Shemaiah was able to hear what she had to say.

"I have been waiting for you," the seeress began. "Along with Zipporah, Moses' wife, who is here by my side, I have been waiting for you." Sensing his confusion, she giggled, then explained that she was the youngest of the seven daughters of Jethro and that Zipporah was her sister. She continued. "Zipporah has come to speak to you about Moses. It is her duty to prepare you. It is my duty to be her voice."

Shemaiah felt a dreadful fear rising up in his body. His mind became a mess of jumbled thoughts. He was in front of a madwoman who spoke words that came from nowhere. He should run away as fast as he could!

But as if she had read his mind, Shuah murmured, "Wait." Lowering her voice even more, she said something in an aside to Keret.

Keret then moved closer to Shemaiah and explained that ever since she was little, Shuah had had the gift of seeing behind the veils. She could enter into the realms of the underworld, where the disembodied spirits live. Some spirits were more developed than others and wanted to help their brethren. Even after their death, these spirits were capable of influencing the things of the world. "These spirits can enter and leave the underworld as they please, and can speak to the living ones. Shuah speaks to them and then delivers their messages to those whom the words must reach." Keret sat back and waited for his mother to continue.

Shuah told Shemaiah that Moses wished to be found because, having died during times of upheaval and transition, his teachings remained unfinished. His spirit had still more to say to people who would be receptive to his message. Speaking ceremoniously, as if giving a proclamation, Shuah declared, "Shemaiah, you must prepare yourself for the task of meeting Moses. You must strengthen your body and also train your mental and imaginative faculties. After these things have been done, you will meet with Moses and will receive valuable information."

Shemaiah was astounded. He had not shared with anyone the dream he dreamed in Gilgal Rephaim. How could this woman know that Gabriel and his father had visited him in that dream, and that he had been commissioned to find Moses?

Speaking slowly, Shuah continued. She recounted stories that Shemaiah did not know. "Jocheved and Amram, Moses' parents, separated when the pharaoh, Tuthmose I, decreed that all newborn Hebrew males should be cast into the Nile. They feared bringing a newborn son into such a world. But an echo from heaven told Amram that he should unite with Jocheved. The voice announced that the time of redemption, which was near, would arrive through the deeds of a son that would be born to them. The spirit of YHWH visited them, transforming their bed into a chariot suitable for hosting the divine presence.

"Jocheved realized from the moment he was born that their son was exceptional, and that their home was always filled with radiance and light. Moses had been born circumcised, which was a sign of his elevated spiritual stature. His physical being was also spiritually transparent, having reached the same elevated level of his soul.[1] All this made it particularly challenging for him to communicate with his kindred, as his words and emotions were so far advanced, they were not always in tune with theirs."

Shuah told Shemaiah that Moses' soul had been brought down from the highest realms by the angel Gabriel. The angelic realm was well acquainted with this mortal being, and contrary to their custom, they did not

---

1. Kaplan, *Meditation and the Bible*, 51.

attempt to interfere or foil his efforts but would always strive to help him complete his special mission in the world.

Shemaiah remained silent, very moved and humbled by the experience.

Then, out of nowhere, Shuah stated, "You received two sapphire stones."

Shemaiah was dumbfounded. *How could she know?* A strong feeling of deference grew in his heart.

"Keep those stones carefully guarded in your mind, between your eyebrows, centered in your mind's eye and in the subtle body that enfolds your soul."[2] As if for emphasis, she opened her blind eyes as wide as she could. "Hold fixed in your heart a desire to meet Moses. To learn from him. When the time arrives for you to meet him, you will hand over to him the sapphire stones." Shuah collapsed against the wall behind her, as if the effort of communicating had emptied her body of all its strength. However, after taking some deep breaths, she rallied. "Moses wants to be known by you. He is a supernal entity and has been waiting for a human interlocutor to help him deliver additional essential teachings to the human realm. He is waiting for you in the meeting place at the top of Mount Nebo. You will find him between the two eyes in the rock. Be scrupulous about finding the eyes in the rock. Pray with a loving heart and he will respond to your need. He will hear your clamor and accept your call." All of this had required an extraordinary effort, and now the seeress became as if mute and numb. Her eyes receded beneath her wrinkled skin.

Shemaiah understood that it was time to go. Aqhat, who had remained outside Shuah's tent waiting, rose to his feet when Shemaiah emerged. Quickly scanning his master's face, he saw that there had been a transformation. It seemed that Shemaiah had regained his life force and his youth. Purpose and determination shone in his face. Though many questions tumbled through Aqhat's mind, out of respect he remained silent and simply waited for Shemaiah to speak.

"I will soon be away on a long journey," Shemaiah said at last. "Come with me, my friend."

Aqhat felt touched. Shemaiah had called him a friend!

"Let us go promptly to Shiloh. There is much to be done," the master said.

Riding the donkeys, it took two days to get back to Shiloh.

---

2. "Somewhere there is a place where the two ends meet and become interlocked. And that is the *subtle body* where one cannot say whether it is matter, or what one calls 'psyche.'" Jung, *Nietzsche's Zarathustra*, 441; also see Purrington, "Carl Jung on the 'Subtle Body.'"

✳✳✳

Shemaiah spoke to his mother explaining in vague terms the purpose of the new journey he must prepare to make. He was not sure where the road would take him; in fact, he had not much to say because all of it was a mystery to him. All he knew was that it was something he was called to do. But Abital did not show any concern about her son's imminent departure nor to the unknowns of the journey that loomed ahead for him. Instead, she found happiness for the fresh vitality he now exuded. This life force had been gone from him for so long! She spoke reassuringly, "Do not worry. I will go to my brethren in the land of Benjamin, where I will wait for your return." Shemaiah agreed that this was a good plan. Wisely, he did not make any promises as to his return, for this was something he could not do.

As his mother helped him in the gathering of provisions, Aqhat suggested that he go back to Keret. "He is a shrewd shepherd," he pointed out. "He knows the ways of the desert and the dangers that lurk."

Shemaiah nodded thoughtfully. Aqhat was right. He should consult an expert. With this plan in mind, he finished packing. Then he asked Abital for her blessing, which she bestowed upon him lovingly.

And so, Shemaiah departed, carrying precious cargo that no one but he knew he possessed. He would guard and keep safe in the sacred space between his eyes and deep within his soul two magnificent and irreplaceable sapphires.

CHAPTER 8

Turmoil in the Royal Palace

Moses Flees Egypt—ca. 1486 BC

IN THE NINETEENTH YEAR of his birth, Kadmiel left the Temple of Khonsû and came to live in the Royal Palace. Soon, he was inducted into the scribal fraternity responsible for tending the Royal Library. Every time he entered into this vault, which held immemorial information and treasured books on astronomy, mathematics, and geometry, it caused the religious fervor he felt inside to deepen. Kadmiel had an inquisitive mind, and his curiosity about all these matters was insatiable. His eagerness to learn was the motivation that kept him burning the lamplight hour after hour in the library.

Scribes and priests used the walls of the Royal Library to diagram critical discussions and keep track of mathematical and astronomical theories as they worked their way through their thought processes. Kadmiel studied these scribblings with interest. He was fond of imagining what it would be like when someday he, too, would be involved in their ruminations and debates. The librarian, seeing the longing in his eyes, offered him support, allowing him access to age-old papyruses.

Kadmiel studied the succession of ancestral kings. He learned that King Userkaf and King Zahure were considered immortal due to the monuments they had built in Saqqara and Abusir. Papyruses chronicled in detail the engravings that had been discovered on the walls of some of their public buildings. One papyrus outlined how King Unis used magic spells to repel danger or evil forces that might lie in the watch. Reportedly, the king engaged in active dialogue with the guardians of the portals to the netherworld as well as with the ferryman who came and went freely into the world of the dead. He knew that this same ferryman would one day take his own soul as it traveled from this world to the next.

Perhaps most importantly, Kadmiel found in this library confirmation of everything Ahtope had taught him. This made him feel both happy and fulfilled. All wisdom seemed a testimony of the greatness of Egypt.

There were moments when Kadmiel missed his mentor keenly. He also came to realize that he wished he knew more about Auserra, his late father. He and his father had met only rarely since the day Auserra had left him in the temple. One memory began to appear in his mind over and over again. He was about seven years of age, already lying in his small bed, which was placed in the corner of a room that was adjacent to the main hall of the house. That particular night, he heard the voice of a man that sounded like the voice of his father. Auserra rarely visited their home. Tempted by curiosity, Kadmiel got up from his bed and scurried to the arch of the doorway, hiding behind the curtain drawn across the threshold of his sleeping room. Auserra and his mother spoke at length in low murmurs.

At a certain point in the conversation, Kadmiel heard his mother invoke the name of YHWH, the Hebrew God. She said, "I wish I knew more. You will have to talk to my brother Elizera." Kadmiel then heard a door opening. His mother exclaimed, "*Wait, don't leave!* Let me get your cloak. Be sure to cover up completely so no one can recognize who you are!"

This odd snippet of memory haunted him now and then. Each time it recurred, it seemed to hold a stronger grip on his imagination. Kadmiel searched avidly all through the library; maybe he would find registries of an encounter between his father or any other Egyptian, with Elizera or other Hebrew priests. Finally, he found some references to a mysterious, sole god in a hymn written by an unnamed scribe. The hymn read:

> *Mysterious of form, gleaming of appearance, the spectacular God with many shapes, whose image is not shown in writings. No one has seen him. . . .*
>
> *He is too mysterious for his majesty to be disclosed, he is too great that men should ask about him, too powerful that he might be known.*[1]

Kadmiel was astonished. Could this be a reference to YHWH, the God of the Israelites? Then, in a second scroll by another scribe, he read:

> *How diverse it is, what thou hast made!*
> *They all are hidden from the face of man.*
> *O single God, like whom there is no other!*
> *Thou didst create the world according to thy desire while thou wert alone. . . .*[2]

1. Pritchard, *Ancient Near Eastern Texts*, 368.
2. Pritchard, *Ancient Near Eastern Texts*, 370.

Yes, he thought. *These writings are different from any I have read before. They speak of a single powerful deity. The meetings between some lector priests and the Hebrew priests in Goshen must have happened. These writings, then, must be a consequence of the interchange between them.*

Kadmiel felt assured that at least two men he knew personally, Auserra and Elizera, had met, more than a decade ago. Trembling with excitement, Kadmiel wanted to know more. The Royal Library was a vault where many secrets of the past lay hidden. He was determined to keep searching. The strict cloister of the Temple of Khonsû, with its exacting rules and formidable routines, was left behind him. In the Royal Library he was able to explore freely and test new ideas.

One night as he lay on his bed in the ample room he shared with other scribes, Kadmiel revisited moments of his life in the temple. He saw images of younger priests complying obediently to the headmaster's instructions. Suddenly he remembered the day that the god Khonsû fell from his pedestal. Four priests were carrying the god back to his place inside the holy of holies when the massive god fell, broke an arm, and an earring jumped from his ear. It happened on the same day Kadmiel left the temple. He realized that he never knew what had happened next.

Kadmiel sat straight up in his bed. He looked around him. Whom should he ask? Whom *could* he ask? For some reason, he was desperate to know the outcome of that dramatic scene. Feeling distressed and confused, Kadmiel rushed toward the outer court. He would go to the temple to try and learn what had happened. It was dark, in the middle of the night, and though he had a destination in mind, Kadmiel wandered aimlessly, as if taken by madness. His mind was relentless, with many questions hunting him. Was everything in place? Had the statue of the god been put back together? Had the young priests been punished? He felt a rush of pity for them. It could have happened to him! Suddenly a voice in his head made him halt.

"Stop at once," the voice shouted. "You fool! Can't you see that the god broke because it is made of clay? That it was crafted by men?"

Kadmiel dropped to the ground. At first he felt lifeless, hollow, emptied. Then, the emptiness was replaced by bolts of panic surging through his entire body. A breach had opened inside of him. Something had cracked. Instinctively, he realized this fissure would be hard to heal. It took all the strength he could muster for Kadmiel to rise and get back to his bed. First his master had died, and now so did the certainties he once carried inside. He had lost his faith in the truth of what he had been taught. He had become a man without faith, a man with no beliefs, a man who belonged to no one and had no place to go. Indeed, would there be any place where he could feel safe?

Days went by. Kadmiel remained in his room, barely eating and talking to no one, not even his closest friends, Menna and Horemheb. He felt desperate. Lonely. But time passed, and Kadmiel regained some of the strength and balance he feared was gone forever. He found his strength in reason. *After all*, he consoled himself, *I am a man of reason.*

He had realized that by thinking and holding the correct thoughts in his mind he could shield his soundness. For this to happen he chose to remain aloof and emotionally uninvolved. Slowly, the ghastly event was buried into oblivion. Kadmiel resumed the scribal work at the library, or so it would be for a while. The gaping wound in his heart remained buried deep inside.

One day, after having spent long hours copying an ancient, challenging papyrus, Kadmiel left the library. He walked down the broad court of the palace with Menna and Horemheb, and as they strolled they were engaged in lively conversation. Without warning, he spotted a strong, impressive man who was standing behind a beautiful line of palm trees and grapevines. The man was dressed like a prince in a short white pleated kilt with a bronze belt wrapped around his waist. Over the man's wide shoulders lay a broad necklace made of pounded, gleaming bronze. He wore a white cloth headwear on his head. Kadmiel sized him up. He looked as if he might be an army general.

"Moses," he guessed, whispering the name to himself, and as if his friends had overheard what he said, they turned their eyes to follow his. Quietly they gathered closer to one another.

Menna and Horemheb were aware that Egypt had been blessed and made victorious in war because of the might of this Moses, who was Queen Hatshepsut's adopted son. Moses was considered a learned man, of power in both words and deeds, and was greatly admired. The two young scribes told Kadmiel something they heard happened: a war had recently broken out between the Egyptians and the Ethiopians. Though the Egyptians fought valiantly, the Ethiopians proved triumphant, and pressed onward in an effort to conquer Egypt. In desperation, the Egyptian generals queried their priests, who consulted their oracles. The answer given to them was that Moses should lead their army. Thus, Moses became commander in chief of the Egyptian military. It wasn't long before he led a surprise attack against the Ethiopians, leading the Egyptian troops into victory.

"Moses," whispered Menna with awe in his voice. "Rammed against the Ethiopian capital city, which was heavily guarded, and *he won*! The king's daughter, Princess Tharbis, immediately became enamored. Admiring Moses' valiant exploits, she offered to deliver the city into his hands if he would marry her in return. Moses agreed, and she fulfilled her promise."

Horemheb concluded the story, saying, "And Moses married her. He consummated their marriage, and she became pregnant and was joyful."

While still engaged in the story, Kadmiel noticed a group of Egyptian soldiers that were moving in their direction. Swiftly, he pulled his friends into hiding behind some boulders. They watched as a lieutenant commander greeted Moses with a ceremonial salute. Moses nodded his head and then was escorted into the throne pavilion, where he would meet Pharaoh Tuthmose III.

"I've heard that Tuthmose doesn't like Moses," Horemheb said, in a deep, solemn voice that foretold evil tidings. "Moses is the greatest general in the land of Egypt; he is great in the eyes of some higher-ranking officials and in the eyes of the people. Tuthmose should be wise and careful and give great honors to the son of the queen. He'd better make him his ally, or who knows what might happen."

As soon as the group of soldiers marched from the pavilion, the three young scribes also continued on their way to the scribes' quarters. They crossed the ramps through the colonnades of square pillars into the first terrace of the palace. Their work had been completed for the day. They realized that they had witnessed a moment of great impact, but of uncertain consequences.

A few days later, Menna came running into the scribes' quarters, breathless and agitated. He signaled to Kadmiel and Horemheb to follow him to a secluded corner near a large window from which they could see farmers plowing the fields.

"The most dreadful thing has just happened!" Menna exclaimed. He pointed toward the countryside and the words poured forth. "*Moses fled Egypt!* Yesterday, in the early hours of the morning, Moses was assaulted. He was taken by surprise while inspecting the Hebrew encampment in Goshen. Strong as he is, he repelled the attacker. No one knows who the attacker was, nor why he did it. All I heard is that an Egyptian watchman, an imperial guard, was found dead, half hidden under the sand, on the same ground where the assault took place. Moses has been charged with the death of the watchman. They say that Tuthmose is furious and wants Moses dead."

All of them knew that the palace was all too often a place of intrigues and conspiracies, and there were times that no one, from the king to the lowest of his servants, was spared. This was indeed a catastrophic development.

Kadmiel alone wondered about one particular element of the story. Why had Moses—the great commander in chief of the Egyptian army—shown any interest whatsoever in visiting the town of the Hebrew slaves? Then Kadmiel remembered that his own father, who was considered one of the great minds in all of Egypt, had entered into the city of Goshen more than once. There, he had met with the Hebrew priests, known as the Levites. Furthermore, whenever Auserra had gone to Goshen, he had done so in stealth. Recalling the night when he overheard his mother and father speaking of YHWH, Kadmiel began to suspect that Auserra went to Goshen to learn about the Hebrew God. He wondered if Moses traveled to Goshen to meet with the Hebrew priests for the same reason. Sadly, since Moses was gone from Egypt, he would never know.

Back in the palace, Kadmiel heard that Queen Hatshepsut was shattered by the news. The Queen had adopted Moses at birth; he was a rightful, righteous son whom she genuinely loved. In fact, Moses was her pride. He had brought much honor to Egypt. Hatshepsut had good reasons not to believe that the dead watchman was Moses' assailant. Neither did she agree with the rumor that Moses had murdered the man. There was a devious plot behind all this, and the queen ordered a thorough investigation.

Queen Hatshepsut and Pharaoh Tuthmose shared the kingdom of Egypt. Both of them coveted the power but agreed to share the duties of their reign and succeeded in complementing each other. Their joint-mandate was prosperous and lasted many years. Under their rule, Egypt became a mighty empire, feared and honored by its neighbors. It all went well until one day the tides seemed to turn against the queen.

With Moses' disappearance, it became clear that Queen Hatshepsut's life, as well as her kingdom, were in peril. Her informers unveiled that the danger resided within the palace. Kadmiel believed this to be true. Out of jealousy and distrust, given that Moses was a rightful contender to the throne, Tuthmose had first ordered a deadly assault on Moses, and then ordered the killing of a watchman to mask the intended murderous attack. The well-organized plot included spreading the word that it was Moses who killed the guard and cowardly fled Egypt. In the palace, the environment was unstable, as if ready to explode. Kadmiel had learned all this from his mother, a Hebrew handmaid who served the queen inside the palace.

Having this inside knowledge made Kadmiel feel segregated, alone, even in danger. He had no friendly ear in which to confide. He hoped that Menna and Horemheb would register all that was happening, and that this event would be recorded for posterity. But instead, a curtain of silence fell heavily over the scribal quarters. It was as if the thing had never happened. Nothing was mentioned nor discussed ever again. Moses had disappeared, no one knew where he was, and no one seemed to comment nor care, only his mother, the queen.

CHAPTER 9

Shemaiah's Journey Begins—1398 BC

THE SUN ROSE BEHIND the stony mountains. Shemaiah woke feeling rested, cheerful, and happy to once again be in Keret's village. Feeling his stomach growl with hunger, he stepped from his tent in search of food. The land was still veiled by a vaporous haze that lent a dreamy, soft appearance to the surroundings. The sky filled rapidly with colors, darkness giving way to hues of orange, yellow, and pink, creating a moving spectacle pleasant to the eyes. Not many places in this otherwise inhospitable region were as beautiful as this one. The oasis was rich with verdant vegetation. The air was filled with the cheerful soundtrack of a nearby brook that was fed by waters tumbling from high up the mountain.

A woman could be seen lighting a fire at the campsite, and Shemaiah's mood brightened even more. He knew this to be a sign of celebration announcing that a visitor had arrived at the settlement, and a meal of welcome and hospitality was being prepared. He knew that when the sun rose higher, the men of the tribe would sacrifice a lamb, and the women would roast a stew of meat and lentils to be shared by everyone after sundown.

Aqhat had great respect for Keret. He told Shemaiah that, being a Shasu, Keret knew every single crack in the desert. "He is an astute traveler who, crossing the southern desert, came from Midian a long time ago. He has been everywhere."

Even so, Shemaiah felt a sense of unease. He had been taught that God forbade the Israelites to interact with the Midianites. Aware of that, Aqhat got ahead in his response, retorting cleverly, "Something good may come to you, my master. He belongs to a house of great tradition in Midian: the house of Jethro. These are the people who helped guide Moses and the Israelites in their journey through the desert." Admiringly, he added, "Keret's eyes are sharp. He can notice a crab hiding under the sand or see a darting hare crossing the field at the blink of an eye."

Shemaiah allowed Aqhat to get him enthused. He felt excitement growing inside and smiled. He needed to feel daring in order to have the motivation to do what had to be done. It was good to stoke the fires of desire—to fan the flames of wanting to explore the world beyond the borders of his little town. He reminded himself that he was a seeker who was now ready to experience new events. His stomach grumbled, reminding him he had still not eaten, and Shemaiah shook himself from his reverie. He crossed a central courtyard that was surrounded by seven large tents made of goat's hair. These were the tents where Keret's family lived. He found Keret sitting at the entrance of one of them. Using a sharp dagger, he was peeling bark from wooden sticks. Shemaiah halted to survey the scene. Having been a guest in the village only recently, he hoped his host would have no qualms about welcoming him again.

Keret, a man of sturdy appearance, had been born and raised in the desert. His face, filled with wrinkles and creases, showed that he had lived many years, although not yet long enough to make him lose the strength in his arms. When Keret noticed that Shemaiah stood before him, his dark eyes sparkled in recognition.

"I don't get too many visits," he said, his voice husky, as if he hadn't spoken much that day yet. Then he gestured for Shemaiah to come closer. Shemaiah nodded and, with a little bow, approached, saying, "I thank you for your hospitality in this noble place."

Not knowing much about his visitor, Keret asked, "Where do you come from?"

"Shiloh."

"Ah!" Keret's eyes sparkled with recognition. "You are a Levite. We, the shepherds from Midian, keep good memories of mighty Moses, son of Amram, the son of Kohath, son of Levi. Speak up. Tell me what brings you here again." Wondering why a young man would wander alone in a place where bandits lurked and wild animals prowled, he added, "And why are you alone?"

"You heard what your mother, Shuah, said. I'm in the desert to find Moses. As I prepared to travel, Aqhat suggested that I seek your help. The desert is unknown territory for me. All I know is that the winds, the sun, and the moon might bring unpredictable changes, making it even more dangerous if one misjudges the clues." Shemaiah peered at the wrinkled face in front of him, trying to guess what the man was thinking.

Keret seemed amused by the candid remarks of the young visitor. Without warning, an intense bout of laughter erupted from his throat and belly. Keret laughed so hard that it made him cough and clutch his abdomen as if it was about to explode. He looked as if he had gone mad.

In shock, Shemaiah moved backward, in slow motion, until Keret shouted, "Stop! Don't go anywhere! If you were my son, I would keep you some more time under my watch. Yes, you are too young for such an endeavor . . . but I will help you." He picked up a stick and used it to strike a bronze bell. Two men who were working in the yard dropped what they were doing and hustled over to Keret. He instructed these men to escort the visitor to the tent where he was lodged, and to serve him bread and fruits, which were the customary food for the morning.

Looking at Shemaiah, he said, "Have some food. Later, we will sit and talk. How long do you plan to stay with us?"

Shemaiah wasn't sure how to answer this question. At this point he was so confused he just wanted to take his belongings and leave, but neither did he want to be rude. Having weighed the options and their consequences, he answered, "Maybe two or three days, if that pleases you and doesn't seem too long a stay in your eyes."

Keret nodded in agreement but said nothing more.

Back in the tent the two men offered him freshly baked bread in a basket filled with figs, dates, and green olives, and then they left. Shemaiah ate hungrily. The food satisfied him, and it also soothed his mind. He then thought to explore the surroundings while he waited for Keret's invitation to talk. A trickling brook was only a few steps away from his tent. As he approached the running waters, he felt the freshness of the air. A soft breeze blew in the spot where the water dropped. Kneeling on the damp ground, he scooped fresh water in his hands and drank with pleasure. Playfully, he bent forward and dunked his head down to his neck into the falling water. Shemaiah remained underwater for a while, then came up, gasping for air. He repeated the ritual a couple of times, as it felt amusing. He then sat on the bank of the brook with his feet submerged, feeling with all his senses the freshness of the cool waters. He lost all sense of urgency while sitting in this place. His mind cleared. There was nothing he should be doing, nowhere more important to go. Nothing could be more important than this moment of total delight.

A person approached. Shemaiah recognized that it was one of the men who had brought him the morning nourishment.

"Keret will meet with you," he said. "He is waiting."

Shemaiah looked with dismay at his garments, which were dripping wet. What would he do? He had brought with him nothing else to wear.

"This is all the clothing I have—"

The guide didn't allow him to continue. "Come with me. We'll take care of this."

He led Shemaiah back to the tent where he handed him a white linen robe. Hurriedly, Shemaiah undressed and donned the dry clothing. He tied his leather sandals around his ankles quickly, and in a matter of moments walked out of the tent and followed his guide.

Keret wasted no time in getting to the point. "Those who saw Moses before his last farewell said he parted ways with Joshua when the Israelites were about to enter into the land and conquered Jericho. Moses left, alone, in the direction of the rising sun, in the land of Reuben, and reached Mount Nebo. You will have to climb the mountain to find the exact spot that Shuah mentioned, the place where there are two eyes in the rock. Be attentive!"

Keret explained that the desert was both magnificent and also dangerous. He warned Shemaiah to remain always watchful, as robbers would try to steal his possessions. He said that Shemaiah would be threatened by predators and wild beasts, and by venomous creatures—snakes, scorpions, spiders, and lizards—all of this was inevitable. "Take this rod with you," he said, extending toward Shemaiah a long walking stick. "It is long enough to lean on and hard enough to deliver a strong blow if need be." Keret showed him a sack full of ashes, instructing, "Take these with you. A handful of ashes thrown into the face of an animal will leave him blinded, sneezing, and helpless." Giving him a pat on the shoulder, he added, "Ashes can be easily made by burning dry wood anywhere." He then reassured him, "You will enter the land of Reuben, a land of very hospitable people. They'll become even more so when they learn that you are a Levite."

And so, having received these instructions, Shemaiah set out from the village walking east. He would cross the Jordan River and enter into the land of Reuben. In this search for Moses, he would reverse the path that the Israelites had traveled eighteen years before, during their conquest of Canaan.

CHAPTER 10

Hatshepsut

The Queen Who Became Pharaoh. Plot Against Moses—1486 BC

QUEEN HATSHEPSUT WAS PROBABLY the purest royal figure alive in Egypt. A willful woman of impeccable regal lineage.

It was written in the walls of the temple at Karnak that she had been fathered by Amun-Ra, the god who created the heavens and the earth. It was also written that one day her father, cloaked under the guise of Tuthmose, entered as furtively as a soft breeze into the royal quarters of Ahmose, the royal queen. The queen was overtaken by the seductive, heavenly fragrance of the presence she believed was her king, and she woke as an irresistible desire for him swelled inside her. Amun-Ra placed the ankh, a symbol of life, to Ahmose's nose, and Hatshepsut was conceived. Khnum, the divine potter who formed the bodies of human children, was instructed to create the body and ka, the life force for the newborn.

Queen Ahmose named her daughter "Hatshepsut," who she believed was meant to be a distinguished woman. Indeed, Hatshepsut grew to be even more exceptional than her mother had hoped she could be. Eventually she became the most renowned woman in the history of the kingdom. Kadmiel was told that in her youth her looks were more beautiful than anyone and anything else in existence.

When she came into power, Hatshepsut ruled over Egypt during unusual times. No ruler before her had shared a double crown, as she did with her stepson Tuthmose III. Under their joint government Egypt became the greatest empire the world had ever known. The queen built and restored impressive monuments and temples, while Tuthmose excelled as a military leader, one of the great warrior kings of Egypt. Even so, neither Hatshepsut nor Tuthmose trusted one another.

It was written that King Tuthmose expressed his complaints to a confidant, saying, "What I relate is no invention: she is astonishing in the sight of men, and an enigma for the hearts of the gods who know it all. But she does not realize it—that no one is for her except herself."[1]

Tuthmose, a man of superior intelligence and military shrewdness, had managed to subdue all the surrounding lands. Triumphant and glorious, he craved all the praise and veneration for himself. He wanted to be remembered as the greatest pharaoh that ever lived, and he believed that only Hatshepsut stood in the way. This was the backstory behind the plot against Moses.

One night, Menna and Horemheb rushed into the scribal quarters and hastily began packing their belongings. Kadmiel looked at them uncomprehendingly. "Are you going somewhere?" The two did not answer him. It seemed that they were determined to avoid any conversation. Kadmiel wondered if they had been sworn to secrecy.

But Menna turned to Kadmiel just before he left the room and said, cryptically, "We have been given a special assignment and will be away for a few days."

Kadmiel was perturbed. This was certainly odd, and Menna had failed to explain what they were about. Chuckling nervously, he grabbed Menna's arm. "But you can tell me, Menna! I'm your friend! You know I can keep a secret."

Menna unhooked his arm abruptly. He and Horemheb left in a rush.

Three days passed. On the night of the third day, Kadmiel's friends reappeared. They looked tired, so tired, in fact, they seemed much older, as if they had aged years rather than days.

"We need to sleep," Menna muttered on his way to his bed. In his eyes Kadmiel read a plea for silence.

Kadmiel honored their need for rest, and sat quietly on his own bed. Perhaps they would tell him what this was all about tomorrow.

It would be two more days before Kadmiel could speak with his friends, but at last they gathered together on the outskirts of the palace, where they sat on the ground beneath a tree in a place where they were in the clear, with nothing in the surroundings that could serve as a hiding place for a spy. The faces of his two dear friends were twisted in sorrow and anguish.

Menna began brusquely. "Difficult times are to come, my friend."

Horemheb nodded in agreement.

1. Luban, *Exodus Chronicles*, 119.

"The headmaster of the library instructed us to find every scroll and document belonging to the queen and destroy them."

Kadmiel was stunned.

"It is a malicious plan to erase her name and deeds from the memory of the people," Horemheb added.

Kadmiel understood their sorrow. They had been forced to perform actions that caused them to suffer an ethical struggle of epic proportions. He could not help but share in the anguish they had suffered. What they had been ordered to do went against all that they held dear. As scribes, they had been trained to record the truth of their history, thereby perpetuating Egypt's greatness for all of posterity. Their purpose was never to distort or destroy but to respect and record with truthfulness and accuracy.

Horemheb was flushed with anxiety. "Let us pray to the god Tutu," he said, "that fierce and hideous monster. Let us ask him to protect our dreams and scare our enemies. Let us keep fresh in our memories all that we have learned these days. Let us commit to always remember the story of our queen so we may rerecord it someday when this nightmare is over."

And so, these three men who were so young and so passionate about their profession prayed and made a pact. They had nothing but admiration for Moses and now they were overcome with compassion and pity for his mother, their queen. No wonder then that they pledged to be keepers of the memories of Queen Hatshepsut.

Menna and Horemheb knew well the story of Hatshepsut. They told Kadmiel that she carried the eloquent title of "king's daughter" because she had been born to a king and his queen. This was an uncommon rank to find among royals. It was perhaps not surprising then that she grew to be a forceful woman who was herself quite proud of this royal lineage. The ambitious princess had understood from a very young age that, in a world ruled by men, her path to power must be carefully designed and flawlessly executed. This included marriage at the age of twelve, when, according to tradition, it was determined that she would marry her stepbrother Tuthmose II. Hatshepsut conformed to the plan.

"The purpose of the marriage was clear in her mind," observed Horemheb. "It would legitimize Tuthmose's ruling of Egypt, as he was the son of a lesser wife. More importantly, the marriage would bring her closer to the crown of Egypt, which was hers legitimately."

Hatshepsut soon would find the means to take control of the throne. Again, in the royal tradition, following Tuthmose II's early demise, the crown of Egypt was handed down to his oldest son and the son of a minor wife, Tuthmose III, who was at this time merely an infant. Hatshepsut, being both his stepmother as well as his aunt, became coregent and governed for him. The queen knew it would take many years before Tuthmose III came of age and became a monarch in his own right. Thus, Hatshepsut surrounded herself with powerful officials, successful military men, and purpose-driven civilians, all of whom supported her visions for Egypt.

And so, both Egypt and the queen thrived. Despite her success and prosperity, she never relinquished a certain fear of oblivion. Following Moses' disappearance, Hatshepsut fell prey to a mysterious illness that no medicine man or magician could cure. Mysterious bruises appeared all over her skin. The bruises covered her face and body, and she lost both her vitality as well as her beauty. Daily, she spent hours immersed in a bath in which calming herbs and milk had been poured by maidservants, but nothing completely soothed the itching and the burning.

One day the magicians entered her suite and announced that the queen had been cursed. "It is the decree of the Seven Hathors," the magicians proclaimed. Hatshepsut saw truth in their words, and all her courage seemed to drain right out of her. The Hathors, who were celestial goddesses that ruled over the length of a person's life, had taken Neferure at a very early age and now Moses was also gone. Obviously, they had come to claim Hatshepsut too.

Hatshepsut was severely ill and felt so powerless she could not even grieve. For the first time in her life, she gave up. Twenty years from her coronation, two years from the day that Moses had vanished into the desert, and fifty-two years to the day after her birth, the queen—confined to her bed and eaten up by the wounds on her body and the scars in her soul—breathed her last.

Tuthmose III continued to rule over Egypt. Throughout his forty-year reign, he decreed and oversaw the desecration of all monuments and references to Queen Hatshepsut. He destroyed statues and paintings that had been created in her image. What he hoped for was that she would be forgotten and her spirit so lost it would be unable to find its way back to Egypt, which was precisely what the queen had feared most. Meanwhile, no one challenged the throne since everyone assumed that Moses was also dead. Thus did the cunning Tuthmose rewrite the history of Egypt and pave the way for his son, Amenhotep II, to rule over Egypt, which he did for twenty-six years.

CHAPTER 11

On the Path to Finding Moses

A Fateful Encounter—ca. 1398 BC

SHEMAIAH WALKED UNCEASINGLY FOR three long days. As the night fell on the third day, he arrived at an arid plain, where several palm trees encircled a well of water. The place was tidy and organized as if it was a spot where people were accustomed to gathering.

"It must belong to someone," he said to himself.

Grateful for having found water, he took a moment to offer thanks to YHWH. After replenishing his canteen, he sprinkled water over his head and body, and felt refreshed. He liked to reminisce about his meeting with Shuah; it filled him with a lively zeal for the journey. He was reassured by her words because they confirmed the dream he had in Gilgal Rephaim. These words erased any doubt that Gabriel had entrusted him with a sacred mission, a task of utmost importance. At nineteen years of age, Shemaiah was aware that he would need help in the road taken, even though he had no way of knowing exactly what difficulties he would face along the way. But on this night as he lay down under the broad leaves of a palm tree and stretched his woolen blanket over him, it was Shuah's voice that he heard ringing in his ears. She was giving him an enigmatic warning, telling him, *"Be prepared!"*

Shemaiah had learned early in his life the special indications that Moses gifted to the Levites. These were rituals that had to be practiced daily and with the utmost care after the age of twenty-five years. The routine included cleansing the body with water as well as the shaving of all hair and washing of every garment he wore.[1] However, a strong desire to please YHWH was

---

1. See Numbers 8:5–7.

nested in his heart, and he had decided to start at an earlier age. Shuah's admonition may have implied this ritualistic cleansing. "Be prepared!" she had told him. And yet Shemaiah suspected that her words referred to more than just these bodily preparations. But what exactly had she meant? He fell asleep pondering this question and, as happened quite frequently, a dream came to him.

In the dream, he was bathing in the River Nahaliel. As he approached the bank, wanting to exit the waters, he saw the shadow of a man in dark clothes. With a strong hold, the man gripped him on the shoulder. His hand was as strong as iron, and it held him so tightly he was unable to move. Shemaiah could not emerge from the water; in fact, he was unable to move in any direction. In total panic, Shemaiah opened his eyes, looked all around him at his surroundings, and saw that there was nothing to fear. There were only palm trees and a life-saving well of water.

Then he realized that fear was an unwanted guest, just as that iron-strong hand had been. It could grip so tightly that it rendered him frozen, petrified, unmoving. He realized that in the past he often had felt trapped and inadequate, and he recognized that he had been fearing this mission for some time. He was worried that he would not be able to find Moses. He was fearful that he would not be able to deliver the message entrusted to him by the angel. He was terrified!

Impulsively, Shemaiah leaped to his feet, gathered his things, and started walking in the direction from where he had come. He had decided to go back home. He had not walked too far when he heard the noise of sheep bleating. It reminded him of his fondness for animals and how much he missed the quiet days shepherding his father's flock. He stood silently and waited for the animals to appear.

Soon enough he saw the herd advancing in his direction, moving briskly but orderly. A young lad and two girls guided the animals. Using only long wooden staffs, they kept the herd together. They didn't seem to have noticed him, so Shemaiah approached. He hadn't spoken to anyone in days, and he was hungry. He was thinking that they might allow him a drink of fresh warm milk.

The young people continued in what seemed a familiar path toward the water well. Shemaiah rushed to offer help. Then, he believed, they would be willing to share some of the precious milk with him. Shemaiah approached the young man first, the proper thing to do, and after disclosing his name, added, "May peace be upon you." He shared that he was from Shiloh and was from the tribe of Levi.

The young boy greeted him in return, saying his name was Joash. He was the son, and the girls two of the daughters, of Ohad, son of Elizur, son of

Shedeur, the head of the tribe of Reuben. This well belonged to their family. The two girls watched with interest from a distance.

Joash called to them. "Dinah, Moriyah. Come." He added nervously, "We have to water the animals before the sun rises high in the sky. It will soon be too hot to pull a pitcher with water. Hurry!" he yelled for emphasis.

The girls ran to their brother. Together they hauled water and then poured it into a stone trough placed on the ground next to the well so that the flock could drink.

Shemaiah was surprised to see that the gutter was built for that purpose. These people were not wanderers, nor were they apprentices. *They must be settlers in that land, for it is obvious that they are well informed*, he thought.

While the animals drank, Shemaiah learned from Joash that the tribe of Reuben had sizable herds that required abundant grazing land. The tribe had settled in the land of Gilead and the surrounding area. In this arid place, the grass stretched unevenly and at some distance from the other. "But this is a piece of land where we don't have to fight with our neighbors," Joash said.

Suddenly, one of the girls began to scream. She pointed at a bush, behind which a poisonous snake crouched in a coil. Moving quickly, Shemaiah hoisted the large rock on which he had been sitting and thrust it with all his might upon the bush. He stayed alert watching for any movement from the snake, but there was none. He approached the scrub with caution. Finding the snake dead, he used his knife to separate the head from the body.

Trying to show composure they didn't feel, the two girls moved toward the men, afraid of being alone. Dinah, the oldest sister, thanked Shemaiah with the customary modesty a woman should show when in the presence of a stranger, averting her face to avoid eye contact. She said, "My father Ohad is indebted to you greatly for what you have done. Would you accept an invitation to meet with him?"

Shemaiah accepted, offering his further help in gathering the flock as they led the way to the city of Kiryatayim.

✳✳✳

The sun reached its zenith as they approached the town on the hill. Along their way Shemaiah had seen men plowing the field behind a pair of oxen linked together by a wooden yoke. The animals pulled the wooden plow, leaving a groove on the soil. They were preparing the clay soil for planting seeds of wheat and barley. It all seemed peaceful and enlivening, giving

Shemaiah a feeling of warmth and welcome. He could see that the area was quieter and more peaceful than Shiloh. Having always been drawn to the tranquility of pastoral life in the fields, Shemaiah felt strangely at home.

As they approached the house of their father, they saw Ohad and a helper cleaning the structure as well as a storage room for weaponry at one side. The people of Israel were always surrounded by seemingly countless mighty enemies armed with metal weapons. Their chariots forged from iron made them almost invincible. The Israelites, on the other hand, were poorly equipped and their weaponry was scarce. They had no army; when at war, the men were expected to supply their own armaments, including shovels, wooden forks, oxgoads, and sharpened jawbones. Joash explained that even in peaceful times, when there were no disagreements or armed clashes between the tribes, his father kept a watchful eye on the village's weaponry. Memories of the conquest of Canaan were still fresh, as it had been a difficult time fraught with fatalities. Ohad himself had lost two dear brothers. As head of the village, Ohad kept stores of several types of weapons: swords, daggers and spears, slings that hurled stones, and a bow or two used to propel arrows. He cleaned them often and made sure that they were in working condition. Joash added, "My father believes that the Almighty is our strongest weapon. And so it was, during the battle in the waters of Merom, when Joshua led the people to victory, under YHWH's design."[2]

Shemaiah looked around and was pleased at the sight of the busy, purposeful villagers. Right next to Ohad, he noticed men cleaning the stables, scooping out the straw bedding where the animals had been stabled for the night, and then spreading their stalls with fresh bedding. As the group got closer to their father's house, Joash called out to his father. Ohad turned and, seeing his children, smiled. Shemaiah could see that here was a strong mid-sized man whose skin had been darkened by years spent working beneath the sun. His most striking feature, however, was his eyes, which were dark, inquisitive, and knowing.

Shemaiah felt the power of Ohad's scrutinizing gaze, but Joash was quick to make a proper introduction and ease the moment of tension. Ohad was not expecting a visitor, and so the appearance of a stranger felt more like the approach of an intruder. He was taken aback by the enthusiasm with which his son presented him and was perturbed by the thinly veiled fascination he read in the faces of his daughters.

However, after hearing that Shemaiah had killed a serpent to protect his daughter, all of his guardedness dissipated, and he thanked him in earnest. He welcomed Shemaiah into his home, going so far as to instruct Joash

2. Joshua 11.

to share his room with the newcomer. That night, Ohad told his wife about what Shemaiah had done to save their daughter, adding thoughtfully that of course now he understood why the girl looked at Shemaiah the way she did. As if boding the future, Ohad stated with sarcasm, resignation, and worry, "No doubt we now have a long-term dweller in town; one who has come to stay."

**

And so it was not at all surprising that during the next two months a betrothal was made and a wedding ceremony planned. Shemaiah and Dinah, Ohad's oldest daughter, were to be married.

It was important to Shemaiah that his mother would attend the ceremony, so the wedding was arranged according to her arrival. Ohad sent three messengers as escorts to keep her safe while she traveled from Shiloh to the land of Gilead. When Abital arrived, she embraced her son, sat at the table of his in-laws-to-be, and enjoyed a savory meal prepared by Dinah's mother. Abital was warmly welcomed by the townspeople, and was happy to be sharing such joyful moments with Shemaiah.

On the day of the wedding, as was customary, Shemaiah came to Ohad's house to claim his bride. He was flanked on either side by Joash and a neighbor friend, whose duty it was to ensure that there was no physical contact between bride and groom.

Dinah was a beautiful sight. She wore a white flowing dress, and a wreath of flowers crowned her head. A white veil covered her face. The procession walked toward the groom's house with much parade fanfare. Along the way well-wishing neighbors who had lined up to admire the bride sang and played little drums and tambourines.

Shemaiah's house had undergone elaborate preparations for the ceremony. There, under a floral canopy, the groom pulled the corner of the white mantle he was wearing to cover Dinah's head. This was a sign for everyone to see that they had chosen each other. After this ritual, the groom and bride left for a private chamber, where they were to know each other. Meanwhile, a feast had been prepared, music was playing, and all were joyful.

Dinah was a graceful girl who had turned fifteen in the winter. Abital, always attentive to her son's legacy as a Levite, was happy to know that all was well and that, according to tradition, Shemaiah had married a maiden. Ten months later, a baby girl was born. The couple named her "Zehava" because she was beautiful and precious as gold.

Shemaiah decided that his family would live in Kiryataim, a city in the land of Gilead, not too far away from Shiloh. Although Shiloh was vital because it housed the Tabernacle, it was a well-known fact that its surroundings were problematic. Bordered by several Canaanite cities, Shiloh's inhabitants were always under the influence of nefarious religious practices as well as frequent military campaigns, all of which put pressure on the inhabitants of the region. Shemaiah preferred the pastoral life of the highlands at the east side of the Jordan River, where he could shepherd the flock. There he would find time for everything: time to tend the animals, time to muse when he walked in contemplation, and time to practice his writing.[3]

With a wife and a child to care for, the mission that the angel Gabriel had given him faded into the background, at least for the time being. Slowly he came to appreciate a new understanding of his place and purpose in life.

Shemaiah was a good listener, someone people liked to talk with. People sought his counsel when they had important decisions to make; despite his youth, he seemed to know how to help them arrive at the best choice. At twenty-two years of age, he carried the wisdom of a much older man.

He felt close to nature and to all living creatures and could read the signs in the sky and know if the rain would come or if a severe drought would hit the land. When he would perceive that the heat of the sun would ignite a fire, he warned the villagers to prepare for the hazard. Shemaiah could also sense when an animal was sick and took care of the illness before it became a threat to the flock. Even more important, he developed an acute awareness of sharing the space he lived in with an Invisible Being, a presence that was always beside him. He trusted the guidance of this invisible companion and felt protected by it.

Dinah gave birth to a second child, a son they named "Aviel," to praise God, the Father of all living things. As the years went by, a sense of serene accomplishment grew inside of Shemaiah, making him feel fulfilled, thankful, and at peace.

3. See Ecclesiastes 3:1–8.

CHAPTER 12

Kadmiel Moves to Goshen

Moses Returns to Egypt—ca. 1445 BC

FOLLOWING HATSHEPSUT'S DEATH, THE atmosphere in the palace became increasingly dark and unpredictable. As with a swarm of vipers, stings could come from any corner at any time. Kadmiel was disturbed by what he saw and by the wild uncertainties that roamed in his mind. He watched Menna and Horemheb languish in despair after having carried out their orders to destroy each scroll and document that contained the name of Hatshepsut. The two friends told Kadmiel of more frightful maneuvers they had witnessed in the royal court. The queen was treasured by the people of Egypt and had earned the respect of many in the palace. Even so, under the immense pressure put on them, more than one officer surrendered their loyalty to the queen. The king's emissaries attempted to eradicate Hatshepsut's story by removing her image from all of Egypt's temples and monuments. It was a systematic campaign to erase her legacy. Menna and Horemheb would never overcome the guilt and the anger they felt; it would haunt them for the rest of their lives. Horemheb committed suicide by hanging. After Horemheb's death, Menna made a vow of silence and retired to a temple in the desert, where he would live out the rest of his days as an ascetic.

Feeling both disgusted and unsafe, Kadmiel disengaged from the work he had once loved. His profession was to seek truthfulness, and he needed truth and credibility to heal his broken spirit. He decided to leave the palace.

He remembered that his father had made a stealth journey to Goshen, a fertile piece of land where the cattle grazed happily, for the purpose of learning what the Hebrew priests had to say about YHWH. Kadmiel decided to follow in Auserra's footsteps. He would go to Goshen, a town that lay on the east side of the Nile. It was the place where the Israelites had been dwelling for two hundred years, ever since the times of Joseph the grand vizier.

When Kadmiel arrived, the Hebrew elders welcomed him with pride and satisfaction. After all, he was a high-ranking lector priest. As a son of a Levite woman, he was given a place to live amongst the people of Levi. It was not long before a group of learned men assembled around him not just to teach him but also to learn the teachings he could offer.

Kadmiel heard stories about the life of the Hebrew ancestors Abraham, Isaac, and Jacob, and of their encounters with YHWH, a complex God that was hard to please. Kadmiel, an Egyptian scribe, found his home in Goshen. He married Hedvah and they begat two sons, Hanan and Eglon. And time passed.

***

It was the beginning of the Shemu season. The spring breezes blew softly, pleasingly, as if heralding good tidings. It was time to harvest the crops. In the fields farmers, laborers, and slaves began work before sunrise and did not quit until the sun was setting. The taskmaster on guard made sure that no one dawdled, as it was essential that the harvest was secured. At the end of the season, the salaried workers and farmers received a wage, the same amount of grain a worker reaped in one day. Slaves and prisoners received the amount of food and shelter that their rulers considered reasonable, and were paid according to their performance. Some women laborers followed the men, gathering bundles of grain into baskets. The local poor, mostly women and children, followed in their wake, scavenging whatever grain had fallen to the ground. Some begged the harvesters for alms. Such was the food chain. The work ethic demanded that in the name of the gracious god Geb, lord of the fruitful earth, nothing—not even a single grain—could be lost. Even the cleaned stalks were left for livestock to feed on.

It was during the early regnal years of Pharaoh Amenhotep II that a series of events unfolded. An old man with a long white beard came into the land of Goshen. He was tall and slender. People could tell he was from a foreign land by the sandals he wore. They were made of leather, unlike the woven sandals made of papyrus favored by wealthy Egyptians. Also, unlike many Egyptians who wore a white skirt wrapped around their midriff, the newcomer wore a simple robe of natural color gathered at the waist with a cord. His head was covered with a light brown piece of cloth. He said that he had come to find Aaron, the son of Amram and Jochebed. He also said his name was Moses.

Hearing this, curious bystanders gathered together. Just that name—*Moses*—stirred neglected bits of narrative buried so deep they felt more mythical than true memories. These memories were of a time when a prince named Moses vanished from Egypt. No one knew with certainty what happened then; what they did know was that the Moses who stood before them had a purity and a simplicity that was far from what they had come to associate with a royal background. Nothing about him hinted at the riches of a life lived inside the walls of the palace. Nothing indicated that he was the lost son of a queen.

Kadmiel was among the group of bystanders. In fact, he had lived in the palace. He had witnessed what had happened inside the royal quarters. And he remembered Moses. He knew that the man standing before them was the long-lost prince. Here, indeed, was the baby whom the great Queen Hatshepsut had adopted as her own son.

Moses crossed the courtyard holding a long wooden shepherd's staff in his hand. He strode energetically toward a small group of men who had gathered in the central square of the town and inquired whether they might know Aaron, the son of Amram the Levite. Kadmiel stepped forward and motioned that Moses should follow, and he led him to Aaron's hut.

Aaron, Moses' oldest brother, came to the door in all haste. His heart rejoiced to know that Moses had finally returned to be with his family. His sister Miriam also hurried to greet him. The three held meetings behind closed doors. Before the night fell, Moses had conveyed to Aaron all that YHWH had instructed him to say. "YHWH has seen the suffering of his people and will take them to freedom," he said. "God will instruct me on the steps to take and you, Aaron, will be my speaker." Aaron thus became an essential partner with Moses in the formation of God's people.

Moses asked to meet with the elders of Israel. They came to Aaron's hut, Kadmiel among them.

"YHWH has sent me unto you," Moses said. "'Ehye Asher Ehye'[1] is his name forever."

"God has remembered you and has seen your affliction in Egypt."

Abruptly he cast his rod to the ground, just as YHWH had instructed him to do, and when he did the rod became a serpent. The elders sprang to their feet in horror. Some who were terrified left the room. But Moses called them back. He calmed them down, saying, "Do not worry, YHWH is with us."

Putting forth his hand, he took the serpent by the tail and it turned into a rod again. But the elders were unable to accept as true what they had

---

1. See Exodus 3:14, "*I Will Be that what I Will Be.*"

seen. They voiced their disbelief, accusing Moses of performing a magic trick like the many they had seen performed by Pharaoh's magicians.

God had forewarned him this would happen, so Moses put his hand into his bosom, and as he took it out, it had become white as snow, covered with leprosy. The elders hid again behind the doors in horror, but yet again did Moses call them back. He reached his hand back into his bosom, and the elders witnessed that the hand spontaneously was healed.

All of this happened as YHWH had foretold.

Now the elders believed in him and offered to arrange a meeting with Pharaoh.

The sun had set behind the mountains, signaling that the day of work was over. The time had come to speak to the people. Grasping the staff of God in his hand and with Aaron and the Hebrew elders at his side, Moses walked resolutely into the center of the courtyard. The men surveyed the courtyard as a small crowd of men, women, and young people gathered. The word had spread around and everyone heard that Moses had returned to Egypt. Although tired from their long day in the fields, they were curious to hear what this self-proclaimed liberator had to say.

Raising the staff up high, Moses commanded silence and the crowd hushed. He announced to the Israelites what God had told him to say. "God says that He remembers you. He knows the hardships you have endured in Egypt." Moses gazed at the people's faces and saw in them bewilderment. "I was sent to lead you out of Egypt."

A sepulchral silence followed.

Then a man in the back of the crowd challenged him, shouting out with defiance, "Who are you? Who do you say sent you? And why should we listen? Why should we risk more punishment?"

Murmurs arose from the crowd as the people shifted their feet and glanced anxiously at one another. Some started to move away. Not everyone knew about Moses. But they knew Aaron, and he was well respected in the community. And they recognized the elders, their guides and teachers, who stood beside Moses.

At this point Aaron stepped in. "This is Moses," he said, "my long-lost brother. We thought he had died in the desert." He nodded in recognition of the fear he saw in the faces of his kinfolk, thereby acknowledging that he understood. Nevertheless, he continued. "Moses has come to free us, as YHWH our God has ordered him to do. He will guide us into the land that was bequeathed to our forefathers. I trust his words."

Kadmiel stood at the edge of the courtyard and watched as the people slowly dispersed. They had heard enough. Their hearts were filled with disbelief. Countless years lived in suffering had left them exhausted, unable to trust, and without hope. They were too tired to listen to what seemed senseless. Too tired to waste the brief amount of time allotted to them to rest and recover. They were simply too tired.

It was true: the task God had entrusted to Moses was arduous, perhaps even impossible. Moses understood the signs: the Israelites were discouraged. Dejected. It would be difficult to earn their trust and win their approval. Moses would have to find another way to reach the hearts of the people.

The next day, Kadmiel convened the elders of Goshen to a meeting. He brought before them some pieces of evidence that he hoped would strengthen their confidence in Moses as a leader. He told them he realized that Moses' origins were uncertain, buried as they were in a past that seemed so distant. It seemed that a shadow of distrust loomed over him and over his actions. He could see in their expressions that he was connecting with them, so he forged on.

"I have in my hands a precious papyrus I once smuggled from the Royal Library. It is the record of adoption of a child named Moses."

A murmur of astonishment filled the room. Kadmiel read from the scroll. A Hebrew child named Hever had been adopted by the king's daughter, who chose to name him "Moses," as he had no father from which to derive a name. The scroll confirmed the story Kadmiel's mother, Orpah, had told him. Hatshepsut, a young and resolute princess, had adopted a child that was found floating inside a basket in the river.

The scroll stated,

> Year three, the third month of Shemu, day twenty, under the Majesty of the King of Upper and Lower Egypt, Tuthmose I, life, prosperity, health!
>
> On this day of the great proclamation to Amun-Ra, Lord of the Thrones of the Two Lands, the shining forth of His divine presence in Karnak—
>
> I, Hatshepsut, King's Daughter of Tuthmose I, say:
>
> "I make Moses, the child drawn from the waters of the Nile, a son of mine. I grant to him all that I possess—lands, herds, servants, gold, and offerings made to Amun—having no son or daughter apart from him.
>
> "Should it come to pass that I bear a son or a daughter, all that I possess shall be divided into equal shares between them at the time of my crossing to the Western Horizon."
>
> Written by the Scribe of the House of Life, in the presence of witnesses numerous and true:
>
> —The Steward of Amun, Djehuty.

—*The Chief Nurse of the Palace, Sitre-In.*

—*The Overseer of Royal Granaries, Nebnefer.*

—*The Chief of the King's Women, Ahmose-Meritamon.*

—*The Divine Father of Amun, Hapuseneb.*

This papyrus is sealed under the authority of the Great Seal of the Temple of Amun-Ra, and placed within the archives of Karnak, that Amun himself may bear witness to its truth for eternity.[2]

Looking up from the parchment, Kadmiel continued telling the story. The child had been left in the river in the hope that a charitable soul would welcome him. Jochebed, the child's mother, was later allowed to take the newborn to her hut and nurse him. When Moses was three years old, Jochebed brought him back into the palace. It had been recorded so it would be known for all posterity that the child had been willingly given to the queen by his biological mother. Hatshepsut would later give birth to a daughter, Neferure, whom she laboriously prepared to be her successor. But Neferure died young, leaving Moses as the heir apparent. Years later, he disappeared following an attempt on his life. No one saw him again until the day he appeared in Goshen.

Eliphaz, the oldest amongst the elders, rose to speak. He said that Moses was born the seventh of Adar of the year 2368, counted from the time of the creation of the world. "It was the harvesting season," he said, "and a rare grouping of stars made an appearance in the sky."

Kadmiel, having learned about the movement of the stars in heaven, nodded in confirmation. "A person born under such a rare constellation was endowed with wondrous powers that made him holy to the gods," he said. "And so it was with Moses. As a child, Moses was greatly blessed. His life was spared at the moment of birth from a sure death, drowned by royal decree into the waters of the Nile. The papyrus I found in the library confirms that he is a princely man of Hebrew origins." Kadmiel looked at the elders with excitement. "I anticipate that extraordinary deeds will continue to happen."

✳✳✳

Meanwhile, Moses didn't seem at all perturbed by the resistance he had encountered. Instead, he decided to make another use of his time. He told his

---

2. Adapted from the Papyrus Ashmolean Museum (commonly known as the "Adoption Papyrus"). The original document records a legal act of adoption and property transfer, dated to the reign of Tuthmose I, and preserved in the Ashmolean Museum, Oxford. For scholarly analyses, see Eyre, "Adoption Papyrus in Social Context"; Cruz-Uribe, "New Look at the Adoption Papyrus."

brother, "You and your sons—Nadab, Abihu, Eleazar, and Ithamar—are to stay with me for many days and nights, during which I will teach you the way to God."

The men prepared food and supplies for a retreat away from Goshen. Aaron led them to a small cabin hidden under a dense mantle of trees and shrubs on the east bank of the river. The next morning, they entered the waters to wash their bodies from head to toe.

"You are to do this every day before going into prayer," said Moses, "for when you come to God, you must be clean of all defilement." Moses spoke of the importance of binding oneself to God through prayer.

Aaron nodded in support.

"Our father, Abraham, got up in the early morning hours and hastened to return to the place where he stood before God.[3] And so should we." They stood in silence, stirred anew by the recollection of the profound wisdom their patriarch had modeled.

Moses instructed them that they should pray during the early hours of the morning and also at night when it was dark and no noises or interruptions would disturb their concentration. Moses taught them how they could do this. How they could discipline their minds to keep distracting thoughts at bay. How they could remain centered and focused in the silence within.

Moses then spoke about the immense power hidden in God's sacred name. He explained, "God created the universe with only one purpose: that of showing His greatness." He pointed toward the fresh stream of water that ran underneath, and to the beautiful plants that benefited from it. "God wants to be recognized in every single form that exists. His magnificent presence fills the world. Even more, God wants to be called by each and every one of His various names, each one an expression of His inclusive wholeness and greatness."

Moses taught the men that every time a sacred name of God was uttered, the world was set in order, such was the limitless power hidden within His names. Moses closed his eyes. He spoke the name that God had shown him, "YHWH," in a voice deep and resonant. Opening his eyes, he invited them to do the same. Then he instructed them on the power of holding and repeating God's name, entwining the letters of the two names that God chose to show him at the burning bush. He explained that one name expressed God's existence hidden up high, while the second expressed His presence in the world. He chanted, "YaHdWnHi," and the men sang with him, repeating the name just loud enough for their ears to hear it once, after which they remained silent, holding the sacred letters in their minds. No

---

3. See Genesis 19:27.

other thought was permitted. Finally breaking the silence, Moses said, "You shall do this every day. As long as God keeps you alive in the world, you shall do this. The sacred names will bond your minds to God. If you elevate your minds with thoughts of Him, you will hear His voice."

From that time on, Aaron and his sons did as they had been taught. They washed their bodies in the early hours of the day and assembled with the Prophet, stilling their minds in contemplation of the holy name. There were many roadblocks to overcome. They realized that thoughts were unruly; if left to roam freely, thoughts would distract them from their spiritual undertaking and keep them attached to earthly concerns. But Moses counseled, "Practice with discipline and you will prevail. Overall remember this: be discreet with what you learn. This practice is only yours, for no one else has been appointed to partake from it. In other words, God chooses whom He wishes to call. You have been chosen to become the soldiers of mighty YHWH. Do your duty and do not lay down your weapon, which is the sword of the divine name."

As the days passed, Moses counseled them on how they were to live in the world. "Make use of no substance so strong that it may cloud your mind, so strong that it may weaken your judgment, or so strong that it may confuse your actions. This would only bring pain and suffering. A healthy body constitutes an efficient instrument for the spirit that abides in it, so you must treat your body with the respect it is due. You may not in any way weaken your health nor shorten your life. The number of years you live is for God alone to decide. Lead a life that is simple, straightforward, and pure. Set a noble example to others. YHWH appointed you to be His soldiers, and I will stand by you as your guide."

Moses, his brother, and his nephews left the cabin of retreat and returned to Goshen. Moses then took it upon himself to teach the descendants of Levi—twenty-two thousand men in total. He prepared them to be teachers and judges of the people. They became his army, and he led them as he had led the army of Egypt in days of old. Aaron and his sons fell second in command, after Moses. They were to guide the Israelites through their journeys, both corporeal and spiritual.

Kadmiel was the most avid of all his students. He learned and registered in detail all that Moses taught as well as what happened during those times so that everything would be recorded for posterity.

CHAPTER 13

Shemaiah's Inner Struggle with YHWH—1390 BC

IT WAS THE MIDDLE of spring, the most fragrant time of the year. Wildflowers of red, yellow, and blue cropped up everywhere, and a green carpet of wheat covered the terraced hills and floors of the valleys. On one particular day, the village stirred early, at the first signs of dawn. Shemaiah left the house swiftly and went outside to release the livestock from the stables. He ate some morsels of bread and a few olives slowly, much in the way he liked to do things. Then he headed to the courtyard, where the women's work was done. Here, the daily bread and the midday meals were prepared, with some women rolling the dough into balls, others flattening the balls with large stones, and still others baking the flatbread on a griddle that had been heated over an open fire. Shemaiah collected what he needed for the day he would spend in the pastures: dried figs, parched wheat, bread, and a canteen of water, and then he left for the fields.

At some distance afar, he spotted his wife Dinah and their daughter Zehava moving slowly toward the compound. Dinah and a friend were carrying the deep earthen bowls used to transport freshly milked milk. Little Zehava walked briskly beside them, skipping gaily, as children do, from here to there. The women stopped under a cluster of acacia trees and poured the fresh milk into goatskin churns that hung suspended from the branches. Zehava began to wag the churns, pushing them back and forth, to make the milk thicken and curdle. Shemaiah would have liked to stand there and admire the choreographed dance of their work but it was time for him to be on his way. He turned around and continued toward the patio, passing by several young people who were laboriously preparing tools for the plowing of the land.

A pair of oxen were already joined with a yoke. Men threw the wooden plow over the back of one of them, and then headed toward a field in the west. Nobody stood by idly. Even the children did their part, taking care of the newly born spring lambs, calves, and goats. These young animals were learning how to graze, and the children took them to a safe place not too far from the village where they could also get supervision from the elders.

Shemaiah instructed his son Aviel on the ways of the shepherd. He would say to him with affection, "Heed my words, and you will become a master. The work of a shepherd is important and demands attention. It should not be dealt with carelessly because the flock depend on us totally." Aviel was only six years old but even so he was attentive, for he liked the way his father spoke to him as if he were an equal. "We provide the flock with food and protection," his father said. "If we fail them, they could die." These were words Aviel would take to heart.

Shemaiah counseled his son repeatedly that the matters might seem easy but required a willful commitment from the shepherd. The flock was innocent, vulnerable, and reliant upon their master. Frequently an animal would put itself in danger, as happened the day a lamb lost her way and fell from a cliff. This occurred in the blink of an eye, demanding promptness and all the physical strength the shepherd could muster. Shemaiah descended downhill at the place where the lamb fell, skillfully dodging the loose rocks that slipped under his feet. He lifted the frantic animal and, carrying her in his arms, returned her to the flock.

Aviel had watched intently as the drama unfolded. Shemaiah concluded the memorable event by taking Aviel's hand and laying it over the lamb's heart so that the child could feel it pounding within its little chest.

"Pay close attention," Shemaiah said to his son. "Then tell me what you feel."

A few minutes later, Aviel cried out in surprise, "Father, father! The heartbeat is slowing down!"

Shemaiah, knowing of the healing effects of a caring touch, smiled. Now he could rest assured that Aviel knew it, too. Reassuringly he said, "She is fine, and now we are too."

Aviel learned much from his father. He learned how to care for the animals and also how to explore the surroundings in search of fresh pasture. Indeed, the shepherd's commitment to the care of his animals was all-consuming. They sometimes put their own lives in danger, as when they had to protect the sheep from lions, leopards, and other wild animals. The shepherds carried a wooden staff for support, but they also had to learn to skillfully manage a club and a sling for protection. Securing a good supply of food and water was a life-and-death concern for them. In the arid terrains of Gilead, this was important. As the years went by, Aviel learned how to differentiate the animals by their wants and needs, as if they were children. In turn, the animals recognized their master and responded to his voice. In becoming a devoted shepherd, Aviel was becoming a partner with the animals under his care.

***

And so, for a few blissful years and in stark contrast to the initial turbulent years of the conquest of the land of Canaan, life in the countryside was uneventful and quiet. Daily routines were carried out without much difficulty. Shemaiah's father-in-law was a respected man and, as head of the Reubenites, people trusted his guidance and came to him to solve their disputes. Shemaiah was also recognized and trusted by his kinfolks. By nature, he was kind and nurturing. He was a natural storyteller, and people enjoyed listening to him. As a Levite who had been trained in the ways of service to YHWH, he knew the answers to many thorny questions.

One day, Ohad approached Shemaiah as he was locking the flock inside the barn. "It has been my long-held dream to build a sanctuary to YHWH in Kiryataim. This is our treasured home in the land of Reuben," he said. Ohad fell silent, his eyes lost in the distance or, perhaps, lost in a dream. "And I want to ensure God's protection for my people, for my family. Most of all, I want to serve mighty YHWH, with no delay." There was some apprehension in Ohad's voice. "But I need to know: you are a Levite. Would you serve in our sanctuary?"

The question took Shemaiah completely by surprise. A hidden hand was playing around with Shemaiah's life, changing the course of his destiny. It had happened before and now, it seemed, it was happening again.

Shemaiah sat on the ground, next to a tree, and took a moment to set his mind in order. As a shepherd, he was totally disengaged from the rituals that constituted the life of a Levite. True, he had left the city of Shiloh prepared to fulfill the mission that the angel Gabriel had assigned to him. He had left behind his widowed mother, who had to survive on her own resources. Then, he allowed his life to take a new turn when he married Dinah and fathered children. Holding his face between his hands, he pondered his obligations. "I have been born a Levite," he reminded himself. Slowly, clear judgment was taking hold of his emotions, his priorities set in order. His mind then became still, and, with a newfound sense of direction, he approached Ohad and agreed to his request. Shemaiah knew that he was a teacher at heart, and that nothing would please him more than this opportunity to serve his people.

Ohad gave Shemaiah the power to do whatever he wanted. Shemaiah chose a small hill as the site for the shrine because then it could be seen from every corner of the city. With the help of some men, he constructed a house of high walls. Stone pillars marked it as a special place. Inside, he built a raised platform on which was placed an altar made of stones. Six steps led up to the platform. The altar was designed as a unique space where the divine and human worlds could interact. It would be the place where ritually slaughtered, sacrificial favors would be offered up to YHWH. This would be done so that the people of Reuben had opportunities to establish, maintain, and restore their relationship with God. Right in front of the main altar, Shemaiah built a small four-horned altar that was dedicated to the burning of grain offerings. Nearby were placed two small vessels for the burning of the most fragrant of incense, aromas to satisfy YHWH.

The sanctuary was almost ready. Even so, Shemaiah was worried. His heart felt heavy with old concerns, more so now that there was a conflicting decision to make. Sitting on the floor, he leaned against a wall, recalling some difficult moments in the life of his people. The Israelites had never totally abandoned the practice of placing teraphim or other household gods in their sanctuaries and places of worship. He always felt conflicted with the Asherah in his mother's house and with the fact that the Israelites worshiped idols despite YHWH's demands and admonitions. YHWH, with a vindictive rage, would hit them with plagues. This wrathful God brought harsh punishments up to the third and fourth generations. Shemaiah feared that with the decision he now was to make—whether to place teraphim and the Asherah in the sanctuary or not—would bring God's punishment upon himself, upon his family, or to anyone standing in proximity to the idols.

The temptation to follow idolatrous ways had been present in the life of the people since early patriarchal times, and the Levites, the priestly class, were forced to deal with this. A few years ago, Shemaiah overheard a heated discussion among the priests in Shiloh. It was late in the afternoon, just before sundown. He and a group of young men were in a room with Eli, an older Levite, who was teaching them prepare the ketoret,[1] a unique blend of herbs and balms as instructed by God to Moses. Twice a day, this blend was to be burned on the altar in front of the ark of the covenant. It was a most sacred duty. Eli's voice suddenly became barely audible while the tone of a discussion in the adjacent room got louder. Shemaiah could hear some sharp, angry voices, some in favor of and others against the worshiping

---

1. See Exodus 30:34–38.

of idols. Shemaiah's heart pounded in fear, expecting that YHWH's anger would be ignited in no time. But it didn't happen and the discussion went on for a long time.

One man argued that Asherah, a protectress of the fields who brought bounty to the earth, should be shown respect. She was in fact YHWH's consort. A fist hit the door, and a voice yelled out, "No one, I say no one, can expel the Asherah from our shrines."

There was a long silence. Then Shemaiah heard the piercing voice of a man who argued solidly that there also was the gruesome issue of Nehushtan, the bronze serpent Moses had built according to YHWH's instruction. "I was only a child," the man said, recalling the scene, "but I remember that day in the Sinai Desert when tension was mounting. I remember people speaking harshly against God and against Moses."

Another voice jumped in, saying, "I remember people complaining, 'Why have you brought us up out of Egypt to die in the wilderness? There is no water, and we abhor this miserable food.' And YHWH sent fiery serpents that bit the people for committing the sin of evil tongue. Many died, and when the Israelites repented, God stopped the plague.[2] But then God Himself ordered Moses to build a serpent of bronze and put it up high on a pole, and whenever a snake bit a person, he would gaze upon the copper snake and remain alive."[3]

"Yes," said the man with the angry voice. "In some mysterious way, all who saw the bronze serpent were healed. It was he, Moses, who built this bronze serpent. He built an idol that is still revered to this day. An idol to whom the Israelites burn fragrant ketoret as if it were a God."

"After all," another man reasoned in a loud voice, "Moses and Aaron never passed a definite judgment on this matter. Now they are dead and can say no more."

Shemaiah remembered feeling torn, as much then as he felt now, by this abhorrent contradiction. It was an incongruence that was hard to comprehend, even more so because it had been orchestrated by God. True to his quiet nature, he avoided getting involved in what were fruitless arguments, but his mind would take no rest.

Shemaiah kept his judgments on these matters to himself. But truth be told, he thought that the idolatrous practices among the Israelites were YHWH's making. They were YHWH's fault. God's mandates were incongruent and conflicting. They went against the principles He had given Moses in Sinai. But why so? Shemaiah did not have an answer to this question. He

---

2. See Numbers 21:7.
3. See Numbers 21:8.

only knew that YHWH was a complex and contradictory entity. An entity that sometimes acted in deceitful, devious ways that confused the people. When led astray, how would the people know which way to follow? And why would they deserve punishment? However, Shemaiah's essential question was this: should he place the common household idols in the sanctuary? The question burned his insides; he wished Moses could answer that question.

Shemaiah remained sitting in the same spot for a very long time, his head hidden between his legs until his back hurt. At last he stood resolutely, as if he had arrived at a decision. Picking up the figures, he decided to place them in the shrine against a wall in the back. These idols were created by the hands of men, so they had the power that men had given them. In the shrine he just built, they would be present. Even so, they would not share the same prominent position as YHWH, the powerful God who led them out of Egypt and fulfilled His promise to bring them into Canaan. One day, Shemaiah assured himself, he would find Moses and ask all his unanswered questions. Shuah, the seeress, told him he should prepare for the encounter. He was determined to do so.

With resolve, Shemaiah placed the teraphim and the Asherah behind the altars, in a place where they could barely be seen. He then anointed the place with the oils Moses had instructed were to be used. He anointed the two altars, one for the burning of incense and another for the burning of offerings. He sprinkled oil on the altars and utensils seven times so that they were properly consecrated. Afterward, slowly and purposefully, Shemaiah consecrated himself. He washed his body and poured some anointing oil on his head, then clothed himself with a white tunic, signifying that he was prepared to serve YHWH as a priest. To complete the ritual, he chose a ram from the animals in the outside yard. It was one of the animals that he loved very much. Placing his hands over the animal's head, he spoke lovingly into his ear, requesting his permission to be slaughtered.

"Dear one," he said, "in your innocence, you give yourself to me, and my heart cries with pain. Atone for us, and may our hearts be renewed. May your soul be blessed in turn in its path to greatness."

Shemaiah made the ram lie on his side and drew a long, sharp knife, in an uninterrupted motion to severe the major structures at the neck. He watched the eyes of the animal drop and knew it had lost consciousness, becoming insensible to pain.[4] He then smeared the tip of his right ear, the thumb of his right hand, and the big toe with the blood of the animal. He sprinkled the remaining blood around the altar. He then allowed the blood

4. See Deuteronomy 12:21, 23–24. Also Chabad.org, "What Is Shechita?"

to run like water into the ground. All this was done according to YHWH's commandment. Then he burned the ketoret of fragrant spices: myrrh and cinnamon, cane, cassia, and olive oil.

Willingly, Shemaiah had set himself apart to the service of a perplexing and incomprehensible God. He did so not without a measure of fear. He was no longer a solitary shepherd but a man who had surrendered himself in service to YHWH.

✳✳✳

The sanctuary was ready. Ohad invited the people of the town, without any distinction, to come and praise YHWH. Shemaiah, looking imposing in his white garb, recounted stories from the past—tales of an unfathomable God who revealed Himself to the Israelites as they stood at the foothills of Mount Sinai. Shemaiah described as vividly as he could these moments of intense commotion and fright. Moments when the people saw God as a vigorous power that could not be approached directly lest they would die. Shemaiah spoke about Moses, an unusual man, who knew how to reach God and talk to Him face-to-face. Shemaiah said, "God promised us in Sinai that we were to become a kingdom of priests. A holy nation."[5] Shemaiah then added that God wanted to be obeyed and His covenant kept. "An Israelite that recognizes he has transgressed may come to the Tabernacle and make an offering to show he has repented. He may ask for forgiveness."

But Shemaiah's heart was contrite and filled with unrest. He knew that the path to God was not clear. He loathed coming before God with burnt offerings, with countless rams and rivers of olive oil. He believed that God should be exalted instead, with acts of justice, with love and acts of mercy. The day would come, he believed, when people would not fear God nor fear punishment, but would long to have a direct, personal relationship with the Creator.[6] He liked to believe this would be possible.

On the day of the inauguration, Shemaiah felt calmer, inwardly reassured that the path he had chosen—despite all his vacillation—was the right one. For the time being, he had chosen to serve the good rather than whatever was contentious or divisive. A time would come when many of his questions would find an answer.

5. See Exodus 19:6.
6. See Micah 6:6–8.

CHAPTER 14

The Ten Plagues of Egypt—ca. 1445 BC

AMENHOTEP II, KING OF Egypt, had turned eighteen years of age when he rose to power. He was a finely developed young man. On the sixth year of his reign, Moses returned to Egypt. Kadmiel wrote of these last days of servitude in Egypt: "It came to pass that the Israelites left Egypt in a massive exodus. But their exit was preceded by a series of dreadful events caused by Pharaoh Amenhotep's daring confrontation with the all-powerful Hebrew God. God's wrath fell on the people of Egypt and their land."

One day, an unidentified old man entered walking confidently into the Royal Palace. His brother walked beside him. It was Moses, who had come to face Pharaoh Amenhotep. He was determined to fulfill YHWH's command to lead the Israelites into the desert so that they could worship their one and only God.

Some of the people who stood in the throne room were old enough to recognize Moses. There he was, Moses, the long-gone prince, the son Queen Hatshepsut had mourned to her dying day—alive! Moses, the victorious general of the Egyptian army—alive!

Aaron stood before Pharaoh. Speaking with solemnity appropriate to the moment, he said, "So said YHWH, God of Israel, 'Send out my people, and let them sacrifice to me in the desert.'"

Pharaoh Amenhotep was astounded. At first he remained quiet. Then he roared, "Who is YHWH that I should heed His voice and let the Israelites out? I do not know YHWH, neither will I let Israel out."[1] Enraged, he ordered the taskmasters, "You shall not give straw and stubble to the Israelites. Let them gather stubble for themselves." He then proclaimed, "Let the labor fall heavy upon their shoulders and let them work at it. They should not

---

1. See Exodus 5:2.

waste our time talking about false matters."[2] And the taskmasters did as the Pharaoh had instructed. The Israelites watched their work and their levies increase even more.

Kadmiel the scribe recorded the subsequent punishments that YHWH rained down on Pharaoh as a consequence of his arrogance. "A horrible and frightful competition blew up between these non-worldly forces, hitting the land and its people," he wrote. "All the most potent godly dominions, from above and from below, challenged each other, initiating a massive fight between veiled forces; everything beyond our human understanding. YHWH turned Moses into a godlike man whose eyes flashed with fire and whose voice boomed forth, deep and thunderous, strong and intense, so that his words reached into every corner of the world. Moses was given superior power, such that he was able to influence natural events. He became the most powerful man in the world. Moses challenged the priests and magicians of Egypt, rendering them unable to placate nature, unable to placate YHWH, the greatest of all gods. Ten terrible plagues fell on the land of Egypt and its people. The days suddenly grew longer, extending to insufferable limits an endless whirlwind of events which allowed for unimaginable damage and destruction.

"The more Pharaoh resisted and opposed YHWH, the worse it became. A harsh dryness fell upon the earth, the waters, and the sky. A climate typically benevolent turned beastly hot. The swift-flowing Nile River became slow and muddy. Finally, what Egypt feared most happened: the two great goddesses of Egypt were punished. Nekhbet and Wadjet, proud cobras of the crown of Egypt, protectresses of the country and of the pharaohs, were slain and cut to pieces by the relentless might of sharp swords. YHWH then punished Nehebkau, the two-headed serpent with numerous arms and coils who guarded the entrance to the underworld. YHWH pierced each and every otherworldly guardian in the Upper and Lower Kingdoms of Egypt. So much blood was spilled, the mouth of the Nile River flooded and the waters were turned to deep red." As it happened, Kadmiel witnessed it all. "On that day, mothers that fed their children and every single person in Egypt woke to find there was no water to drink. The waters were filled with blood.

"Nothing escaped punishment. Every living body, every plant, and every tree suffered. An invasion of frogs, lice, and flies lasted many months.[3] Boils and pustulant ulcers lacerated the skin of people and animals. Hail and locusts lashed throughout the land. The plagues, guided by an invisible and unerring hand, rained down on them. Even Amun-Ra, the great god

2. See Exodus 5:7–9.
3. See Exodus 7 to Exodus 11.

of the sun, was brought to his knees. The world sank into the darkest darkness that had ever been experienced. The blackness filled every cranny and crevasse throughout the land. YHWH had displayed His immense power over nature, over the heavens and the earth.

"Pharaoh Amenhotep remained stubbornly wreathed in his pride and arrogance. He would not let the Israelites go," Kadmiel wrote. "But then suddenly, out of the immense darkness that enclosed the land, a bolt of lightning shone. A bright light no eye could behold splintered the clouds in the sky." Kadmiel could feel his heart beating strongly against his chest as he described the scene. "And through this crack came in a stampede a throng of big black elephants that crossed the sky as if they were clouds. They created a deafening, rumbling sound. Then, a dark and enormous winged being appeared from behind them. It was Samael, the Angel of Death, whom YHWH sent to every Egyptian house to kill each firstborn child."

And so it was that every firstborn in Egypt perished. The firstborn of the pharaoh sitting on his throne, the firstborn of the maidservants working behind the mills, and the firstborn of the cattle in the fields. Pharaoh Amenhotep watched his firstborn son, Webensenu, die in the arms of his mother. Only the Israelites were spared this terrible punishment. A sacrificial lamb was slaughtered and its blood was smeared on the doorposts and lintels of their homes. This served as a sign for the Angel of Death to bypass their houses.

A great outcry such as had never been heard before arose throughout Egypt.[4] Amenemhat, high priest of Amun, kept his head lowered and his thoughts to himself. Having been versed on the profound secrets and ancestral knowledge stored in the temples, of course he knew the reason for these deaths. A long time ago, Pharaoh Tuthmose I had ordered the killing of all newborn Hebrew males. The high priest knew that hidden behind the veil in the timeless eternity where the gods dwell it was necessary that Ma'at, the goddess of truth and justice, acquiesce to YHWH. And Ma'at did render her verdict according to His will: the death of all firstborn children at the hands of the Angel of Death was an impartial, dispassionate consequence, merely compensation for the killing of the Hebrew male children that had been perpetrated in the past. The cycle of an overpowering natural law—the law of cause and effect—had been displayed to its full force. At last the balance of forces, the natural ebb and flow of life, was restored. Kadmiel concluded with his voice thinned in a whisper: "YHWH prevailed over the gods of Egypt." And as he spoke, a dense, crushing sorrow washed over his entire being.

4. See Exodus 11; Exodus 12.

CHAPTER 15

Shemaiah

Opening of the Spiritual Channels—1390 BC

MANY YEARS PASSED SINCE the day Shemaiah arrived in Kiryatayim. They were years of self-discovery and maturation. Shemaiah became a father and grew in understanding and tolerance of the cycles of life. After building the sanctuary, he became even more introspective. He enjoyed long walks into the desert fields, always by himself; this helped to calm his restless mind. He kept in touch with nature, and this nourished his soul; it became a source for fortuitous but magnificent discoveries.

One day he walked to a small brook. The air was fresh, the water clean, and the pastures on either side were plush and soft. He stood motionless for some time, observing the cattle grazing peacefully. Shemaiah, having a high sensitivity toward animals, didn't want to disturb their tranquility. He knew that while pasturing the animals could be frightened by any shadowy presence in their proximities. He simply desired to partake of the serenity of their environment. Moving softly, he sat by the water, took off his sandals, and enjoyed its coolness bathing his feet. As he watched the flow of the brook, the sound of gurgling water and smell of fresh grass immersed him in a dreamy mood. He pulled a thick leaf from a nearby plant and placed it in his mouth, playfully chewing on it.

Much to his surprise, his tongue started to feel numb. Soon he realized that he could not sense the bitter taste of the leaf. He took a closer look at the plant. He had seen it before. He recognized its yellow flowers and triangular, fleshy leaves with serrated edges. The plant seemed to have the power to numb sensations in his mouth. *It must be the substance inside the leaves of the plant*, he thought. It was a transparent, sticky fluid, much thicker than water.

Feeling a rush of excitement, Shemaiah washed two round stones and pressed more plant leaves between them. The sticky fluid oozed out, and he continued pressing gently until it became thinner and smoother. He then scratched the side of his left leg with his knife. A small amount of blood sprang from the wound. Taking some of the leaf substance onto the knife, Shemaiah placed it over the small wound, eager to see what would happen. Then he waited, sitting on the ground as he snacked on bread and green olives. After a brief interval, the wound stopped bleeding and the redness surrounding it faded. It seemed that the sticky extract had the ability to speed healing. Shemaiah packed up some of the leaves. He wanted to continue watching the effect of the ointment on the wounds of animals. He reasoned that the balm could probably be kept fresh for many days if covered by a sheet of clean goatskin.

In time, he used this miraculous ointment to heal scratches and abrasions on his two young children. He realized that the balm could numb different kinds of pain: it would numb an aching tooth or heal a bump in the body. It could also be swallowed to bring relief to a swelling stomach. Soon the word was spread, and people would speak in awe of the healing Balm of Gilead.

Shemaiah became revered as a wise man. People believed that his life was inspired by God. And Shemaiah would make himself available for every question brought to him by his community, and answered to the best of his abilities. Even so, his heart ached. He was keenly aware of his incompleteness, his imperfection, and his frailty. The balm he had discovered could numb physical pain but did not heal spiritual or emotional hurts. It could not make people whole.

Shemaiah longed to know more. He wanted to learn what could bring true and everlasting healing to humankind. He believed that the knowledge he wished to achieve was hidden somewhere in the world. Instinctively, he sensed that this was the kind of knowing only a man like Moses had achieved. But Moses seemed to exist no more.

Every day he thought of the great Prophet. He wondered about the strong incongruities in a man who had put his life at the service of God but then also chose to act in ways that displeased Him, thus God took him away before he was able to complete his mission.

He had heard a story retold hundreds of times about why Moses was punished in this way. It was a consequence of Moses ignoring God's command at Meribah. God had instructed Moses to strike with one blow a rock at Meribah so that water would pour forth and satisfy the thirst of the people. But Moses struck the rock twice; even worse, when the water poured out he did not praise God for the miraculous event, leading the Israelites to

credit Moses for the miracle. Since no man should make himself look as if
he had the powers of God, Moses was punished harshly by being prevented
from entering into the promised land.[1] Because of this, Shemaiah was always careful to praise YHWH, ever fearful of His wrath, knowing that, even
so, there was never a guarantee of being safe.

✳✳✳

Over time, Shemaiah developed more skills as a healer and as a spiritual
leader. He would spend time pondering the nature of God as a massive force
that could be threatening in its presence and full of contradictions. And
what about the human condition? Humans were frail. They needed guidance
and seemed to lack insight. People were contending with a mysterious force
that, even though He brought abundance to their lives, ruled the world with
forceful commands and a weighty hand. These difficult questions wouldn't
let Shemaiah rest. God seemed confusing, enigmatic, and contradictory.
And then there were his questions about Moses. Moses disappeared one
day; everyone believed he died but the angel Gabriel said no, he said Moses
was waiting . . .

Shemaiah stayed busy as a strategy for quieting the inquisitorial chatter in his mind, and remained locked within himself. He wondered: maybe
the time had come to complete his task. Perhaps it was indeed time to find
Moses and deliver to him the two stones that were missing from the ark.
Maybe it was time for him to pose his questions and get some answers.

As if on cue, Shemaiah heard the echo of Shuah's voice telling him to
"*Be prepared!*"

Yes. It was time to get prepared.

He was once again ready to leave behind a comfortable life and go
forth into the desert wasteland. At last, he felt ready to seek answers to the
questions that haunted his mind. This was the next phase in his calling.

Shemaiah started to spend longer periods of time alone. He left his
home to sleep in the shade of the trees or in caves throughout the countryside, craving the company of silence. When he lay on a blanket in some
unknown place, he would focus his gaze into the vast vault of the skies, as if
he might see what lay behind the clouds. His mind found relief in contemplation, and his thoughts followed his soul as it raised up toward infinity.

Shemaiah rested in the awareness of a void that existed but which
would never come into earthly life. It was an expanse, another dimension
that existed beyond all that he knew about the world. It was a space of

---

1. See Numbers 20:9–12.

calmness, a sanctuary within as much as a sanctuary without. Shemaiah allowed himself to repose in the calmness of the sanctuary within. Little by little, day by day, he felt that the more he rested in this inner sanctuary, the more he was transformed. He imagined this as a state of being where man and God, finite and infinite, were joined as one. A state where they were not separated.

Sometimes, to his inner sight, the sanctuary within resembled the Tabernacle Moses had built. The place where YHWH was said to dwell amidst humanity. Shemaiah had a far-reaching idea: he believed the Tabernacle was also in his heart. No one but the high priests had ever seen the Tabernacle. Nevertheless, Shemaiah had seen it while in contemplation, projected on the screen of his mind. In time, Shemaiah could also view with his mind's eye the innermost chambers of the Tabernacle. It appeared as a structure built with the noblest wood of acacia, its walls covered in gold. He wondered: would the actual Tabernacle resemble these visions?

Enthralled by the majesty of the Tabernacle he perceived in his mind's eye, Shemaiah continued in his contemplation. The Holy Ark of his inner Tabernacle was splendorous. It was coated in gold, both within and without. Two Cherubim were seated above the lid of the ark, with their wings spread upwards and facing each other.[2] The indescribable beauty of it all rendered him speechless. Could this be true? His own mind doubted what he had seen, in total disbelief. Still, he chose to remain alert, attentive, and aware, all in loving contemplation of the vision that was being offered up to him.

Shemaiah came to realize that in the sanctuary within his heart he was never alone. There, existing outside the boundaries of time, lived an Invisible Being. Could it be the same all-encompassing, stirring Presence he had felt at the births of his children?

Shemaiah practiced entering into this living space by becoming natural and transparent. By letting his mind flow like water. When he was in there, every question had its reply. The answers, precious and precise, came to him with absolute accuracy. He had been told from birth that God dwelled everywhere, in every corner, every crevice, every crease of the world. He asked himself, *This Invisible Being—is this God?* The answer came to him immediately as an inner knowing. *Yes. This is God. And He can be reached in this inner sanctuary with the inner vision of the heart.* Shemaiah understood then that God is experienceable as an emotion. He learned that God stands real and identifiable within this unique, silent, personal place of perception.

2. See Exodus 25:20.

Being a scribe, he devoted time to record on white parchments made of calfskin every word he "heard" in his head. Sometimes the words appeared in beautiful colors, and he described even this in minute detail.

One night as he lay alone beneath the stars, without warning his mind became calm, natural, transparent, and his heart felt at peace. A significant presence started to outline itself on the screen of his mind. It was a figure he had seen before. He watched and saw a long white robe shining with a golden glow. Then, a pair of soft brown eyes looked at him with loving resolve.

"I'm Gabriel," the presence said.

Yes, Shemaiah knew who he was.

"The time has come for you to fulfill your mission. Place the girdle around your loins, the sandals on your feet. Take your staff and the rod in hand and prepare to go to a place I will show you. There, you will find Moses."

The angel's appearance was to remind him of a mission that once filled his heart with excitement and dread. Now, ten years later, the angel was telling him that he was ready to move forward. Many things had to be set in order before his departure, and he went through each, one by one. This was a special moment in his life. He was an essential link in a chain of events. Moses was waiting, and he was ready to fulfill his part.

Lost in his musings while lying on the blanket, a dark shadow appeared and hovered over him. It moved swiftly, coming from the left but then also from above as well as from behind. Shemaiah was startled but when he tried to move, his limbs were paralyzed. With great effort he was able to shake his shoulders, struggling to shoo away the ghostly figure. His limbs began to jerk and spasm ineffectively, to no avail. The more he struggled, the more the ghostly shadow attached itself to him. Shemaiah tried to scream, but his voice would cast no sound. Caught in terror, Shemaiah realized that he was at his hour of death.

A dark, deep voice spoke, saying, "So, you think you are great—special among men? Your thoughts created me; they have invited me to your side. I am the product of your pride and your arrogance."

This remark startled and alarmed him. He had not realized that he nursed a sense of specialness, pride, and arrogance within him. More so, he had never imagined that these thoughts, of which he was unaware, had such power of creation—that with his imagination he would bring to life such horrific beings.

The dark voice continued, saying, "I'm also the product of your fear and mistrust."

Shemaiah was apprehensive. He feared that other creatures would appear while he was wrestling with this dark shadow. Fear was taking over, feeding on his insecurities, bringing all sorts of negative injunctions and accusatory remarks into his mind. He had landed in a dark and deep abyss. A mixture of anger and sadness cropped up, but the angrier he became, the more strength the shadow figure gained, and the harder their struggle. Finally worn out and tired, Shemaiah fell into a passive state. Memories of life in Shiloh came to mind, and he recalled times with his mother and days of childhood while his father was still alive. His father had left them, and then Shemaiah left his mother. Now he was to die, leaving his wife and children behind, leaving the flock. He realized with pain that he did not want to leave them. He didn't want to go on a mission, much less did he want to die.

Tears filled his eyes. He cried for all that was lost in the past and for all that he would be losing in the future. Shemaiah mourned with anger and sadness, and as he drowned in these miserable, uncomfortable emotions a voice demanded, "Pride and arrogance, fear and mistrust, sadness and grief: it all has to go."

"Why?" he protested in defiance.

Where had that voice come from? And why must he comply? Why must he leave everything behind? Why again?

An answer vibrant and precise came to him. "To take this path, you must give up all identifications. You are now being stripped naked of all that you know about yourself, all that you remember, everything you believe you are meant to become. Learn to live without it all."

Everything turned to black. Shemaiah felt as if he was hanging in nothingness. Suddenly, he heard a soft, rhythmical beat. He realized that he was sliding into a space that was lit by a soft white light, which he recognized for what it was: Shemaiah had entered into the sanctuary and could sense the Invisible Presence. It was He who had spoken.

Sudden relaxation flowed through his limbs. His mind relaxed too, becoming natural and transparent, like the water in a brook that springs freely from its natural source. The shadows disappeared as suddenly as they had arrived. They were genuinely nonexistent. They were merely potent creations of fear as it played with his mind.

A new perspective dawned over him. And while he waited, he continued to empty his mind, cleansing lingering thoughts and haunting feelings and preparing himself to become a deserving vessel of what was to come.

CHAPTER 16

Moses Leads the People Out of Egypt and into the Desert—1446 BC

THE ACTIVITY IN THE streets of Goshen was feverish in preparation for a massive departure. Since the years when Joseph was grand vizier of Egypt, the Hebrews had settled in Goshen and built a town where they grew and developed. Houses made of mudbrick bordered the narrow streets, one next to the other, and families would live in close proximity, helping each other. Many years before, the sons of Jacob had come down into Egypt, escaping hunger and penury. The years went by and the Hebrews multiplied; they were fruitful and increased, sometimes merging with other people and laborers. The Hebrews worked in the fields, in quarries or mines of gold. Some became servants in Egyptian households where they lived. For most of them, Goshen was their home.

It was during the reign of Tuthmose I that the pharaoh spoke to his people and warned them, "Behold, the people of the children of Israel are more numerous and stronger than we are. Get ready, let us deal shrewdly with them, lest they increase, and a war befall us, and they join the barbaric Amu, wage war against us, and depart from the land."[1]

The pharaoh took severe measures to protect his kingdom, disowning Joseph, the much-respected grand vizier, and ordering the killing of all newborn Hebrew males. The Hebrews were enslaved, and a crushing workload was imposed on them. They lost all civil privileges, and their lives became miserable.[2] Moses emerged to offer hope for the future. Trusting his words was a gamble the Hebrews were challenged to take.

---

1. See Exodus 1:9–10. "Amu" is an Egyptian term for West-Asiatics, often Canaanites/Amorites; sometimes associated in later periods with the Hyksos.
2. See Exodus 1:11–14.

The Hebrews had not much time to discuss or digest the matter. If they were to leave Egypt, they would have to do so quickly; there would be no looking back. The pull of this massive undertaking was so overpowering it seemed to annul all personal feelings of grief or remorse. On the same night that Samael, the Angel of Death, passed with a scythe in his hand hitting the land of Egypt, the Hebrews were instructed to offer a lamb in sacrifice to YHWH. They were to eat the flesh of the lamb and smear its blood on the doorposts of their houses. The Hebrews ate in haste this meal. They ate with their loins girded, the shoes on their feet, and the staffs in their hands. Then they took the dough of their breads before it had leavened, with their kneading bowls bound up in their clothes and on their shoulders as Moses had ordered them to do.[3]

The Egyptians were also in a hurry, afraid that more punishment would hit the land. Articles of silver, gold, and clothing were offered to the Hebrews.[4] Wool, linen, and fine woods. They took with them all they could carry, as well as their animals and other goods.

The Hebrews left Egypt 210 years after the sons of Jacob arrived in the land, 430 years after the Patriarch Abraham's sojourn in Egypt. Moses took Joseph's bones out of Egypt as the Patriarch had requested in his hour of death, and so they left as a unified soul. All the angelic legions of YHWH, the Upper and the Lower, left as one body, harnessing a power too great to be resisted. This diverse conglomerate of people were not to be called Hebrews anymore, but rather Israelites, as they constituted a new single nation under the rule of Moses. The Israelites moved forward as a massive block which YHWH had strengthened. They marched firmly on a path that God had paved with sapphires, bordered with the colors of twelve precious stones, one for each tribe.

✳✳✳

Many years had passed since the exodus of the Israelites from Egypt, and one cold night in the desert, Kadmiel sat by a fire with his grandson. Having been born in the desert, Zakai knew nothing more than life in these arid steppes. Now at thirteen years of age, Zakai had questions he needed to ask of his grandfather.

"But grandfather, the pharaoh was a proud and arrogant man. I've heard you describe him so well, I sometimes believe I know him. He would

3. See Exodus 12.
4. See Exodus 12:36.

not cease prodding God with his negatives. But I wonder: what made him change his mind?"

Kadmiel allowed himself the smile of a proud grandfather. "You are right, my child. Let me tell you this. I was in the palace on the day Tia'a, queen of Egypt, took the lead to expel the Israelites from Egypt. Overpowered by deep grief and rage, the queen stormed into the throne room yelling, 'Those despicable Habiru! They are opportunistic and deceitful! They always were! Send them out!' Tia'a seemed to be the only royal who understood and feared the continuation of YHWH's reprisal. The plagues were a merciless, ruthless display of strength and power in the war between the gods of Egypt and YHWH, the God of the Israelites. The Egyptian priests agreed. They conceded that YHWH had prevailed. It was time to open the gates and allow the Hebrew slaves to leave Egypt." Kadmiel paused, as if he was looking back in time. "Of course, Moses was in haste. He knew that the Israelites must leave Egypt immediately, lest Pharaoh change his mind." Kadmiel's voice softened, and his eyes sought the middle distance. "Dear, dear grandson. I will say this over and over again. As a historian I praise guarding with precision memories of the past, lest some future pharaoh or some people might try to deny that it ever happened." As he spoke, memories of the horrific desecration of Hatshepsut's monuments played themselves out in his mind. Overcome with emotion, Kadmiel declared, with a proud intonation in his voice, "And it was on the sixth regnal year of Pharaoh Amenhotep II that almighty YHWH prevailed over Amun and over all the gods of Egypt. The exodus began on the fifteenth day of Nissan, the year 2448 of creation, in the middle of the day, after the Angel of Death struck off the firstborns of Egypt. Six hundred thousand men and their wives, children, and flocks crossed the border into the desert. I, and every member of our treasured family, was among that crowd. We will always remember."

CHAPTER 17

On the Path to Finding Moses

On the Path to Finding Moses—1386 BC

SHEMAIAH WAS READY TO fulfill Gabriel's commands. He returned to Kirya-taim and packed some belongings: his shepherd's staff and his blanket, the water canteen, the knife, and a little bag with some figs, olives, and bread. People had seen him leave before, so no one thought this time it would be any different, not even Ohad, who greeted him warmly when Shemaiah entered his house.

"Peace be with you," said Shemaiah.

Ohad nodded with gratitude and asked, "It is early in the morning; you are just in time to take the flock into the countryside, aren't you? Something vital must bring you here. Do you have any concerns?"

Shemaiah answered, "I'm requesting your permission to leave Kirya-taim." Ohad frowned, but Shemaiah continued. "I am ready to fulfill the mandate that YHWH has entrusted to me. I have made my preparations to execute this mission. In fact, I must leave."

Ohad, unsure of Shemaiah's intentions, appeared to be deeply disturbed. "Have you spoken to Dinah?" Ohad knew the pain Shemaiah's departure would cause her.

Shemaiah answered softly, "No, I have not. I will do so only after you give me your blessing. I'm asking that you take good care of her and the children."

Ohad was astute and judicious. He knew that men sometimes needed to explore the world, seek new horizons, for doing so would sometimes restore their lives and renew the tribe. He had watched Shemaiah grow in wisdom and knowledge through the years. He had seen him heal sick people and provide thoughtful answers to difficult questions about God.

Ohad loved Shemaiah, which is why he trusted that his son-in-law would know what he was doing. He gave him his blessing, saying only, "I only hope you'll know when to return."

With this, Shemaiah next approached his wife, who was milking the cows as was her custom every morning. Calling her aside, he said, "My dear one, you have been good to me. You are a trustful friend and a loving wife. But I must go. I must fulfill my mission." Dinah's countenance grew pale.

For some time now, Shemaiah had been setting himself apart, avoiding small talk around the family quarters. She believed it had all started when he built the shrine to YHWH, and she harbored secret thoughts that building the sanctuary on the hill had not done him any good. She remembered the day when he had walked into the house. His face looked contorted, transfixed with distress as he had just placed the Asherah and the teraphim in the sanctuary. It was obvious that he felt torn apart inside. He had told her that it was as if he was of two minds: one that knew that which was true and he should follow, and another that lived in falsehood but nevertheless also influenced his actions. At the time Dinah did not understand his worries. To her, his mission had been fulfilled. Couldn't he appreciate that all was good, that his children and the animals were well fed, and that there was plenty of work for all? Now, Dinah realized that Shemaiah was lost to her. In fact, she had lost him long ago.

The next morning, Shemaiah gently embraced his children, who peeked at him through sleepy eyes. "I will be back," he promised, and then was rendered mute by the lump in his throat. His children believed him for he had always been true to his word. Dinah watched silently as he prepared to leave. He claimed that he was to obey a mandate from YHWH. Had it come to him in a dream? Maybe it did. Shemaiah always dreamed—who else dreamed as often as he? Better for everyone if he left swiftly. With sadness in her heart, she bid him farewell.

And so, in the early hours of the morning, Shemaiah left Kiryataim. He walked steadily, journeying without pause until the end of the day, when at last he spread a blanket beneath a solitary palm tree and quickly fell asleep. When the sun rose, Shemaiah woke to see a torch of fire coloring the skies in splendid hues of orange, yellow, and red. At a distance, he saw the silhouette of two rams playfully goring one other. Behind them stood the mountains in profile. Which one was the mountain from which Moses caught a glimpse of the promised land? His wish today was that he would find someone who could show him which of the mountains was Mount Nebo.

Shemaiah recalled Shuah's words: "Moses will be there, in his meeting place at the head of the mountain. There, between the two eyes in the rock, you will find Moses. Only if you can see where the eyes are can the entrance be shown to you. Clear your mind, and be prepared!" Repeating these words energized him enough to resume his journey. Shemaiah rose, ate lightly, and set his feet walking toward those distant mountains. He traveled east, then north toward the plains of Moab. Trusting that all he had left behind—Dinah and their children, the flock, and the shrine—would be watched over by Ohad, Shemaiah strode forth.

He had been walking for many hours, but the scenery had not changed. The mountainous profile remained at a fixed distance. Not a single living creature crossed his path. Shemaiah ate some morsels of dry bread and drank a bit of water. He now realized he had left Kiryataim rather abruptly, as if in haste, as if he was running away from something. He realized that he had no clue which path to follow. Anxiety flooded his body. He felt the contraction of his entrails as he gazed over the vast expanse that stretched before him.

Many times during his younger years, he heard that Moses requested help from his father-in-law Jethro in guiding the Israelites through the wilderness. Jethro was well acquainted with the region, and Moses trusted that he would teach them where to camp safely in the desert.

Shemaiah knew that the oases in the desert were few and far between, and that only experienced nomads knew their location and how to get to them. Here he was alone, with no one at his side. He felt as if he was lost. It was essential that he find an oasis. Better still, it was critical that he find a fellow traveler from whom he could buy some provisions.

Fear overtook him. He did not know where to go, nor did he know how he could turn around and head back. Realizing the enormity of his mission, and realizing that he had set for himself an impossible task, he fell prostrate on the ground and prayed to YHWH. Desperation engulfed him. A wild, plaintive cry came from deep within and there he lay until sleep overtook him.

With the morning light, he was awakened by a soft, humid touch. He opened his eyes to a midsized dog leaning over him. The dog sniffed him with gentle curiosity and then licked his face. Shemaiah petted the dog before rising to a seated position. He was confused. Where was he? What had happened? In a flash, he remembered being alone in the desert and in desperate need of help. He took a quick survey of the surroundings but saw no one to whom this shepherding dog might belong. They sat together, the dog and he, as Shemaiah stroked his fine head. The animal responded by licking his hand.

After some time, the dog got up and, looking back at Shemaiah as if inviting him to come along, started to move away. Reasoning that dog had come as if in answer to his cry for help, and grateful for the companionship,

Shemaiah decided that he would follow. The pair walked a very long way to finally arrive at a cliff, where they stood on an enormous boulder that protruded out over a deep ravine. Shemaiah looked into the valley below. As far as his eyes could see, there were vast expanses of rocks and dry, crusty soil with a thick, mixed grove scattered here and there.

Where was he? Feeling even more fearful and disoriented, he held tightly to his shepherd's staff, his water canteen, and the bag of food. The dog quickened his pace. Shemaiah did not want to lose his companion, so he followed him between a few palm trees, where they began a long descent by following a trail that wound its way between the rocks. Though the path was steep and challenging, the dog seemed familiar with it. Shemaiah kept his attention fixed on the difficult trail, measuring carefully every step he took.

When they made it to the bottom of the cliff, the dog turned left and entered a cavern that was secluded below boulders that protruded from up above. It was a natural grotto carved deep into the rocky mountain. The dog barked, as if to call to someone. A thin man appeared from the moody thickness of dark green trees and shrubs. He was wrapped in a black cloak. His skin was olive; his hair and beard were long and curly. His dark eyes were large and expressive. Smiling, the man bent over to welcome the dog. Looking at Shemaiah, he said, "Peace be with you. And may I ask: what is your name?"

Shemaiah was not sure how he should answer. Should he let him know he was an Israelite? Or should he say that he was a shepherd who had lost his way? It was well known that the desert steppes were dangerous. Many who roamed through them were often outlaws or tinkers of dubious reputation. Was this person trustworthy?

Shemaiah answered tentatively. "I'm a shepherd who lost his way."

"We have many of these," the man said, nodding while he sized up Shemaiah. "But there must be a god that is protecting you. Most men who stray this way have perished." With that he pointed toward a white mound of bones and skulls. As if having come to a decision, he added, "If your god protects you in this way, then I will too. Come with me."

Beckoning him to follow, the man turned and led Shemaiah into the forest. As they walked among the trees, the temperature dropped and Shemaiah felt a cooling freshness upon his skin. They approached a pond that was encircled by exceptionally tall boulders. The stones created a rocky rooftop that crowned the life-sustaining waters. The thick forest provided protection for the entrance to the oasis. Hidden as it was underneath the huge boulders, the precious setting was nearly impenetrable.

"Hungry?"

"Yes."

Shemaiah didn't know what time it was since he couldn't see the sun in the sky, but he guessed it should be an afternoon hour. Although there were some morsels of dry bread left in his bag, neither he nor the dog had eaten.

"You haven't told me your name, stranger. What should I call you?" The dark-haired man smiled with amusement.

"Shemaiah."

"Ah. An Israelite, I can tell. I'm Epher."

They entered a brown tent made of goat's hair. The canvas was supported by a line of central poles running up the middle; the back and sides were supported by shorter poles.

"This is my home," Epher said, tidying a bit as he went along.

He gathered up some plants and, using his hand, scooped red seeds from them. These were edible plants—peeled cactus leaves and fruits. Pointing toward a large stone, he showed Shemaiah where to sit and then gave him the seeds.

"Eat; this is good."

He ate with relish and drank what water remained in his canteen. His host joined him in the meal. While they ate, Shemaiah took a closer look at Epher. He could not venture a guess as to his age because his skin was as wrinkled as that of an old man, but his energetic gait and gestures gave him the look of a much younger man. Shemaiah recognized something of himself in Epher. Though silent, he seemed a straightforward person. Fleetingly, he wondered how Epher spent his days, but then his mind quickly went to more pressing matters. Did Epher know the desert and, if so, did he know which of the mountains was Mount Nebo?

That night, the two men sat beside a fire and got to know one another. Epher said that he was a Midianite. He had lived in this secluded place by himself longer than he could remember, saying, "I found this place because, much like you, a god wanted me to survive."

He revealed an aspect of the story of the conquest of Canaan that happened right around the time Shemaiah was born. It was a story that Shemaiah vaguely remembered.

Toward the end of the forty years of the children of Israel's wandering in the wilderness, the Midianites allied themselves with the Moabites in an attempt to exterminate the Israelites. They conspired together to curse Israel and anger YHWH. Their plot was to bring Israel to its knees by making use of the cunning grace and irresistible beauty of the Midianite women. The women would seduce the Israelites and then entice them to serve their own idols. The story told by Epher made Shemaiah feel apprehensive and insecure. It didn't seem a good omen. Nevertheless, he sat quietly and listened.

Epher described how Moses sent twelve thousand men to fight the Midianites. Moses' army was led by Phinehas the priest, fanatic, and zealot. "The Midianites were defeated and most all of their males, including their five kings—Evi, Rekem, Zur, Hur, and Reba—were killed. I was fifteen years old. By some great stroke of luck, I escaped the massacre. The Israelites set on fire all the cities and fortresses of the Midianites. They carried the women and children into captivity and seized their cattle and goods. Moses then ordered every Midianite male child and every woman to be slain, sparing only the female children." Closing his eyes as if wanting to forget the unspeakable scenes he had witnessed, Epher explained, "I knew I was supposed to be killed, which is why I ran away. I became a nomad living in a tent and remaining as far as I could from the site of that war until one day I discovered this blessed place. Here is where I will stay until I die."

Shemaiah could not help but be appalled. He himself did not remember much of these tales, as he had been a mere child when they happened. He did recall that the idol worshipers amongst the Israelites were punished with a plague and died by the thousands. Still, he did not know that God ordered Moses to take vengeance on the Midianites. The Israelites fought against Midian, killing every man, burning their towns, and taking all the plunder and spoils, including the people and animals.[1]

Those were times of war. Times of fear. And now Shemaiah feared for his own life. Epher had offered him hospitality, but what if this man still held a grudge by what had happened? Shemaiah tried to read his host's face. Was he in danger?

But Epher seemed lost in his thoughts, evoking events from a distant but impersonal past, as if they happened to somebody else. Then Epher continued his monologue, speaking aloud a web of intangible reflections regarding the ease by which people became enraged, and how quickly fury against their fellow human beings could be roused.

As if he could read Shemaiah's mind, he soothed, "You have nothing to worry about. This is why I'm telling you the story: to get it out of our way. I never understood nor do I condone the haste with which a man can turn anger against a neighbor—it's a brutal cycle that is sometimes unending. This is why I decided to part ways with people, all the people, and became a loner. One may never know what gets stirred inside one's fellow man. I believe it is easier and safer to live by myself. It is already quite difficult to deal with what within me may one day become violent—and without me even knowing the reasons why. I could even end up hurting someone." Epher seemed perturbed by the idea. He remained quiet for some time, and

1. See Numbers 31.

then, as an afterthought, observed, "Dealing with my own self is more than enough."

Epher stood up. Silently, he went back to the tent. Shemaiah followed. It was time to lie down and sleep.

✱✱✱

This first encounter with Epher had been tough, and Shemaiah felt the need to be on his own. He sat outside the tent again, keeping his own counsel as his mind recreated the horrible scenes of death and destruction that his host had described. He remembered how difficult it had been experiencing the dark, menacing shadow that attacked him as he slept alone under the trees in the countryside that surrounded Kiryataim. This, he now realized, was a projection of a dark side within himself, a strong force fed by his insecurities. A force that thrived in his feelings of anger and fear. That darkness within could turn, in just an instant, to hurt others and himself. But on the other hand, Shemaiah had also experienced a Being that was powerful and wise, with no earthly attachments or concerns. A Being that nurtured a vision of the future as well as a total, comprehensive understanding of life. It bothered him that this timeless Being would sometimes stand away, distant and remote from the world of living creatures, uninterested in its dramas and arguments and conflicts. Still, at times, Shemaiah felt the closeness of this Being, as when he had a dream, or a vision, and even more so when he was immersed in nature.

As thoughts of this Being flitted through his mind, Shemaiah wondered again if this Being was God. Thoughts about the paradoxical nature of God continued to haunt him. Specific questions turned endlessly in Shemaiah's head. How could God have created such a magnificent world to then also create beings that quickly became beasts of prey? Humans could become insensitive monsters and thoughtlessly kill their fellow men by the thousands.

And then, God Himself . . . He was a puzzle. In Sinai, He had issued an authoritative command that no one should ever kill. And yet sometime later He commanded the Israelites to slay the Midianites and erase them from the face of the earth! Shemaiah could not tolerate the incongruence. It was too heavy a burden. *Who is this God?* he asked himself. *Who is YHWH, the God the Israelites live to serve?* He needed to find answers. Amidst this tormenting confusion, Shemaiah was also taken by an enormous sadness. He felt mournful, for himself, for his children, and for the human condition.

All were forced to experience the actions of an indomitable God who was incomprehensible, mysterious, and perplexing.

As he questioned God's motives, a terrible fear started to grow inside of him. He felt afraid of God's wrath. Afraid that God would punish his presumptuousness. He felt engulfed by an absolute terror of being destroyed, right there, on the spot. Shemaiah fell to his knees and, crouching, hid his face between his legs. So he remained until the fear subsided and he felt emptied, exhausted, and spent, both physically and emotionally. Slowly he rose from the ground and entered the tent, where he lay down on his blanket and fell into a deep sleep.

CHAPTER 18

The Israelite Encampment in the Desert—ca. 1446 BC

LIFE IN THE DESERT was rough, and so was the movement of such a massive group of people, their animals, and belongings. The caravan moved slowly, like a wave of thick magma through the sands. Once they had arrived at the chosen resting spot in the desert, Moses dictated clear coordinates on where the crowd was to be located. Kadmiel's writings detailed the organization of the encampment as directed to Moses by YHWH.

It took more than a year to build the definite structure of the campsite, with the Sanctuary standing in its midst. Through the years, the encampment would be dismantled and set up time and again according to the exact same pattern, which was a mystical configuration that God had dictated to Moses.

Moses had once commanded the most powerful army in the world. Now, having the conquest of the land of Canaan as his goal, he made the most out of this experience as he structured new lines of command in a masterly way, organized like an army. He chose the most capable men from all of Israel and turned them into leaders guiding thousands, hundreds, fifties, and tens of thousands of people.[1] For the most part, the people willingly followed orders given by their chieftains. When occasional brawls erupted among them, they acceded to the judgments over their petty grievances.

Each time the camp dismantled, the large crowd would again move slowly and heavily across the desert. A pillar of cloud by day and a pillar of fire by night were the guides the people followed.[2] These pillars hovered at all times directly above the Tabernacle. The Israelites traveled until the

1. See Exodus 18:25.
2. See Exodus 13:21–22.

cloud set itself to rest.[3] Only then would they allow themselves to stop moving. In this way they proceeded at God's command. The pace was slow, with
women, children, and the sick riding on donkeys but everyone else on foot.
Tents and belongings were loaded into carts pulled by oxen or lugged on the
backs of camels.

The camels were the most precious of laborers, as they could haul
massive loads upon their packsaddles with ease. Their distinctive bellows
ringing out all across the camp enlivened the atmosphere and brought comfort to the weary travelers. Most importantly, camels could go days without
water, unlike donkeys or other livestock, which would quickly die if left
unattended under the harsh heat and drought of the desert.

Four months after setting out of Egypt, they reached an oasis in the
wilderness of Paran called Jotbathah. It was late on the night of the twenti-
eth day of the month. The slopes of a mountain covered with lush vegetation
could be seen beneath the rising sun. The mountaintop was bathed in rays
of an ocher light, the steep hillsides colored by darker shadows. Trickling
brooks of water crisscrossed the land.[4] The Israelites camped safely in this
expansive oasis, a fabulous site with enough water to both satisfy the animals and the humans.

With the first rays of light, the men began unpacking the tents and
setting up the camp. The women emptied bundles that were stacked high
on the camels. The Levites labored for many days and nights to set up the
Tabernacle, God's holy abode.

The camp would be often visited by other desert dwellers—people
seeking shelter or a place to water their camels before moving on. Moses
showed his gift of leadership and administrative skills by establishing clear
rulings. He put Joshua, his lieutenant, in charge of the wells of water: some
were designated to serve the Israelites; others, the wandering travelers. Joshua made sure that the watering stations were locked during the night. This
was to make certain that the water could not be stolen by bandits who hid
in the mountains. These marauders seized any opportunity to steal sheep,
camels, sometimes even unattended children. It was unusual for them to
attack during the day, but because they were known to wreak devastating
harm during the night, Joshua established a steady watch at all hours.

The encampment at Jotbathah thrived. The people were happy to finally be somewhere that felt like home, and they settled in. However, after only
a few months, Moses once again gave the order to move. That night at the
fire, Kadmiel spoke to some disgruntled neighbors, sharing what he and the

3. See Numbers 10:11–12.
4. See Deuteronomy 10:7.

elders had learned. "The caravan will be heading to Kadesh-Barnea, a large oasis in the Desert of Paran. Moses has sent scouts into the region, and they brought him news of a fertile valley with flowing springs of water, where the desert and its parched ground is transformed into a beautiful green."[5]

Thus, the Israelites left Jotbathah and trekked to Abronah; then they left Abronah to camp in Ezion-Geber; and after that they were to head toward Kadesh-Barnea. It was a seemingly endless pilgrimage that stirred feelings of disconnection and uprootedness. To the people, the goal of establishing a homeland seemed ever more elusive and remote.

The encampment in Ezion-Geber, a beautiful plain by the sea, was buzzing with activity before sunrise. Young and old worked side by side, folding tents, packing utensils, and herding animals. The women prepared the food for the next leg of their journey. The sheep and the cows had to be milked before their departure, lest they become swollen and irritated along the way. The sounds of people calling and shouting and moving around filled the campsite as everyone worked to meet the timeline set by Moses.

The blast of the silver trumpets was the sign that it was time for everyone to set out on their new journey. The first trumpet blast let the tribes camping on the east know that they were to set out. The sound of a second blast signified the departure of the camps to the south.[6] The dismantling of the Tabernacle could only be performed by the Levites, who were trained by Moses to honor the majesty of the sacred space shared with God. They were taught to meticulously wash themselves before entering the tent and wear priestly clothes with which to cover their human nakedness, particularly the most impudent parts.[7] God's canons of holiness were high. All the other tribes had been strictly warned not to approach the Tent of Meeting as they were in danger of overlooking these specific rules and might, as a consequence, die.[8]

5. See Psalm 107:35.
6. See Numbers 10: 1–7.
7. See Exodus 28:42–43; Exodus 30:19–21.
8. See Numbers 1:51; Numbers 18:21–22.

CHAPTER 19

Shemaiah and Epher

On the Nature of Man and God—1386 BC

EPHER WAS NOT A talkative man, but since he treated his guest with kindness and respect, Shemaiah felt welcomed and safe. That night, when Shemaiah was about to lie down on his blanket to sleep, Epher handed him a soft cushion made of goat's hair to put under his head. They were strangers to each other, but they shared the living space inside the small tent harmoniously.

Two days passed, and Shemaiah felt emotionally healed and serene. He enjoyed the stillness of this beautiful oasis, the freshness of the air, and the availability of water. In ways that he did not quite understand, Shemaiah sensed that this quiet, gentle, unobtrusive man was teaching him much. Epher didn't seem to hold any bitterness in his heart. He was a descendant of Midian, also a son of their forefather Abraham with his second wife Keturah, and so it was that Midianites and Israelites became bound by ties of blood. The Midianites knew YHWH but also worshiped other gods, including Baal Peor and Ashtoreth, the queen of heaven. As the days passed, Shemaiah was puzzled to discover that, contrary to his expectations, Epher the Midianite wasn't a wicked man. He was reverent and mindful in every way.

Shemaiah learned not to distrust all Midianites. He had watched Epher clean the tent, bathe his body, wash his dog. He had watched him collect the food and cut the branches of some plants as well as pick little fruits from bushes. All this he did with care and respect. He never took too much nor in haste, taking only just enough to satisfy his needs. Shemaiah heard Epher chanting often, always in a murmur, repeating chords that were soothing to the ear. He thought of asking what the sound was about, but then he chose not to, thereby sparing him from innocently making an indiscreet inquiry.

One morning Shemaiah woke up feeling confident enough to continue his journey. He sensed that it was time to leave, and he believed that Epher would probably feel the same way. He approached Epher to find out what would be the best pathway to take.

Epher was seated right by the pond of water outside the tent. The dog was at his side. He held a knife in his hand with which he peeled the outer layer of a cactus leaf. After preparing a few stems of the plant, he laid them carefully on a bed of foliage. Shemaiah, being reluctant to disturb his privacy, approached softly.

Standing at a short distance, he said, "I want to thank you, master and friend, for your kind hospitality. I wish I could offer you something in return." In earnest, he added, "I might be able to do so someday."

Epher turned in surprise, as he had not felt his guest approaching him. "That is my sacred duty, dear friend. Please take a seat next to me." With a smile, he added, "I know we have not talked much. But if there is something you need to know, I'll give you my best answer."

Shemaiah explained that he had been assigned the task of finding Moses, the lost Prophet. Many years had passed since Moses left the people of Israel behind; some people believed he had died, but he knew he did not. With this, Shemaiah feared he might have said too much, and so he fell quiet. He was unsure of what more to share. Should he speak about the dream with the angel? No—he preferred to hold that private.

As they sat by the small fire eating some fleshy shoots and fruits, Epher resumed the conversation. "So you think Moses is alive? Nobody has ever found him." He fell into a pensive reverie. "But you may be right. It might very well be that he is alive. It is known to all that Moses was a man of God. I have always wondered why a man of such spiritual magnificence was taken from the world. He could offer much help. And if, according to your suspicions, he's still alive, why did he part ways with Israel on the threshold of entering the promised land?"

Epher's appearance had changed. He now seemed much older. His voice sounded deeper, his face shone with a glow, and his eyes seemed serene. He looked as if his mind had gone into a place where he was all alone. Shemaiah wondered if Epher was now in that other realm. The place that was like a temple and where the Invisible and Protective Being dwelt. But he didn't say a word as he did not have an answer to Epher's questions. They were the very same queries that puzzled him.

A soft breeze touched Shemaiah on the skin. He began to speak wholeheartedly. "I was only a child when Moses left, but my father told me some stories about him . . ." Jumping to his feet, he muttered an excuse and walked away. He needed a moment to reconsider opening up to his host. He wasn't sure if it would be wise to share his feelings with a complete stranger. Should he expose his questioning of the God of Israel to a Midianite, a worshiper of Baal Peor? The burden felt too heavy, but on the other hand, Epher had proven to be a kind man. The long years lived in solitude had turned him into a thoughtful and receptive person. Besides, Shemaiah needed some release for his pent-up feelings. He returned to Epher, and Shemaiah bowed his head in recognition and continued speaking. "Moses' last words before he died were about God. He said that the deeds of YHWH, the Mighty Rock, are perfect, for all His ways are just. He called YHWH a faithful God, righteous and upright.[1] But I disagree . . ." Shemaiah raised his voice. "My eyes have seen Nehushtan, the bronze idol in the shape of a snake that Moses built while they were in the desert." Raising the tone of defiance in his voice even more, he affirmed, "Moses built the idol following YHWH's orders. I'm a Levite, and I have seen how the Israelites bring offerings and fall prostrate before Nehushtan. I have seen them seek the protection of the Asherah, and I have placed their teraphim in an altar in the sanctuary of YHWH."

Epher remained silent. It seemed to Shemaiah that he was listening impassively and nonjudgmentally.

Feeling too agitated to remain seated, Shemaiah rose to his feet. Standing tall, he continued, "Moses also said that if ever there was destruction, it was not because of YHWH but because of us, His children. It was because of our defects. It was because we were a crooked and twisted generation.[2] But again, I, Shemaiah, disagree." He continued in a trembling voice. "YHWH ordered the total destruction of the Midianites, the destruction of your people, dear Epher. He did not order the killing of the ten, twenty, or one hundred people who were guilty of committing adultery. He ordered everyone to be killed, whether guilty or not."

Epher, in reaction to the memory, closed his eyes. Shemaiah seemed disjointed as he articulated the question that was at the very core of his predicament. The question that burned inside his soul.

"What kind of God is this?" he shouted. "A God that defiles His own commandments! Wasn't it He who commanded that we should not make images in the likeness of the living beings that move on the earth or in the sky? Wasn't it He who commanded we should not kill? How, in the face of these contradictions, am I to trust that God is, as we have been told by Moses, righteous and upright?" Shemaiah, feeling shattered by his confession, collapsed in a heap. Feeling as if he were choking on the painful mixture of anger and sorrow that rose to his throat, he wept. After some time

1. See Deuteronomy 32:4.
2. See Deuteronomy 32:5.

a wry grimace twisted on his face and he concluded, "We are bound to an incomprehensible God. A God who has warned us of His power. A God who declared that *no one can be delivered from My hand.* Yes, I know we are bound to Him. But I say: there is more to know about the overpowering nature of God. And so I must find Moses because he is the one who knows the answers that I seek."

There was a long silence. No more words were uttered because there was nothing more to say.

Finally, Shemaiah asked Epher, "Do you know in what direction I should travel to get to Mount Nebo?"

"Yes, I do." In a soft voice, Epher added, "I will lead you to the foot of the mountain. But I'm not coming up with you. It is known that the mountain is very well guarded by powerful angels and by seraphim." Hesitantly, as if gauging what words he should use, Epher continued, "The Angel of Death stands there, *right there* between the ground and the first heaven. He brandishes a drawn sword, while dreadful horned ogres and demons form a protective ring around him. They are the ghosts of those who were killed and are not at peace. These unhappy spirits of the dead always escort the Angel of Death, the cruel snatcher of souls that smites and destroys human beings." Pausing a moment to catch a breath, Epher repeated for emphasis, "I am not coming up with you. I will not be killed by his sword."[3]

Though Epher's fear caused Shemaiah to feel rather shaken inside, he could not argue with Epher's restraint. He had to agree that this task of finding Moses was his and only his.

∗∗∗

Shemaiah fasted on that day and also on the next, and that night he could not fall asleep. He could not delude himself: he was afraid of the task given him by Gabriel. He knew that God created the Angel of Death during the twilight of the sixth day of creation, and that heaven was the Angel's abode. An unruly idea crept into his mind. Could it be that the Angel of Death partnered with God? This wild thought confused him even more.

The Angel of Death was God's twelve-winged emissary. He was responsible for the fall of Adam, and he was continually engaged in a fight

---

3. The "Angel of the Lord," a cruel snatcher of souls who "smites" and "destroys" human beings (cf. 2 Samuel 24:16; Isaiah 37:36), is called "the destroyer" (Exodus 12:23; 2 Samuel 24:16) and is described as standing between earth and heaven with a drawn sword in his hand (1 Chronicles 21:15–16).

with Adam's descendants.[4] It was said that the Angel of Death would stand near the head of the dying, holding a drawn sword from which a drop of bitter gall was suspended. As soon as the dying person would see the Angel, he would be seized with a convulsion that would cause his mouth to open, and thus the Angel would throw the drop into the open mouth. This drop of bitter gall, Shemaiah heard, is what causes death. The person would turn putrid. His face would become yellow. As soon as he tastes that drop, he feels death.[5] The soul would then escape through the open mouth.

Epher's words were as a warning, making Shemaiah realize that the Angel of Death stood on the path that leads to Moses with his sword drawn and ready. He knew that he would die unless he could provide an offering that would please this Angel. But what would suffice? There were no suitable animals nearby—no ram or sheep, not even a bird. Should he collect some grains and burn them in a fire to invite the Angel's protection? Or perhaps— was it possible—the better thing to do was ask for God's protection?

Shemaiah felt torn inside as he realized the bizarreness of life. God, the Protector, had created an ominous Angel. Now he didn't know whom he should serve with his offering. Whose grace was he calling for—God's or the Angel of Death? Shemaiah felt trapped, powerless, and incapable of thinking clearly. Most of all, he felt a sinking feeling of being unable to avoid death.

On the night of the second day of fasting, Shemaiah had a dream in which Shuah the clairvoyant woman came to him. In his dream, she predicted, "Tomorrow you'll be on your way to Nebo. You are on a path of ascension, and there you'll find opposition. Nothing important in life comes without conflict and resistance, and so it will be this time. This journey is fraught with difficulties that you must overcome one at a time, so listen carefully." Shuah continued, "Moses now sits in heaven. He sits near the throne of God the Father and King of the Universe. Seven of God's mightiest, most impenetrable angels surround and protect Moses. They will try to obstruct your mission. The Angel of Death is the first angel that you will have to face; make no mistake about it, he is prepared to succeed. But it does not have to be so; indeed, he will succeed only if you believe that you can die. Hear me, Shemaiah! The Angel of Death will succeed only if you were to believe that there is such a thing as death. Do as I say: take your shepherd's staff and engrave in it the Ineffable Name. This will be your scepter and your armor. Hold it in front of you and it will serve as a shield. Then you'll be further on

---

4. Pirķe Rabbi Eleazar 13, in Sefaria, "Pirķe Rabbi Eleazar 13."
5. Talmud, *Avodah Zarah* 20b:2

in your path of ascension. Do as I say! Now, I bid you farewell. From now on I will not be by your side. Conquer the fear of death, and then you'll find others waiting for you on the other side of the veil. They will guide you and give you further counsel."

Shemaiah woke from the dream with a soft rocking sensation in his body, and, as soon as that sensation vanished, he opened his eyes. Taking hold of the shepherd's staff, he did what Shuah had instructed. When he became totally absorbed in the carving of the sacred letters of the Ineffable Name, the paralyzing fear and anger vanished. New ideas in the form of words danced across his mind. They were words he had never heard before. In a low murmur, he repeated these words.

"God is my shepherd, I shall lack nothing. He revives my soul. Though I walk in the valley of the shadow of death, I will fear no evil, for He is with me; His staff will comfort me."[6] Shemaiah felt strengthened for the journey.

6. See Psalm 23:1–3.

CHAPTER 20

The Tabernacle in the Desert
—ca. 1444 BC

THE LEVITES WERE THE descendants of Gershon, Kohath, and Merari, sons of Levi. They had been entrusted to be Moses' loyal sentinels. Thus, eight thousand men who were always poised to shield God's honor rallied for Moses. They assisted the high priests in tending the Tabernacle and became warrior priests, honor guards, and gatekeepers.

Kadmiel and his sons Hanan and Eglon were descendants of Kohath, the most important Levitical clan. They were in charge of the Ark of the Covenant. This was a matter of pride, not only because they shared the same family roots of Moses and Aaron but even more so because the Ark of the Covenant they tended to was the physical representation of YHWH's presence among the people.

The day they were to set out for Kadesh-Barnea, the work began much earlier than ever. There was a feeling of vibrant expectancy among the people. Kadmiel felt particularly enthusiastic and opened up to share his excitement with his children and anyone who would like to hear: "Kadesh-Barnea is an exceptional landmark! Abraham, our great ancestor, dwelt there for some time.[1] In Egypt I heard it said that it is a land of opportunities, a fruitful place. That is where Hagar the Egyptian slave bore Abraham a child, Ishmael,[2] and later Sarah, his barren wife, also bore him Isaac, when she was ninety years old!"

Hanan, Kadmiel's eldest son, absorbed his father's positiveness about the next destination, and approached his work cheerfully. He entered the Tabernacle through the pair of magnificent draperies that covered the

1. See Genesis 20:1.
2. See Genesis 16:14–15.

entrance toward the east.[3] The drapes had been crafted by skilled embroiderers from the best wools in the world. Beautiful hues of turquoise, scarlet, and purple were interlaced with white twisted linen.

Once inside the courtyard, Hanan paused before the bronze altar and the laver that was placed in front of the Holy of Holies. Each was large and heavy. It would require men of great physical strength to lift and carry these treasured items. Next to them stood the most sacred structure in the edifice, the Holy of Holies, inside of which were housed the Ark of the Covenant, the altar of incense, table of the bread of presence, and a lampstand of seven lights.

The Levites started disassembling the tent that covered the Holy of Holies in a procedure that was as precise as it was rigorous. More than one hundred men began to lift and fold all four layers of coverings. First, they dismantled the most massive of the coverings. Made of porpoise skin, this layer protected the Tabernacle from rain and the morning dew. Once the porpoise skin had been folded to exacting measurements, the men turned their attention to the second layer. This layer was made of ram skin that had been dyed red. The third covering that had to be removed and folded was made of goat's hair. Finally, the innermost layer was taken down and folded. This layer was made of white linen, considered the most beautiful material known to exist in all the world.

Once all four of the coverings had been folded, the men took down the pillars, bars, boards, sockets, and ropes that held the tent coverings in place. Each part, being essential to the whole, was handled with care. It was stored, labeled, and safeguarded so that it would be ready the next time the Tabernacle was to be assembled. The whole process involved laborious, exacting, painstaking work, and Hanan took great care of tallying and listing the objects to ensure nothing was left behind or misplaced. The components of the Tabernacle were a precious load that, if mishandled, could result in the death of any person deemed reckless in his duties.

The final piece of the process was the loading of the sacred objects into heavy wagons pulled by pairs of strong oxen. The men moved slowly, carrying the long golden poles of the Ark which rested heavily on their shoulders. The Ark had been packed and hidden under a large cover made of skins and blue cloth. It was carefully concealed even from the eyes of those who carried it. When, finally, the Ark had been carefully stowed for the journey, the caravan began its slow crawl through the desert.

3. See Exodus 27:9–19.

A few days later the Israelites reached Kadesh-Barnea. They established the encampment rapidly. The Levites reinstalled the Tabernacle with all its components. All was well.

Aaron and his sons were actively involved in setting up the Tent of Meeting, a place of absolute repose that was always quiet and serene, filled with exquisite aromas emanating from the rarest incenses. The Tent consisted of two rooms divided by a beautiful, thick curtain that was skillfully crafted with representations of winged angelic beings known as the Cherubim. These celestial images were embroidered with twisted linens in colors of blue, crimson, and purple. The largest room in the sacred Tent housed the bronze candlestick, the altar of incense, and the table of the bread of the presence. The smaller room, the Holy of Holies, was a place of real wonder because it harbored the powerful presence of God. The Holy of Holies also housed the portable throne from where God spoke to Moses: the Ark of the Testimony. This ark was a massive chest made of gold. Depicted on the canopy were two Cherubim, their wings spread wide, seated facing each other. God had promised Moses, "I will arrange My meetings with you there, and I will speak with you from atop the ark cover between the two Cherubim that are upon the Ark of the Testimony."[4] With reverence, Hanan reached out the tip of his finger to touch the fabric of the curtain of the Tent of Meeting. Seldom had he ever had the chance to stand so close to the sacred objects in this room.

The moment the Tent was set, the cloud established its position above and the people were reassured that the glory of God was once again filling the Tabernacle.[5] As it happened, the Israelites would remain amid the beautiful oases and copious water wells of Kadesh-Barnea for the longest duration of any of their encampments.[6]

---

4. See Exodus 25:22.
5. See Exodus 40:34.
6. See Deuteronomy 1:46; Deuteronomy 2:14.

CHAPTER 21

Trials on the Path to Moses

Emergence of the False Self—1386 BC

SHEMAIAH WOKE UP EARLY that morning in what he believed was the beginning of a new time in his life. His family and priestly duties were now behind him; the time had come to fulfill a mandate that had been dictated by the angel Gabriel. This moment had evolved in total concurrence with the yearnings of his soul. Deep within himself, he held a strong desire to find Moses. He imagined talking to the great Master, he visualized himself posing difficult questions about God, and he envisioned Moses answering those questions willingly. Several issues concerned him and, in time, they had become even broader, more defiant, and complex. In fact, would Moses agree to enter into such dialogue?

The more Shemaiah reflected on his concerns about the nature of God, the more he realized that YHWH was neither fair nor was He reasonable. Shemaiah had been told that God created humans in His image and likeness but no, this could not be so—there was that other side of God that indicated God and men were not alike. God did not understand men. He was a distant, portentous, phenomenal force with whom no reasonable interchange was possible.

Feeling overwhelmed by his conflicting thoughts, Shemaiah shook his head and hid his face between his hands. YHWH escaped every depiction the human mind could offer, every explanation, and Shemaiah needed to imagine that Moses had the answers. *Moses saw God face-to-face*, he reminded himself. *He must know.*

What is God's nature? Why did God create the world? Does God have an interest in humanity? What purpose do humans serve? These are the pressing questions that drove Shemaiah up a treacherous mountain so that he might obtain the answers.

Epher and Shemaiah prepared to set out upon the road. Shemaiah cut across the bushes that encircled the oasis, looking around, exploring the environment. The sky was beautifully tinted in bright orange. An infinite number of thin clouds infused that sky with a soft texture. It all looked so peaceful, so promising. He held tightly to the staff and placed all his hopes upon it. This staff contained the promise of protection and a sign that nothing could go wrong. Epher finished preparing the peeled shoots of cactus and grains and filled the canteens with fresh water. Shemaiah placed the food in his bag, his knife and blanket, and hoisted the bag across his shoulder.

A look passed between them, and Shemaiah nodded. Epher stepped out, leading the way across the wall of foliage. He was headed toward the arid lands surrounding the oasis. The land that crumbled into the sands of an almost-endless desert. Shemaiah felt uneasy. At every turn of the head, the landscape looked the same to his eyes. How did Epher know which way to go? But Epher seemed confident.

As if sensing Shemaiah's concern, he said, "We are going east, toward the sun, and then we'll turn to the left, heading north."

A barking sound made them turn. Epher's dog was running to catch up to them. Shemaiah looked at Epher with questions in his eyes. Pointing to the animal, Epher said, "This has happened before. He will follow us for some time but when the heat becomes unbearable, he will return to the comfort of the shade at home."

They resumed their hike as a trio. Sure enough, not too far away, as if this had been rehearsed, the dog, panting heavily, looked up at his master. Then he turned and headed back to the camp.

The men had been on the road for some time when they saw a small caravan crossing their path. People were riding on donkeys and camels, and the sharp metallic sound of little bells was heard as they moved.

"These must be Shasu Bedouins," said Epher in a low murmur. "I recognize the sound of their bells. The sound is meant to shoo away any bad spirit crossing in their way. There must be a settlement nearby." Gesturing with his hand, he indicated that Shemaiah and he would slow their pace.

The Shasu were seminomadic herders, and Shemaiah did not know much about them. Were they safe? Or were they at risk? He studied the passing group for signs of danger. The caravan was composed of four men and two women, all dressed in light-colored robes. The women's dresses were striped in red, black, and white, and they wore white turbans on their heads. The men's faces were covered with full, dark beards, and they were dressed in ragged white robes, and also wore white turbans on their heads.

As was the custom, Epher approached the oldest man of the group and, with ceremony, asked if he knew of a place where they could rest and spend the night. The man slowed his donkey long enough to point toward the direction from where they were coming. He said that only five hundred cubits to the north they would find a small creek with palm trees. This was the right place to rest. Pointing toward a woman who was moaning softly, he added by way of explanation, "We are in much hurry. This pregnant woman might soon be in labor." They resumed their pace and continued along their way.

That night and all the nights that followed, Shemaiah sat beside Epher telling him stories of the past. He recalled his younger years in Shiloh and his adult life in Kiryataim. He also spoke about the Israelites in their exodus from Egypt and in their quest for the promised land. He described how they wandered forty years in the desert searching for the land YHWH had promised to their ancestors. Shemaiah wanted his Midianite friend to understand and perhaps even empathize with the struggles of his people. Epher listened with great attention to the stories of how the Israelites transformed and amalgamated through time to become a nation.

On the fifth day, as soon as the sun came up and daylight awakened them, they rose, ate some grains, and drank some water. Once again, Epher initiated their march.

"Today," he said, "we will arrive at the foot of Mount Nebo."

Shemaiah felt the clutch of fear in his stomach, as he realized that they were approaching his destination and he would have to part ways with Epher. He was not ready to say goodbye to his guide. From that moment on, Shemaiah, lost inside of himself, walked in silence. He used this time to set his mind in order, but feelings of fear overpowered his reasoning. His knuckles turned white from clutching the staff engraved with the holy name.

Epher's gait slowed. He indicated that Shemaiah should take the lead. Shemaiah raised his eyes; right there in front of them stood the majestic Mount Nebo.

"Please. Stay with me tonight," he pleaded.

Epher nodded.

They spread their blankets on the ground beside some bushes. They ate and drank, then lay themselves down to sleep. As soon as he sprawled on his blanket, Shemaiah's head perked up with a vibrant life of its own. Tortuous thoughts filled his mind. Having met Epher, a kind and thoughtful Midianite, raised doubts about whether and where justice existed in the world. He now wrestled with the uncertainty that God would protect him in his venture. Thoughts of the unpredictability and volatility of an all-powerful YHWH who, time and again, changed His ways bombarded his mind. In a moment of much brittleness, his mind had turned against him and became an accusatory tool that dissected everything and offered no certainties on which to stand. The mind argued that there was nothing he could rely on, making him doubt everything he had learned, questioning how he had lived so utterly devoted to the service of an unreliable God whom no one except Moses had ever seen!

He remembered a story about Moses' ascension to Mount Sinai. He had climbed alone; his companions Joshua, Aaron, and the elders had been instructed to stay behind. There in Sinai is where Moses confronted God. Moses saw Him face-to-face and received the laws God wanted to deliver to the people. But who was to say it had not been Moses himself who composed the Ten Commandments?

Shemaiah argued with himself. *Despite having been given these laws to govern almost every aspect of life—these powerful notions that are sometimes hard to follow because they are at odds with human nature—men are even yet still monstrous. Even today, men kill one other. Even today, men covet one another's wives. Nothing has changed.*

With some bitterness, he voiced again the imperfections of his God. "Look at this: YHWH transgressed His own commandments on the day He instructed Moses to build Nehushtan, the bronze serpent. He transgressed His own commandments the moment He commanded that the Levites kill their brothers. When He could have shown wisdom and mercy, YHWH did not." An unanswered question hung in the center of his mind. "If Moses was His child, His chosen one, why didn't He show forgiveness and give him a second chance? Where is God's fatherly love?"

At that moment, Shemaiah understood that he should not expect YHWH to be a protective father in the same way an earthly father was. YHWH did not share Shemaiah's personal cares and concerns. Why should he? YHWH was not human.[1] His nature was different from ours. And Moses must have realized this when they met face-to-face. This insight made Shemaiah feel bereft and lonely.

Torturous questions about God continued to form in his mind. These concerns were his and his alone; there was no one with whom he could share them. "You are a man without a God," a sudden voice inside his head said mockingly. "There is no God, nor is there an Angel of Death. Life is what a man accomplishes in the world, what a man can do with his time, what he can understand, the challenges he can overcome. All this only if

1. See Job 9:32–33.

that man is lucky enough not to perish while trying." The voice turned even more sarcastic. "Hear this, you human. Life ends when a person dies. Death is inflicted upon him by an enemy that pierces his body, or by terrible illness, or by a beast that consumes his flesh. No God pulling strings. Death is the blind, thoughtless consequence of a person's actions. This is all there is to know about life and death. Nothing more." The thought went on and on, a circular loop repeating endlessly in his mind. *There is nothing above. We humans are the flesh that we are, the flesh that we nurse, the flesh that will one day crumble and decay. Look around and you will know there is nothing more than us; we are alone in the world.*

Unexpectedly, Shemaiah felt a sense of relief. It was a strange sensation because it opened him up to feel fearless, daring, and audacious. There was no need to weigh one's steps or to try to avoid angering a God that was the creation of the imagination of humans. Having to rely on an external supernatural force weakened him. It made him feel unsure of himself and of which path to take. It made him afraid of inciting anger in the nonexistent God. But now that the truth had emerged, bold and clear, he had a definite objective on which he could focus: serving himself. Serving his own living body. Making it strive and survive until, one day, the end would come. It was true: the ending was inescapable. But until then the path was his to develop and his to follow. The task was straightforward and precise. He now knew who it was he should pay attention to. Whose interests he should fend for. Only his own.

Shemaiah stood tall in this new understanding, ready to achieve that which he desired and completely assured that he would get to the top of the mountain. Little did he know that what was growing inside of him was a dangerously puffed-up false sense of self. An audacious, intrepid ego, over-confident and filled with pride, and all of it was heightened by the power of his youthful age. The prideful self had no doubts that he would find Moses. He would complete his journey and then return to Kiryataim where his people would honor him as a hero. He would be loved and respected, and remembered for generations to come. To the false self, life was ruled by luck, everything was a matter of luck, and luck was at the side of those who dare.

Thus, feeling energetic and inspired, Shemaiah came to Epher. He thanked him for his dedication and for supporting him this far and said he was ready to part ways.

Epher nodded. He understood. "There is yet a stretch of the path that we should cross together, then I will let you on your own," he said, and quickened his pace.

When the night fell, Epher announced that they had arrived at the foot of Mount Nebo. That night the two men slept under a starry sky. They were surrounded by a strange silence that seemed quieter than ever. Not even the winds of the desert could be heard blowing across the sand.

CHAPTER 22

The Levites

Moses' Priestly Sentinels—ca. 1444 BC

KADMIEL WORKED CLOSELY WITH Moses and knew him well. He saw in Moses a charismatic leader deserving of trust. Abital recalled that Kadmiel once told Zakai that the mere presence of Moses was edifying. Kadmiel said, "He makes me believe that there is a purpose in the path we travel, a purpose that justifies the difficulties we face constantly. Moses has a gift, of this I can assure you! He had the gift of interpreting God's commandments when they were handed down from above, and now he is able to render them into concrete rules that show themselves to us as inspired laws that will guide us throughout our lives."

Kadmiel believed that his calling in life was to record what Moses said and did, so he chronicled the day when Aaron and his four sons, all descendants of Levi, were ordained by Moses to become the priestly class.[1]

"Initially," Kadmiel wrote, "God intended to invest the priesthood in all firstborn sons of Israel. But the people took a big step backward and defiled themselves by choosing to worship a golden calf. They turned their back on YHWH even after having witnessed God's magnificence when manifested in Mount Sinai, and turned instead to worshiping an idol." Because of this shameful action, God chose the tribe of Levi, which was the only tribe that had remained faithful to YHWH, to become His priests.

Moses instructed the newly formed priestly class on how to carry out the cult of God and how to offer guidance to the people. The Levites were to fulfill a variety of functions in the Tabernacle as well as teach and heal

---

1. See Numbers 8:16–18.

the people. Moses selected his older brother Aaron and Aaron's four sons as high priests to lead the priesthood.[2]

He presided over the public ceremony of priestly consecration. First, the five men were cleansed with water. Then, Aaron was dressed in a white coat, on top of which Moses put the ephod, a luxurious apron of wool and linen, lavishly embroidered in gold, blue, purple, and scarlet yarns. Moses tied a woven band around Aaron's waist to hold the ephod securely in place. Moses then placed the priestly breastplate adorned with twelve precious stones, one for each tribe, over the ephod. These were the Urim and Thummim, the oracular stones with which the high priest was to query the will of God. The people watched in silence as Moses poured anointing oil over Aaron's head. One final step consecrated Aaron for priestly work: Moses set a turban on Aaron's head, on the front of which was placed a golden plate, a holy crown. Then Aaron's sons stepped forward. They were clothed with white tunics and girded with a girdle, anointed in oil, and crowned with tall hats. All of these things were done in accordance with God's instructions.[3] When the ceremony was concluded, the men were confined in isolation inside the Tabernacle, YHWH's abode, where they remained secluded for seven days and seven nights.

The Tabernacle was a stronghold carefully guarded by all the Levites. No one else was allowed to come close; in fact, nobody tried to. Nevertheless, Kadmiel envisioned in his mind's eye the events that would occur inside the Tabernacle as he relived precious moments of his own training in the Temple of Khonsû. These memories remained embedded forever in his body, his mind, and soul.

As time went by, the teachings and social structure provided by Moses became more extensive and robust. Life on the encampment was well ordered, revolving as it did around a routine that included daily rituals in the service to YHWH. The Tabernacle sat amid the camp, and the priests worked untiringly in the fulfillment of their duties. The smells of roasted flesh or grain and the smoke ascending to heaven, along with the soothing sound of the shofars, marked the area as a rare place where earth and heaven touched. The fire and smoke of daily offerings served to remind the people that the living God sat among them.

Moses continued training the Levites with the same strict disciplinary tactics he once used in training the mighty Egyptian army. Every morning, a large stream of priests clad in long robes of white linen would walk toward the Tabernacle. Kadmiel and Hanan joined their fellow Levites as

2. See Exodus 28:1.
3. See Exodus 28, 29; Leviticus 8.

they gathered in rigorous fulfillment of their obligations. The tent of the Tabernacle, an imposing structure, shone in splendor. Built of the gifts of the people, all goods that were brought out of Egypt—gold, silver, brass, fine linens, goat's hair and skin, wood, oil, and incense—every bit of it was intended to honor YHWH with the best they could offer.[4]

The Levites worked arduously ordering and cleaning, and at the end of the day they consecrated the sanctuary and its vessels with holy oil. The glory of God, that awe-inspiring manifestation of sound, fire, and lightning that the people witnessed at the top of Mount Sinai, now rested in repose at the foot of the mountain inside the Tabernacle.[5]

Witnessing YHWH's epiphany in Sinai had frightened the people, but now they felt reassured. Moses had promised them that God, despite His overpowering show of magnificence, was not to be feared. The Levites became a class of their own. The priests performed with the utmost care all the rituals commanded by God and did so day after day, year after year. Kadmiel recorded in the scroll that on the first day of his investiture Aaron the high priest approached the holy altar and prepared the animal offerings that had been chosen for sacrifice: a bull calf as a sin offering and a ram as a burnt offering. These offerings were made to atone for the high priest and the priests, an expression of their complete devotion and their commitment to God.

Aaron also prepared the animals brought by the people to be offered in their names—a he-goat, a calf, and a lamb—and performed the people's sacrifice. All was done as God had commanded.[6] In the end, Aaron lit incense of exceptional quality in an effort to further please YHWH. The offerings were made so that the physical and spiritual realms were bridged. They were intended to mend any discord between the human and the heavenly world, and to repair disagreements between the Israelites and their Creator.

✳✳✳

Kadmiel's love and admiration for Moses grew by the day, so when rumors and gossip began to be heard in criticism of Moses, Kadmiel was concerned.[7] Kadmiel himself was also an unusual man. He had been a man of influence in Egypt. He was intelligent and well educated. He was tall and imposing and had lived a long life, longer than most of his fellow men. Moses saw in

4. See Exodus 35:4–29.
5. See Exodus 25:8.
6. See Leviticus 9:7.
7. See Numbers 21:5.

him a capacity for deep and transforming insight as well as clarity of vision. Moses singled him out to be one of seventy elders, the wisest men in every tribe. These men were God-fearers, men of substance and truth, who were impervious to monetary gain.[8] Side by side with Moses, these elders led the troublesome, diverse multitude that had followed their leader out of Egypt. The encampment in Kadesh was fully established. As Moses had foreseen, the years of wandering the desert made the memories of Egypt and enslavement remain behind. Here, every person worked diligently at their chores, be it cultivating the fields or herding the flock.

The Israelites plowed the fields and planted wheat, barley, and millet which were used for baking bread, cooking porridge, gruel, or other such dishes. They cultivated legumes, including peas and beans as well as seeds such as sesame and flax. They also cultivated several kinds of spices, including dill, cumin, and coriander.

Herding was the second-most-important occupation, and it was carried on mostly for their own consumption. The Israelites had become a seminomadic or sedentary society, and shepherds led their animals, mostly goats and sheep, along the territory while maintaining a home base in the base camp.[9] An occasional caravan would cross the region bringing cotton and linen and other goods from Egypt, and the Israelites would trade them for spices, olives, fertilizers, or any other local goods when available.[10]

The Tabernacle was fully functioning as well. YHWH rested quietly, a sign that He was pleased with the activity carried by His people, and the people felt reassured and happy. One ordinary day, Kadmiel and the elders had gathered in the outer court of the Tabernacle to take care of daily issues. Kadmiel returned home, looking unusually animated. He said to his son Hanan, "The elders and I were engaged in the discussion of what punishment should be inflicted on a man who viciously attacks another. Suddenly, in ways difficult to explain, the atmosphere in the room changed. I turned around and saw that Moses had entered the room. His face seemed transfigured, as if he had been transported to faraway regions. I had seen that look before. It is how Moses looks after meeting with God in the Tabernacle."[11] Softly, then, in a hushed whisper, he told his son, "God's presence in one's life has a transformative effect." Kadmiel remained quiet. He covered his face with his hands, as if needing to set his thoughts in order, then he continued. "Today, when Moses entered the room, I felt stirred up with a mixture of

8. See Exodus 18:21 (author's paraphrase).
9. Borowski, *Daily Life in Biblical Times*, 20–30.
10. Borowski, *Daily Life in Biblical Times*, 56.
11. See Exodus 34:29–31.

emotions. Joy. Awe. Fear. They all came back to me, as if I was once again there . . . at that moment . . . at the foot of the Mount Sinai. Through God's descent upon this great man, God has touched us, too. That is the gift and this is the truth, my son. Today I understood, and Moses has helped me grasp, that God lies behind and beyond everything we see, hear, and touch."

Kadmiel, the son of Auserra, a prominent Egyptian priest, was filled with greater spirit and wisdom because of Moses, a Hebrew priest.[12] Kadmiel felt the greatness and the universal reach of YHWH and felt an even deeper calling to join Moses and Aaron and help them develop rituals by which the newly established priestly caste would conduct themselves to find favor in the eyes of YHWH.[13]

"Rituals are necessary to establish a connection. An inner connection with God. It will bring good fortune to everyone involved," he affirmed. "All that I learned in the temples of Egypt has served me in this new venture, my son. It has borne fruits." Kadmiel then told Hanan, "Nothing exists without a purpose, not even things that seem incompatible or antagonistic. Everything—listen well my son—everything that exists is God's making. It belongs to God's plan for the world, and we all play a part in His plan. Let's be thankful for that."

12. See Numbers 11:16–17.
13. See Exodus 28:2–3.

CHAPTER 23

Trials on the Path to Moses

Encounter with the Angel of Death—1386 BC

AT DAWN, WHEN THE sun came out, Epher bid his friend farewell and reversed course, starting out on the long trail back home. Shemaiah sat on a stone for some time watching Epher as his form faded into the distance. He felt calm and hopeful, and he rejoiced for the new, courageous self that had emerged just in time.

He turned his head toward the mountain and looked up to the top. It would take two or maybe even three days to get there. He considered the amount of food and water in his bag, realized it wasn't much, but dismissed the thought, refusing to allow worry into his thoughts. It was not necessary to think about all this. He would be able to handle it. With a little luck on his side, he would get all that was needed to sustain himself while he sought and found Moses.

Shemaiah stood up straight. As if to underscore his determination, he squared his shoulders. Then, leaning on his staff, he started walking toward the mountain. It was a massive body of rocks in the colors of the desert. He started his climb, placing his feet on stones that seemed likely to hold his weight. When he came to the larger boulders, he used them to rest for a moment. This was, after all, his first day climbing the mountain. So he climbed for many hours until he reached an enormous boulder that was protected by shrubbery. He decided to spend the night in this place.

He drank some water. There were some shoots of cactus leaf Epher had packed, but he didn't eat them. He would save the small bit of food for later. He slept on the large, protruding boulder, carefully gauging his movements so as not to roll off and plunge down the mountain.

On the second day, the climbing became more comfortable. Here, he encountered longer trails on flat land, and they seemed to have been trod-den before. Believing this foretold a remarkable journey, Shemaiah was ju-bilant. But the longer trails had no trees, therefore there were no spots where he could rest in the shade. Soon the heat of a merciless sun would take its toll on him. He began to feel that his head was spinning. He stumbled. He fell to the ground. His body plunged down a steep slope, and by the time he stopped rolling, he had lost consciousness.

When he revived and came to, he was hurting all over his body. He had landed in a bed of rough shrubbery. The branches had left scratches all over his skin but, fortunately, the shrubbery had protected his bones from being broken. Shemaiah did not know how long he had been lying there. Realizing that he had lost his staff, his bag, and the canteen of water, he got up to search for his belongings. Pain seared throughout his body with every movement. A loud, menacing laugh filled the air. Looking up, Shemaiah saw a group of ragged beings with hideous long and twisted, grimacing faces. Their threatening eyes stared fixedly at him as they moved forward. The figures drew closer and closer, blood dripping from their sharp teeth while spewing menacing tongues of flames coming out of their mouths. Overwhelmed by horror, he tried to find ways to protect himself from these emaciated, starving ghouls that seemed subjected to a perpetual hunger. A thought entered his mind and Shemaiah could no longer avoid the shocking truth: these were the faces of transgressors who were subjected to eternal judgment and damnation.

A flash of recognition told him he had reached the Gehinnom Valley. He was standing in the abode of the death, the destination of the wicked, and thus, he was an offender. "I must be dead," he said aloud. "And here in Gehinnom, my soul will be cleansed of all my faulty behaviors."

A gigantic, majestic figure wrapped in flames now appeared before him. An intense luminosity radiated from its eyeballs. The imposing figure had enormous wings that when extended increased the fire, stoking the flames even higher. Shemaiah recognized that this frightening apparition was an angel.

Shemaiah looked to his right and to his left. He saw hosts of fiery flames in such infinite numbers, they went on and on until they were lost in the distance. A storm of fierce winds whirled constantly in a funnel around the angel. The crash of thunder and rumble of earthquakes roiled all around where the angel hovered. A cavernous, resonant voice roared forth from the flames.

"So you say there is no Angel of Death?" The evil, spine-chilling laugh was heard again, turning Shemaiah's blood to ice. "Do you truly believe that you create your thoughts, that they are your creation, yours alone?" The voice snickered in derision. "Who put those thoughts of self-importance into your head?" The voice hammered on mercilessly. "Do you know? Do you? Do you really *want* to know?"

Terrified, Shemaiah fell face down on the ground. He buried his head beneath his arms.

The voice roared, "My name is Samael. I am the Angel of Death and I am here to take you."

And then, the great commotion ceased. In an instant, everything became silent. Without looking up or rising from the ground, Shemaiah grabbed a handful of earth and smeared it over his head as a sign of remorse. He trembled in fear at what might come next.

Oddly, the stillness was even more overpowering than the rage had been. He felt utterly overwhelmed. He was paralyzed, unable to move a muscle. As he remained prostrate he saw with his peripheral vision that an aura of light descended all the way to where he lay on the ground. He discovered that he was able to lift his head, and so he timidly raised his eyes toward the Angel. He saw that a large white cloud was covering the portentous figure. A radiant halo encircled the cloud. Beyond the halo came a softer, less threatening voice. The words that were spoken careened and echoed all around the rocky mountainside.

"Take a look at your life. Let it roll before your eyes. Remember who you were, and see the person you have become."

Shemaiah witnessed his life unfold before his eyes in seconds. He saw himself as a child, running around the house in Shiloh; there was his mother and their servants Aqhat and Yassib. He saw his father talking, as he often did, to the flock. He felt again the pain and the insecurity that Zakai's death brought to him. To the family. He saw the town of Jericho on the day he came to search the surrounding fields for his father's shofar.

The dream in which Zakai and the angel Gabriel had given him the task of finding Moses replayed before his mind's eye. He recognized the conflicting feelings he had experienced. He had been both thrilled and frightened. Then, abruptly, the scene changed and images of his wife Dinah, their daughter Zehava, and son Aviel flooded his mind. These images were much too painful. His dear ones! They were so far away!

Bitter tears filled Shemaiah's eyes as he took a hard look at himself. Who *was* he?

Gabriel had assigned him an honorable task because he, Shemaiah, had walked a spiritual path in fear of God and out of love for his fellow men. But now things had changed. He knew he had changed. He had become a new creature. Something had emerged from deep inside. A new creature that was strangely fearless and somewhat soulless.

The thought occurred to him: what charges would be brought against him?

As if on cue, Samael's thunderous voice announced, "Three of the indicting angels—Uzza, Azza, and Azzael—came forth before the Holy One to lodge a complaint. They said, 'Lord of the Universe, what are the merits of this person named Shemaiah, whom You have chosen to reach for heights no other man has ever attempted? Is it not enough that the law was given to Moses and that he brought it down to these inferior beings? And what other secrets might the Holy One share with these humans that He has not shared with us?'" The cavernous voice paused as if it, too, needed time to consider the enormity of these questions so boldly presented to the Lord. "Shemaiah, the prosecutors were determined to damage your spiritual path by making your mind roam autonomously. They filled it with chatter, thereby creating obstacles that would interfere with your ability to discern wisdom from above. You believed them, and you became arrogant because you felt such false sense of empowerment."

Shemaiah understood now. The indicting angels had inspired those conceited thoughts that had flooded his mind. They went even further by feeding his arrogant condemnations of God, and by making these prideful thoughts stronger every day. And then anger—his anger had nurtured the distortions brought about by the mind, and it became a vicious cycle. His angry mind felt entitled to rule over Shemaiah's life. His angry mind worked to sever every connection between his spirit and God. And thus, Shemaiah had become a man with no God. A man who believed in serving himself. A Godless man who sought a heroic life in which he would be invincible and invulnerable, forever.

By the time the cavernous voice fell silent, a side of Shemaiah that had grown dormant was springing back to life. It was reminding him of his true inner quest. He remembered the words that Shuah had spoken to him in a dream. She had told him that he would find opposition on this path of ascension he would undertake. She had warned him that the journey would be fraught with difficulties, and that God's angels would try to obstruct his mission. She had predicted that he would face the Angel of Death first, and the Angel would prevail only if Shemaiah believed that there is such a thing as death. Shuah had advised him to "take the shepherd's staff and engrave in it, with extreme care and devotion, the Ineffable Name. This will make the Angel of Death flee in terror."

The remembrance of these words made Shemaiah feel protected, and his energies were renewed. He looked around for his staff. He spotted it partially hidden behind a large stone. He rose to his feet, bent and took hold of the staff, lifted it over his head, and thrust the Ineffable Name toward the Angel of Death.

When the Angel recognized the power in the Name, he left without a trace. Samael had, without any doubt, fulfilled the will of God and had helped Shemaiah be transformed. Shemaiah had evolved into a selfless man. It was God's will that Shemaiah would stay alive.

CHAPTER 24

Moses and the Rebellion of Korach

KADMIEL SPENT LONG HOURS in the Tabernacle, keeping track of the daily routines and making sure that supplies needed were available and in place. He could not help but notice that Eglon, his youngest son, who was usually talkative and cheerful, stood apart. One day, Eglon raced through his work and then left the Tabernacle without saying a word. Kadmiel finished cleaning the silver pans in which the incense had been burned and then headed toward his tent.

The night set in and as soon as the first morning rays kindled the sky, the encampment dawned into a great commotion. A crowd assembled in the outskirts of the Levite quarters, where a man named Korach was shouting out, demanding the presence of Moses. Kadmiel watched the scene with worry creasing his forehead. Many people gathered around Korach, some of them leaders in the community. Among those in the crowd were Dathan and Abiram, two men known for their deceitfulness and belligerence. Kadmiel was stunned to see Eglon among this rabble.

Korach shouted, "Moses, you have gone too far, choosing your family members as priests. You selected Aaron and his sons to the exclusion of anyone else! Listen, Moses, the whole community is holy, everyone is, and the Lord is in our midst. Why do you set yourselves above the Lord's assembly by elevating your brother above us?"[1]

Kadmiel, uncertain of where this dispute could lead, did not know what, if anything, he should do. The atmosphere turned scorching hot as if the community itself were about to explode. Hanan appeared from behind, rushing toward his father to protect him in the event of an uprising. Kadmiel was an old man who would need protection if violence erupted.

---

1. See Numbers 16.

Kadmiel looked at his son with gratitude and reached out to grasp his arm. "Let us not get worried, my son. Moses will know how to handle this quarrel. Korach is also angry because his cousin Elizaphan has been chosen rather than himself as head of the family of Kohath, a position Korach thinks is rightfully his."

They waited for what seemed a long time before Moses and Aaron emerged from their tents. Moses was holding the rod of God firmly in his hand. His countenance conveyed serenity. Seeing this, Kadmiel's entire being was flooded with relief. He turned to Hanan and said, "Ah! Moses knows what to do. He has heard God's message and he knows how this will end."

Hanan looked at his father with concern. He did not share Kadmiel's complete confidence that all would be well.

The crowd quieted. Moses spoke.

"You have seen the staff of Aaron that blossomed and produced almonds."

Heads nodded. They had seen this miraculous staff, for it had been placed in front of the Ark of Covenant as a reminder that Aaron had been chosen by God to be His high priest.

"Only one person can be the high priest. Only one person is fit to assume this sacred post. As we all know, Aaron is the one who was ordained by heaven to be our high priest." Moses then looked to Korach. He commanded him and his men to come back the next day. Inexplicably, he added, "Bring pans. Pans on which you will make an offering of incense to God. Aaron will be there too," he said, shifting his gaze to scan the crowd, making eye contact with as many as would look him in the eye. "God will accept the offering of the one He deems worthy." His voice deepened with gravity as he concluded, "In this trial, only one will survive."

Saying no more, Moses and Aaron turned from the crowd and disappeared inside their tents.

Korach, believing he represented the discontent of many, spent the night canvassing on his behalf. He went from tribe to tribe seeking support. His all-night campaign lured many to his cause.

The next day, 250 followers of Korach came to the Sanctuary, each of them bearing incense-filled pans. A crowd gathered around the insurgents. Some were merely curious, others were quite contented with the way things were, and still others were also disgruntled and itching for change. Aaron stood waiting at the entrance of the Tent of Meeting. He too held a fire pan in his hands.

Suddenly, a flame appeared in the sky. There, before the entire assembly, the flame burned with an intensity that made some of the people flee. Those who remained watched as an intense fire consumed the offerings of the 250 men. When the conflagration was over, only one pan of incense remained unconsumed, a sign that God had accepted Aaron's offering.

Moses raised his voice to instruct all of the spectators to move away from Korach and his followers. Immediately after Moses gave this warning, a thunderous uproar rumbled and erupted from underneath the earth. The ground split open, the earth opened its mouth, and Korach and his followers were swallowed whole.

Kadmiel collapsed against the mast of a nearby tent. The scene that played out before his eyes was shocking. People desperate to escape the ravenous earth ran every which way, pushing, shoving, trampling anyone who stood in their way. Hanan watched in horror as his brother Eglon struggled to stay aboveground. Impulsively, in a wild attempt to save his brother, Hanan ran against the current of the fleeing crowd. Against all odds, he was able to get close enough to grab Eglon by the arm. He dug in his heels and leaned back, trying with all his might to prevent Eglon from sliding into the gaping mouth of the crater. But the weight of Eglon's body caused Hanan to lose his footing. Together, then, the brothers fell to the ground. Kadmiel screamed in horror as he watched his sons tumble, one after another, to their deaths.

At the end of that dreadful day, Kadmiel sat on the ground of his tent, his face painfully contracted in unspeakable sorrow. He scooped a handful of tear-soaked dust into his hand and sprinkled the dust over his head. Softly, in a shattered tone, the primordial sound of a brokenhearted father, he whispered, "Dust we are and to dust we will return."[2] Then, although doing so stabbed a fresh new wound in his already-ravaged heart, he tore a hole in his robe. This, the universal sign of mourning observed by his people, would mark him as one who had lost irreplaceable loved ones. The pain in Kadmiel's heart was immense and even though his suffering mind tried to reason the pain away, arguing that he should accept his loss because this was God's will, he felt bereaved.

Kadmiel's daughter Bathia, Hanan's wife Elah, and Hanan's children Zakai and Naamah sat on the floor by his side. Together, all of them would tear their clothes, spread dust on their heads, and spend the prescribed seven days of mourning while little Daliah, Hanan's one-year-old daughter, slept in the arms of a compassionate neighbor.

A wailing lament could be heard coming from every corner of the encampment. Grief was everywhere as the Israelites mourned the dead.

A few evenings later, after everyone had lain down to sleep, Kadmiel heard in the darkness the sound of muffled sobs. He found Zakai was sitting with his elbows on his knees and his head clasped between his arms. Deep

---

2. See Genesis 3:19.

wells of sadness sprang from his eyes. Kadmiel touched his thin shoulder and lowered himself to the ground to sit beside his grandson. His own heart was throbbing with sorrow, but his grandson needed him at this moment. His grandson must come before his own grief.

"I know," he said in a soft, consoling voice. "The pain is too big to describe." The moment was intimate, as was the pain they shared. "It does not seem fair. Your Uncle Eglon may have invited God's wrath, but your father did not. Why, then? Why your father, too?" Kadmiel's voice betrayed his own tears. "Hanan was a God-fearing man," he said in protest. Grandfather and grandson, both of them weeping in great sorrow, embraced.

At last, Zakai was able to speak. Quietly, and with resolve showing in his eyes, he said, "With the death of my father, a burdensome weight falls over my shoulders. I am now the sole sustainer of the family. But hear me, grandfather: as much as I cannot understand God's reasons, still I place all my trust in Him. I need His support. I need Him now more than ever before." Kadmiel knew that Zakai was dealing with the ageless, terrible paradox that human beings confronted for generations, and that now, although it seemed far too soon, it was Zakai's turn to experience it as well. At such a young age he had been made aware of needing the support of his Executioner. Zakai was now locked in the ancient stalemate.

Kadmiel felt a wrench in his heart because he was familiar with these contradictory feelings. But he nodded in support because they were together in this. Zakai had lost his father; he had lost two sons. It seemed unjust and undeserved, and yet somehow Kadmiel sensed that it was neither.

In the hopes that his words would be helpful, Kadmiel decided to open up his heart. The lad, who was especially sensitive by nature, had just turned fourteen years of age. Kadmiel believed he was mature enough to hear this message even during a time of profound pain and sorrow. And so Kadmiel spoke softly and with all the care and skill he could muster.

"Dear grandson, I have learned throughout my journey in life that even if the path seems narrow and fraught with dangers, we should not feel either discouraged or frightened. The world is a narrow bridge, but we must not be afraid.[3] If we remain calm and have clarity, we will find our direction and our purpose. There is an invisible hand holding and guarding us during even the darkest of moments." Kadmiel was silent as he delved into his heart. New thoughts clamored to emerge, like fresh water from a fountain pouring through too narrow an opening. "Be strong and take heart, Zakai. Remain confident of this: one day, even though we walk a rough trail, we will be able to recognize and understand God's goodness. Yes, my dear son.

---

3. Nachman, *Likutey Moharan*, Part II (Tinyana), lesson 48, 9:156–57.

I am confident of this—that I will see the goodness of God here, in the world that we live in. There is only one thing that I ask from God, and this I will always seek: that I may dwell in His house all the days of my life. Be confident, Zakai, and trust."[4]

4. See Psalm 27.

CHAPTER 25

Trials on the Path to Moses

The Invisible Being—1386 BC

SHEMAIAH TURNED HIS EYES to the mountain he must scale. He followed the long, winding path all the way to its peak and sighed. His body, having been bruised in the fall, ached everywhere. Nevertheless, he held tight to his belongings and, slowly and painfully, put one foot forward and then the next. Only his profound longing to find Moses enabled him to push his physical pain aside and keep climbing.

Memories of the days when he strolled the mountains, pasturing the flock, came to his mind. "If I had animals to care for, this journey would be easier," he thought. "At least I would have company." This stream of thoughts, while helping him pass the time, also distracted him from paying careful attention to the trail. He stumbled and nearly fell to the ground. He shook his head to erase the memories. "Better pay close attention to the terrain," he told himself. "This part of the path is very uneven." It was important that he maintained mindfulness during every step he took. All along the way, he must remain aware of his surroundings, of every stone, every turn, every little mound that conceals a sinkhole.

The earth colored in an orangey-red was parched and filled with stones. At some point the path became not as steep and challenging as it had been at the beginning. That was a good thing because at the same time, Shemaiah sensed the stifling heat of an inclement sun beating down on his head. He paused to sip water from his canteen. To his right he noticed shrubs and bushes, some of which sported flowers in bloom. These were tzalafim, plants of capers. Tightly rooted in the crevices of the rocks, these plants blossomed with beautiful white flowers adorned with violet stamens and pistils. Small leaves sprouted from reddish-colored stems and were fortified at the joint by tiny hooks. No animal, not even a camel, would eat this plant. But some of the other bushes were blooming with olive-green-colored fruits the size of a small seed. Happy with this finding, Shemaiah pulled out his knife and bent to prune the fruits from a bush. After working some time to harvest the little fruits, he realized that not too far in the distance were a number of thin, tall cacti. These were the kind of cactus plants that were capable of storing water inside their fleshy stems and in some pockets near the roots. The discoveries made Shemaiah feel as if he were in the company of faithful friends. He remembered the days when he and Epher gathered stems from noble plants like these, and then peeled and received nourishment from them.

Life is good, he thought appreciatively, and he walked toward the cacti to cut some stems. He then sat on a rock and peeled them, preparing them for storage. Shemaiah ate some of what he had collected, then readied himself to resume the climb.

He had been walking some distance when he perceived movement under a large stone. Was this the tail of a snake or a lizard? YHWH had forbidden these crawling animals to be eaten; however, he thought, maybe they would guide him to larger openings in the mountain. Maybe even a cave where he could find shelter for the night. He used a stick to poke the spot where he had seen movement, and a lizard emerged. Swiftly he followed the lizard all the way to a cranny that cut into the side of the mountain. As he approached the stony wall, Shemaiah was surprised to see a number of tall stakes standing one next to the other, as if they formed a screen erected for the purpose of hiding the space behind it. Using a large stone, he banged repeatedly on one of the stakes until it broke. He stretched an arm through the hole but it waved around in emptiness. Eagerly, he pounded the adjacent stakes until they too cracked open. Here, then, was an entrance to a well-concealed cavity. Shemaiah entered the cave and found that it was large enough to accommodate two people. A big smile lit his face.

He looked around, exploring the curvature of the cave. He had to make sure it was safe. He threw a stone into a corner, and a lizard in hiding scurried out and fled the cave in terror. Shemaiah smiled again. This was indeed a lucky break. He rejoiced. On this day he had found food, water, and now shelter. What that told him was that he would be able to survive alone on the mountain.

Without giving it much thought because it just seemed the natural, right thing to do, he went outside and prepared a small altar, using stones that were right there at his fingertips. On this altar he placed the remnants of all the food still in his bag. He wanted to make an offering of gratitude to YHWH. As there was no fire, he poured the water that was left in his canteen over the seeds and plants on the altar as an oblation to, and a demonstration of trust in, God. He had confidence that he would be protected just as the Israelites had been protected when they were in the Wilderness of Sin, and God had fed them with manna and quail sent from the heavens. He knew for sure that all that was needed would be provided.

The night had not yet fallen but Shemaiah felt very tired. His body and mind suddenly could not go on. He retired to the cave, placed the new fruit seeds he had collected in a corner, then spread his blanket over the ground and set his staff and knife next to the blanket. They were the only tools for self-defense that he had, and he knew he'd better not lose them.

All of the sudden his body started shaking violently, in spasms of fear and grief. Much had happened to him in a short period. He had forsaken the security of home and the support of his fellow man; he had wandered in the desert left to his luck; he'd plunged down a steep slope and lost consciousness; he recovered to experience a brush with Samael the Angel of Death. The images of this close encounter with death played themselves in his mind. *Indeed,* he thought, *I could have died.*

"No, you didn't die. It would not happen," said a voice inside his head.

He was reminded once again of something Shuah had said: "The Angel of Death will only succeed if you believe that you can die."

"Liar!" he yelled into the vast silence.

At this point he realized that the ordeal he was going through was taking a heavy toll on him. Shemaiah felt a wave of anger rising from deep inside. "Shuah was playing with words," he said bitterly.

"No, she was not," asserted the voice in his head.

The voice seemed so real that he turned his head and looked around to see where it came from, but there was nothing, there was no one. He was alone. Shemaiah settled himself on the blanket trying to calm himself down, breathing softly and deeply, until feeling slightly numbed. Suddenly he realized that he had reentered the inner sanctuary, another realm of consciousness where he could be alert and aware without being totally awake. Shemaiah recognized the place. He felt at peace. Lying there quietly, he waited for the Invisible Being to appear. Shemaiah had heard His voice but had never seen His likeness.

A soft voice called his name repeatedly. Looking intently, he saw the outline of a man dressed in colorful garb, secured with a string tied around his waist. The figure, barely discernible in the darkness, looked imposing, floating in the air. *Is this an apparition?* Shemaiah asked himself. Fearing the worst, he sat up quickly and took hold of his staff, seeking protection. Soon he realized that it was not a ghost but rather the ineffable Being that lived in the sanctuary.

The Being now hovered in front of him, and Shemaiah felt calm and secure, in a state of reverie.

"Come with me," the Being invited him. "I will help you get rid of these shackles that constrain you." He then repeated ageless words in a soft voice that seemed to gently wrap itself around Shemaiah. "The world is a narrow path, a confined passage through a valley between mountains which obscure the view. The main thing to remember if you are to continue on this journey is not to be afraid. Not to be afraid at all."[1]

Shemaiah was overcome by a sense of wonderment but, in no time, his doubting mind tried to retake control, and so he asked, "Is this real? How can I go with Him? Where to?" He felt the soft touch of an Invisible hand on his forehead, and, before new thoughts could set in and derail his mind, his thinking stopped. His mind was halted as if held by a fist of iron, remaining perfectly still and attentive. He had never before experienced this.

Shemaiah and the Being now walked side by side until they reached a lake of clear waters. They entered the lake, but the view all around them became clouded by fog. Instinctively, Shemaiah wanted to stop; he was afraid to continue farther. He looked around and saw that they were not alone. Other people were wandering aimlessly in the fog, sometimes bumping against each other. They seemed unable to find their way across the lake.

Shemaiah turned to look back toward where he came from. Far in the distance he saw his body at rest. He realized the meaning: even though his body was lying motionless on the ground, he was simultaneously also able to walk with the Being and move forward.

"You have left your body and the limitations it puts upon you," the Being explained. "You have chosen to come out of the dark and leave ignorance behind. You have chosen to abandon the cult of appearances that engulfs what is real."

Shemaiah asked, "Please tell me, have I died?"

"This is one way of thinking about what is happening; but, you tell me: are you really dead? Have you vanished? Did you die with your body? Do you know your name? Do you remember your parents, your wife, your children, and all others?"

Shemaiah realized that yes, he did remember. He remembered them all. He realized that he was existing without his body. Something remained alive regardless of the body. He understood now that he was deathless. Shuah had been right! The Angel of Death could only kill him if he believed there was an end to life.

---

1. Nachman, *Likutey Moharan Tinyana (Part II)*, 173.

"So," he said tentatively, "dying means getting stripped from a body which is left behind. Dying will be painless if the person is willing and ready at the moment of the departure to merge with Spirit." This insight encouraged him to dwell in the space that existed inside of him, which was rooted in Spirit. The Spirit that he was.

Shemaiah decided that he could now cut through the fog and cross over the lake. As he did, he realized that the figure dressed in the multicolored garb had disappeared. Baffled, he looked around but did not see Him anywhere.

"It was a ghost after all," he said to himself, but kept walking through the fog. As soon as he emerged on the other side, he saw that his own vestment had changed into a multicolored robe. In total surprise, he bowed down his head and struggled to collect his thoughts. He was neither dreaming, nor had he died. A new, clear understanding defined itself in his mind. He and his incorporeal companion, the Invisible Being, had become unified. From now on, they would act in unison. Shemaiah had achieved a broader perspective of that which is commonly known as reality. "The task of life is to achieve unity of the conscious mind with spirit," he said to himself. "This is the purpose of the human experience. We are meant to gain insight and increase our understanding, and so to partake willingly and actively in God's plan for the world."

CHAPTER 26

The Shofar

Moses' Instrument of Redemption—ca. 1444 BC

AFTER KADMIEL'S DEATH, ZAKAI'S life changed dramatically. He assumed the responsibilities as head of the family in addition to his priestly duties without complaint, even though deep inside, what he enjoyed most was the solitude of the pastoral life. For him, life in the encampment was too busy, too complex. He yearned for time to sit by himself. Time to meditate. Time to be in nature and play his flute.

When his father was alive, he liked to join him in guiding the animals around the desert fields in search of the freshest shrubbery on which they might graze. Father and son would sit together and play music while they watched over the flock. Zakai was soothed by the peacefulness that emanated from the docile animals. He always savored the serenity of the surroundings.

Every now and then Zakai would sit alone, playing on the shofar that the angel had given to his father. He was a skilled musician and would make the ram's horn sing in many different ways: some sounds were long and straight while others where short and quick, in playful successions. But the sounds he liked most emerged softly, like a wailing lament rising from the depths of a yearning soul. People in the vicinity would often stop to listen.

One day inside the encampment, a small crowd formed around Zakai as he played his shofar. Moses, who was strolling around the camp, listened and watched from a distance. The sonority was magnificent. It reminded him of a sound he would never forget: the music of the great shofar coming down from heaven. The people had heard it, too, on the day they stood waiting at the foot of Mount Sinai for God's revelation. Moses perceived that

Zakai was bringing forth music that stemmed from the beyond. These were sounds that could only be coming from angels.

Moses went to the elders and spoke to them about Zakai's father having been a vehicle for what was now being manifested through Zakai. "I want the sound of the shofar to be part of our journey," Moses said. "As the sound rises to heaven, it will express our conscious choice—our human voice pleading for redemption. This is a sign of an exceptional moment for humanity."

Kadmiel wrote that in times of redemption the threat of death would disappear and all the disunion in the world, the very basis of discord and evil, would vanish. So while the elders listened, Kadmiel recorded Moses' instructions. First, Moses entrusted Zakai with the construction of shofarim. Second, knowing that there was a hidden power in that sound that he wanted to harness, he instructed that the horns were to be played by the Levites whenever the people journeyed through the desert. Third, the shofar would be used as an instrument of praise and worship as well as a tool of warfare and protection because it was capable of cleansing the environment and driving away evil forces and, at the same time, raising the vibrational frequency of the energy field in the Israelite encampment. Kadmiel observed that the higher frequency it provided to the surroundings, the more it increased the people's ability to remain open and receptive to the guidance that came from above, and he was in awe. "That is the power of sounds such as these."

Zakai assembled a group of Levites to help him build the instruments. As soon as the word spread, the Israelites embraced the idea with enthusiasm. A large number of horns removed from the heads of animals that had been ritually slaughtered were brought by the people and laid in a pile before Zakai's tent. He inspected each, choosing horns of rams, goats, and gazelles that were naturally hollow. Then the Levites worked together at boiling the horns in water and cleaning away any tissue that may have remained lodged inside. Everyone worked diligently to open the narrow end so that a mouthpiece could be fashioned through which the blown air would bring forth music.

When the instruments had been built, Zakai trained the Levites how to blow the horns and coax from them beautiful sounds. This became his life's work. He was a proud player of the shofar and the tutor of those who would keep the tradition alive.

CHAPTER 27

Trials on the Path

The Path of Ascension—1386 BC

SHEMAIAH HAD LEARNED THAT in the beginning God created heaven and earth. The earth was formless and empty, and an uncanny darkness covered the face of the deep.[1] God's spirit floated over the dark waters which filled the unfathomable depths. These waters were divided to become the waters from above and the waters below. And when a massive vastness surrounded the waters below, it became solidified. This is how the world was created. Then, in a process of continuous differentiation, all living and nonliving bodies were born. But from the waters above, unbounded consciousness emerged, and later, the reflective, bounded human mind would come into being. YHWH held this lake of primeval waters above, so the restricted, embodied mind could return to it and be nourished and refreshed, forever.

***

Shemaiah remained in the stillness of the waters above, where he and the Invisible Being had merged into one. His mind and senses rested inside the well of clear waters, fully alert and awakened, but in complete silence. For an instant, he wished this could be his final destination; it was easy to live in such a blissful state. The waters surrounded and protected him; his soul was reminded of the days he was conceived and then developed inside his mother's womb. With his birth into the world, his consciousness emerged into the flesh and the struggles of the world. He wished he could stay here, in this blissful state forever! But something prodded him from the inside,

---

1. See Genesis 1:1–2.

reminding him that he must continue and that he would do so as a function of his newfound understanding and trust.

Despite being aware of the complexities of this new path, Shemaiah chose to surrender to the calling. From now on, his life would unfold simultaneously in two intertwined realms: the realm of matter and the realm of spirit. He would exist in full awareness of both without severing his bonds with either. Keeping a connection with these two worlds would allow him to become a true man of God, just like Moses had been. Then, he would return to serve again in the world below. He would share all he had learned and all that he had yet to discover. Keeping this connection was the challenge. It was the key. *This* was the task. And it was essential that he continue moving forward.

Shemaiah's mind rose to a different level of awareness and understanding. He languished no more in a never-ending stream of doubts and insecurities, feeling unsure of which thought to follow or what action to take. He knew he was being led by a hidden hand: caring and compassionate but also forceful and firm. He trusted that all that he needed would be provided.

Time and space now seemed to have vanished. So, too, did the need to eat or sleep. No distance was too long, no place too remote. He could be wherever he needed to be in an instant, and effortlessly, as he traveled with his mind at the speed of thought.

The urge to find Moses started to prod him once again, but that impulse, a need in itself, represented a limitation born of lingering doubts. Shemaiah realized that there still were limitations that he needed to overcome.

He heard a voice echoing through space. "You will not get there," said the voice. "You are still unprepared." Then a different voice taunted harshly, "What does a man born to a woman do here?"

An angel with a fiery sword in his hand appeared in front of him, blocking the way. Shuah's advice replayed in his mind, and Shemaiah felt no fear. Indeed, he was to expect more intromissions from the angelic realm.

Serenely, he replied, "I'm on my way to find Moses, who is waiting for me. I have something to give to him."

A conflagration rose up. It engulfed the angelic figure and threatened to destroy everything around him. Then the voice, reverberating loudly, as if raised from all four corners of the world, roared, "Who told you to come? And what is this you have in your possession that Moses the great Prophet would find lacking in heaven? You are but flesh and blood! Answer now, or all is over."

Shemaiah stood quietly, considering the angel's words. The angel was right. He was a man of flesh and blood. But it was also true that he had a mission to accomplish. By remaining focused and clear in his intention,

Shemaiah's understanding and cognizance was able to be expanded. He did not freeze in this moment of confrontation. Instead, words of praise filled his thoughts, and he immediately knew these were the words he had to say to the angel.

"Holy Master Uriel, captain of the Hosts of God. You who stand at the gates of Eden with a fiery sword, you who are the truthful protector of those who serve YHWH, hear what I say: the angel Gabriel has assigned me a mission. I am to deliver two stones of sapphire to Moses. Gabriel said, 'These two stones you shall guard carefully, as they are sacred. In the Ark that sits in Shiloh, these two pieces are missing. Moses is waiting. He knows that you will bring them to him.'"

The fire began to subside. It was a signal that Uriel had been satisfied with Shemaiah's explanation.

"Continue. I will be your protector. I will be the unseen guardian that stands at your front and shields you on your way."

Uriel vanished. A stele of fragrant white smoke was all that he left behind.

Once again, Shemaiah set forth on his journey, carrying the two stones of radiant sapphire firmly engraved on his heart and in his mind. He arrived at a place in the bed of the lake that was filled with corals and plants. The site was beautiful, pleasant, and calm. It was a chamber fit for a king. There, he saw the likeness of a man sitting on a splendid throne made of corals in shades of muted oranges and rosy reds. This was a man of exquisite beauty. He radiated a regal aura of purples, magenta, and gold. Clearly, this was also an angel.

Shemaiah wanted nothing more but to stand there in admiration of the magnificent figure. Suddenly, boxes that looked like coffins floated out from behind the throne and came to rest at his feet. Pointing to the boxes, the angel spoke. "This that lays at your feet is sacred knowledge. It comprises all that has been created, since the very beginning until the end of times. It holds all that is known and everything that is yet to become known."

Shemaiah did not yet fully understand, but ventured to ask, "Who are you? What is your name?"

"I am the angel Raziel, he who holds the secrets of YHWH and records all there is to know. You, Shemaiah, are a scribe. You stand at the roots of my tree. Slowly, you will climb upward to join me in my work, but only if you allow yourself to be led."

Shemaiah observed that the cover of one coffin was opening. Rays of bright white light shone from inside, illuminating thousands of letters that rose to the surface of the waters, then drifted down so that other letters could rise to the surface, and then these, too, would fall and be replaced.

A myriad of words was being formed from the letters that rose and fell on this parchment of water. Shemaiah had never seen anything like it. Right before his eyes, an undulating series of letters formed words that aligned themselves into sentences that fell into sequences that created paragraphs.

"What is this that is written?" Shemaiah pondered, and Raziel looked at him with kindness and compassion.

"Know that from now on, you will hear the voice of God with renewed understanding. You will know, and you will see with clarity like never before, and you will record on this watery parchment what you learn. And you will no longer be called 'Shemaiah,' as you ripened and you have changed. It is fitting that you are called by a new name. From now own, you are to be known as 'Shemaiahu,' which means 'he who listens to God.'"

Shemaiahu saw a watery piece of parchment suspended right in front of him.

"This is your tool," he heard Raziel say in a hushed whisper. "It is right inside of you. It is your soul. Once the message is formed and understood with the subtle mind, it will attach itself and remain bonded to the watery parchment of the soul forever! And every letter, every image you conceive, will become a rung in a pathway that is there for you to climb and explore in multiple, unimagined dimensions.

"Everything you will learn in this particular journey—and beyond—becomes an opportunity to expand human consciousness. It is the subtle mind inside of you, that which first differentiates experience and gives shape to an idea. The idea will then become attached to this universal, magnificent, fluid parchment. It will travel like a ripple, carried by boundless waters in the living substance that gives meaning to nature and sustains all humans, all creatures. Within this subtle field the idea will reach all living things in every corner of the world. Know, Shemaiahu, that nothing is meant to be lost. Therefore, always listen attentively, act upon what you understand, and be assured that it will remain inscribed forever and will reach someone, somewhere, at some point in time."

Then, as he bid Shemaiahu farewell, the angel repeated, "Remember: these waters are a vault. All that needs to be known is there; everything available to those who seek—available to those who do the work of accessing the supernatural script that lays hidden in the depth of the primordial living substance."

Shemaiahu the scribe wanted to bring to the world what he had just experienced. His goal was to share it for the sake of generations to come. He now understood that the most vital work involves the expansion of human consciousness, and the tool to accomplish it lay deep within. Here, deep inside, is the spiritual body, which encloses the subtle mind and its capacity to bring forth renewed understanding of God's plan for the world. Shemaiahu understood that the partnership between man and God is what brings purpose and meaning to life.

Raziel had said that the subtle mind connects with the universal fluid parchment from which all vitality flows, into every corner of existence. The subtle mind brings goodness and growth to those who dare to link and work from within it.

CHAPTER 28

Death of Moses

The Conquest of Canaan—1406 BC

THIRTY-EIGHT CONTINUOUS YEARS PASSED since the Israelites arrived at Kadesh-Barnea, and now they were on the move again, hauling their belongings laboriously along the arid terrain. The caravan traveled steadily toward the northeast, bordering the mountains in the land of Edom until entering the land of Moab. Having become unaccustomed to the nomadic way of life, they were to struggle again.

Zakai held the reins of a camel which carried Elah and Daliah, his mother and younger sister. The air was so dense, he felt that he could faint at any moment. Taking the canteen of water, he removed the long turban that heated his head and spread the precious liquid on his hair to cool it down. This he did not do very frequently as water was scarce. He then gave the camel's reins a jerk to make the beast move faster, and the rest of the animals following behind also quickened their pace.

Even in the suffocating heat, Zakai was enthralled by the view that opened before his eyes. As the caravan approached the Jordan River from the southeast, trickling brooks of water appeared. He saw hills high and lush with beautiful vegetation. *Rain must fall often*, he thought. *This is a blessed soil*. He had never seen such an abundance of green pasture and fruit in the trees and wished they would stay here.

But Moses had other plans. YHWH had ordered them to occupy Canaan, across the River Jordan. The Israelites were to drive out all the inhabitants of the land, destroy their temples, destroy their molten idols, and demolish their high places. "You shall clear out the land and settle in it, for

I have given you the land to occupy it,"[1] God commanded and cautioned Moses against letting anyone remain alive. He warned in very clear terms, "Those whom you leave over will be as spikes in your eyes and thorns in your sides, and they will harass you in the land in which you settle."[2]

Moses was a skilled strategist. He knew that his tribal warriors were not capable of besetting the walled cities of Canaan. Much less were they able to stand up in the open fields and confront the heavily armed Canaanites and their chariots. With this in mind, he instructed Joshua, his trusted aide, "Call Caleb and Eliezer, officers of the people, and tell them to stop their advancement. We are not entering head-on into the land of Canaan but will do so indirectly."[3]

The Israelites moved toward the fringes of the desert, turning to the west.[4] There, they rammed the only weak link in the border, the realm of Sihon, king of the Amorites. They conquered the city and pushed northwards to settle in Gilead.[5] Afterward, the Israelites continued north toward Bashan where they took possession of that land.[6] Then they journeyed south and encamped in the plains of Moab, across the Jordan from Jericho,[7] and settled in Shittim. This would be their last encampment at the end of forty years of wandering in the wilderness before crossing the river and entering Canaan.

While they were at Shittim, a plague spread like a curse all across the land. Twenty-four thousand people died because of the epidemic.[8] "So many senseless deaths!" neighbors cried to one another. "Since we settled in Moab, things have changed for the worse," they observed.

But one morning Zakai woke to a colossal uproar. Jumping out of bed, he left the tent and rushed to the place where a crowd had gathered screaming loudly and gesturing toward the tent of Zimri, son of Salu, chief of a house of the tribe of Shimon.

"What is going on?" he asked those standing around him.

A woman who looked quite agitated leaned toward him. "Zimri has been showing off a Midianite princess; last night, he brought her into his

---

1. See Numbers 33:51–53.
2. See Numbers 33:55.
3. Herzog and Gichon, *Battles of the Bible*, 43.
4. See Numbers 21:4.
5. Herzog and Gichon, *Battles of the Bible*, 43; see Numbers 21:21–25.
6. See Numbers 21:33–35.
7. See Numbers 22:1.
8. See Numbers 25:9.

family tent to lay with her! What an insolence! Phinehas has just entered the tent, carrying a long spear in his hand."

Piercing screams were heard. In one stroke, Phinehas drove his spear through the interlaced bodies of Zimri and the princess,[9] then emerged from the tent. The blood that dripped from the spike stained his hands and robe. His eyes were filled with a kind of madness.

Some days later, the plague ceased completely. The zealous retribution delivered by Phinehas, grandson of Aaron, had restored the covenant between YHWH and his people.

***

In Moab, the Israelites were drawn into a licentious way of life, engaging in adulterous encounters with beautiful women.[10] Soon it would be known that the king ordered the Moabite women to lure the best young men into sacrificing to their gods; this, he knew, would infuriate YHWH. The women, of course, did as the king had instructed. They lured the men with their perfumes, feeding them luscious foods and plying them with intoxicating drinks that made them lose control and bow down to Baal Peor. The men forgot their commitment to YHWH and a horrendous plague descended all over the land. "YHWH is incensed against us," the Israelites muttered. "This plague comes straight from God."[11]

After the massive burial of twenty-four thousand people, Moses ordered a count of the survivors. Every male from age twenty upward and able to serve in the army was included in the census. There were 601,730 such people. As had been commanded by God, Moses gave each a portion of the land, and to each tribe he bestowed the land according to their numbers.[12] The Levites, who were also counted, numbered twenty-three thousand males aged one month and upward, but they received no inheritance of land[13] as they were to serve and dwell amongst their brethren.

Moses then praised Phinehas in front of the people. "Phinehas, son of Eleazar, son of Aaron, you turned back YHWH's wrath. Because of your zeal, He did not wipe out all of His people. God grants you a covenant of

9. See Numbers 25:7–8.
10. See Numbers 25:1–2.
11. See Numbers 25:3.
12. See Numbers 26:1–56.
13. See Numbers 26:57–63.

eternal priesthood. In your faithfulness and might, you have atoned for the Israelites."[14]

Some days later Moses gathered the high priest Eleazar, Joshua, and Caleb—his three most trusted men. "My time has come," he said. "I will soon depart from the world to meet the Angel of Death. God spoke to me during the night. He said, 'Go up to Mount Nebo and watch the land of Canaan, which I am giving to the children of Israel as a possession.'[15] He said that I will die on the mountain, and then I will be gathered with my ancestors." Moses' voice broke as he added, "Just as Aaron, my brother, was gathered at Mount Hor."

Moses accepted God's judgment and prepared to fulfill his destiny. He entered the sacred Tent of Meeting alone hoping to encounter God. The question in his heart reflected the immense worry that loomed over him: who would lead the Israelites to their final destination? And God answered, "Take for yourself Joshua, the son of Nun, a man of spirit. You shall lay your hand upon him.[16] I will be with him as I have been with you,[17] and he will lead the people."

Moses took Joshua and presented him first before Eleazar, the high priest. Next, before the entire congregation, he laid his hands upon Joshua's head and shoulders and instructed him to guide the people, saying, "These people are to always serve YHWH and follow His commands."[18]

Then Moses, the great Prophet, the godly man, simply walked away. He entered alone into the desert, heading toward the mountain of Nebo in Abarim, and nobody would ever see him again.

Zakai stood alongside other Levites and watched the silhouette of the Prophet vanish in the distance. Not much was said and nobody knew what had happened. Moses had been an elusive man who stood apart from the people, and Zakai resented that. He had witnessed the greatness of this man when he guided his people out of Egypt with strength and valor. Moses had led them out of bondage with an admiringly unequivocal force. Zakai would have liked to know him better.

The Levites had proven their loyalty to him. They were always ready to defend Moses' honor. They had been his guardians and now they felt abandoned. Some showed surprise; others disappointment; still others, feeling

14. See Numbers 25: 11–13.

15. See Deuteronomy 32:49.

16. See Numbers 27:18–23.

17. See Joshua 1:5.

18. See Numbers 28–30.

rejected, were angry. Some, like Zakai, fought the bitter aftertaste that comes when people do not feel appreciated.

"Where did Moses go?" one man was overheard repeating again and again, as if each time he expected an answer.

"You heard him anoint Joshua to be our leader," someone else said impatiently. "He went away to meet Samael, the Angel of Death. Moses is gone forever."

Another man affirmed, "I saw a cloud standing over him all of a sudden and then he disappeared into the valley."[19]

Still others said that God buried him in the valley of Moab, near Beth Peor, with His own hands.[20]

Eleazar stood before them. He spoke loudly and clearly, so everyone would hear and know that there was a deliberate purpose behind all this. That it was intentional. "No living person will ever know the place of Moses' burial."

And the people mourned for thirty days, until the time of weeping and mourning was over.[21]

19. Josephus, *Antiquities of the Jews* 4.8.
20. See Deuteronomy 34:6.
21. See Deuteronomy 34:8.

CHAPTER 29

Shemaiahu's Encounter with Moses—1386 BC

MOVING SLOWLY AND SMOOTHLY through dense fluid, Shemaiahu continued the path of ascension. At last he reached a summit. He stood at the edge, able to gaze at the valley below. The view was dim and a bit blurry, as if he were peering through frosted glass. After overcoming the sense of unsteadiness that overtook his body, he was able to scan the entire valley below, where he discerned an impressive variety of creatures, plants, and animals. A profound admiration for the magnificence of YHWH's creation surged through his entire being. He shuddered in awe.

A soft breeze coming from behind made him turn around. There he saw a ladder, tall and wide, constructed of pure white marble. The foot of the ladder was set upon the earth, and the top of it reached all the way to heaven. Angels dressed in white light ascended and descended the ladder while singing praises to God in celebration of His creation.

They sang: "*How many are your works, Lord! In wisdom you made them all; the earth is full of your creatures. There is the sea, vast and spacious, teeming with creatures beyond number—living things both large and small. All creatures look to you to give them food at the proper time. When you hide your face, they are terrified. When you send your Spirit, they are created, and you renew the face of the ground.*"[1]

The ladder, the choir of angels, and the glorious hymn of praise sealed within Shemaiahu the certainty that all was well. God the Creator never deserts His creatures.

Two angels now moved toward him. In silence, they gestured for him to follow. The three of them climbed the ladder until they reached a place

1. See Psalm 104.

where the air was fresh and bracing. From this vantage point Shemaiahu was able to distinguish in the background the silhouette of Mount Nebo. Was this a sign that he was in fact following the footsteps of the Prophet? A big smile of appreciation spread across his face. Yes! He was.

They resumed their climb. As they did, the white marble ladder seemed to lengthen. Not only did the ladder increase in height but, like branches growing out from the trunk, new ladders sprouted in all directions. Shemaiahu conjectured that this indicated that there were many other paths he could follow, but he kept his focus on his goal, which was to locate the eyes that were hidden between the rocks.

Steadily he climbed, keeping his focus. And then—there they were! There before him, just barely discernible among the large boulders, he perceived what seemed to be the features of a human face.

Shuah's words came as an echo. *"He will be there, at his meeting place at the head of the mountain. There, between the two eyes in the rock. Only those who can see the eyes will find Moses."*

As if responding to his thoughts, the branch of the ladder on which he stood shifted its position to the left. The ladder was now lined up in front of an opening that resembled the socket of an eye. Trembling with excitement, Shemaiahu was just about to step off his ladder when he noticed two angels approaching. He paused and waited.

"Welcome," they said in greeting. "The time has come."

With one on either side, they guided Shemaiahu through a corridor at the end of which was a spacious foyer. The surrounding walls were made of lapis lazuli veined in gold. A soft, radiant light shone from the room inside. Clearly, this was a sacred place.

The three of them moved along the corridor and into the foyer until they reached a square pillar situated exactly at the midpoint and immediately behind the two eye-shaped openings. Shemaiahu studied the pillar. It was stamped with an image that resembled one big eye, the center of which was not a pupil but a gigantic diamond that glittered with light. On the floor beneath the eye was a shallow, circular pool of fresh, clear waters. Shemaiahu bent forward and peered into the pond. He expected to see his face mirrored in the water, but to his surprise the face of an old man was reflected back at him. It was a fine-looking face. Soft white curls and a thin white beard framed this friendly face, a face that was animated by pinpricks of light that danced from deep within round, dark eyes.

Wordlessly, the angels let Shemaiahu know that the old man was Joseph, he whose bones were taken by the Israelites when they left Egypt. "Turn your gaze upward and see for yourself," they conveyed to him.

Shemaiahu straightened to see a man clad in a long white robe. It was Joseph. He, too, spoke without words. His tone was grave, for he was there to deliver a warning. "Because Moses is a being too intense to behold, you will not be alone when you meet Moses. I will be there."

Joseph gestured toward the pond, instructing Shemaiahu to wash his hands and feet. From that moment on, a series of events developed so quickly, Shemaiahu could barely remember all that happened as he was being prepared for the encounter with Moses.

The angels extended their wings and shielded Shemaiahu beneath them in such a way that Shemaiahu recognized that he was undergoing purification. He was becoming balanced. He felt a sense of wellbeing growing inside of him. Then the angels presented him with a white robe with which to clothe himself. Shemaiahu felt a great surge of gratitude for the mentoring, the nurturing, and the comfort he was being provided.

He bowed his head and murmured, "Will it take long?"

Joseph pointed to the diamond in the pillar, and a thought formed in Shemaiahu's mind. *Wait*, the thought commanded.

A cloud of light surrounded by a halo flowed from the diamond. Shemaiahu saw the blurry likeness of a man inside the haloed light. The next instant Shemaiahu lost sight of his surroundings. He sensed that he was suspended in the air although not actually in motion. He was being transported into a place he had never been before. It was a place that was radiant and warm. Joseph must have never left his side because Shemaiah could hear his reassuring, soothing voice repeating, "You are safe; you are safe." Shemaiahu submitted to the experience and surrendered to the serenity of the moment.

At last he understood that the figure outlined inside the haloed light was Moses. The image was indistinct, like an aura around a lamp, but the center was clear and defined. Shemaiah realized that, although some of the physical features of the man Moses once was could be discerned, he was now looking at his essence, an essence that had remained sealed upon Moses' spirit even after the soul had lifted from his body.

Shemaiahu dropped to his knees in reverence.

"Rise," boomed a thunderous voice. "Do not kneel in my dispensable presence. You should only kneel before God."

Shemaiahu leaped to his feet.

With vehemence he responded, "Dear Master, I have something for you. I brought you two sapphires sent by the angel Gabriel, who instructed me to deliver the stones into your hands."

A burst of laughter rang forth and careened across the room. "Into my *hands*?"

Great peals of laughter again filled the air, and confusion surged through Shemaiahu.

As if he had perceived the young man's uneasiness, Moses hastened to explain, "I have no hands with which to grasp or hold! No. Let the sapphires flow out from where they have been lodged. Let them fill the gap between us. Then they can insert themselves into the place where they properly belong."

Shemaiahu felt a jolt deep in the center of his body. Immediately he saw two astonishingly beautiful stones emerging from the center of his own essence. After the stones emerged from his body they swirled and danced through the air, as if they had been made ecstatic by freedom. The radiance of the stones pulsated and grew more and more intense as they edged closer to the Prophet. When they reached Moses, they thrummed with one last bright celebratory explosion before being absorbed into his halo.

With kindness in his voice, Moses said, "The knowledge contained in those stones was delivered to me at Mount Sinai. These are the essential teachings that were never conveyed to your people while I lived amongst them. The Israelites were not yet capable of understanding their meaning because the notion of slavery still filled their minds. But you, Shemaiahu— you are different. You have followed a path of ascension into the subtler realms. You have allowed yourself to be led. You have trod the difficult, painful road of ascent and have detached yourself from the restrictive impulses that confine human nature. You left behind anger and greed—both of them such difficult adversaries!

"Now—ask! Because I will teach you only what your heart needs to know."

Startled, Shemaiahu wrested his attention to his mind. To what was inside.

Throughout this process of self-searching he already learned that the essential questions, carefully articulated, could come not from the mind but only from the depths of the human soul. Even so, he felt uncertain, and his first question was awkwardly vague.

"Man of God," he began, "the divine Providence is your bride and stands firmly beside you. I am a Levite, a child of Jacob, the forefather who struggled with an angel of God. Although my nature is lower than his, I ask, on his behalf, for your instruction. You are the greatest man—a master who knows God face-to-face. I have come to hear what you can teach me, and thereby rise above my limitations." Dimly aware that his request might come across as sounding pretentious, Shemaiahu lowered his voice as a counterbalancing sign of humility. Then, summoning another mighty effort, he tried again to form a question. "Man of God, I am a man seeking Him. Can you please tell me what God is?" He paused in fear. He was afraid of the words he had just uttered. He forged ahead in an effort to explain himself. "I am here to learn how to better serve Him. How to understand His will." Crushed by the weight of such a bold request, Shemaiahu fell with his face to the ground.

CHAPTER 30

Conquering Jericho

The Death of Zakai—1404 BC

AFTER MOSES' DEATH, JOSHUA took over the leadership of the Israelites. He became the mastermind behind the conquest of the Canaanite heartland. A shrewd strategist, Joshua designed a plan in two stages: the crossing of the river followed by the securing of a fortified position on a bridgehead inside the conquered territory. This would be a place to retreat if necessary.

The region Joshua chose for crossing the Jordan was close to the Dead Sea, skirting the land of Moab. The river in this place could be crossed in many places, allowing for different routes of entry, with numerous tracks that led to the central highlands. A critical landmark was the city of Jericho, a lush tropical garden in the middle of a vast savanna to the west of the Jordan River. Jericho was an old walled town that had supplied the needs of the caravans and voyagers that traveled along the Jordan River for hundreds of years. Secure behind its walls, towers, and fortifications, Jericho stood with defiance and pride, and Joshua sent two undercover spies to explore the city.

The spies entered a hostel lodged behind the city walls. It was owned by an astute, skillful woman named Rahab. The woman agreed to collaborate with them, but only after securing their promise that she and her family would be safeguarded during the siege of the city. She offered them food and shelter. Looking at them intently, she warned, "We must be careful. No one knows you are here, but I don't know for how long. Ask what you need to know but swear to me in the name of your God that you'll be kind to my father's household. Give me a sure sign."

After the men promised they would spare her family with their belongings, Rahab told them what she knew.[1] "The people of the land are fearful of the Israelites and their terrible God," she said. "We heard that YHWH dried up the waters of the Sea of Reeds so the Israelites could cross over when they left Egypt, and we heard how the kings of the Amorites were utterly destroyed. The people in the city are overwhelmed, demoralized by fear."[2]

The king of Jericho got word that two Israelites were lodging in the hostel and sent a party of men to detain them. But Rahab hid the spies beneath a stack of hay up in the roof. After the king's men had left, they escaped by a rope hung from a window in the town wall. She gave them provisions for the road and instructed, "Go out to the hill country and hide there for three days. After that, you may go on your own way."[3]

The spies gave her a scarlet cord to hang from the window in her house as a sign of protection. They instructed her to gather her family and wait inside the house. "As long as all of you stay indoors," they told her, "you will be spared." They hurried to Joshua and reported what they had learned. "God has put the entire land under our control. The inhabitants of the land will melt right in front of us!"[4]

Joshua found a vantage point on a high boulder from where he could watch the troop formation, and announced in a loud voice, "Get ready to cross the river at any time. God has given us the land of Canaan. It is in our hands."

Zakai lined readily with the troops. He believed Joshua's prediction to be true. That it would be a day filled with wonders, a day to remember. As Joshua instructed, he secured a short sword, tempered and sharpened, to his belt. Then, he hung over his shoulder a worn wooden sack that contained his most beloved possession, the shofar that his father received as a gift from heaven.

The Israelites continued getting into formation in preparation for the crossing of the Jordan River. A trumpet blast announced that the time to advance toward the city had come. The multitude of soldiers started moving as one in a massive surge of people entering the river as they had been ordered to do.

Miraculously, the riverbed dried up to accommodate the foot soldiers. It would remain dry until the priests with the Ark of the Covenant passed over and the Israelites reached the other side. On the other side,

---

1. See Joshua 2:12–14.
2. See Joshua 2:10–11.
3. See Joshua 2:16.
4. See Joshua 2:24.

twelve Levites set twelve large stones where the Ark was placed. This site was named Gilgal Rephaim, and the rocks would remain standing memorials for years to come.

A loud voice instructed the people to gather again, each man with his tribe, in preparation for the capture of Jericho. Marching in a disciplined formation, the Israelites followed the Ark as they circled the city. The procession marched continuously for seven days. Seven priests blew their shofars, and Zakai stood proudly amongst them.

The group marched around the city in accord with God's instructions. The first six consecutive days, they circled the city once. But on the seventh day, they circled the city seven times. The priests blew the ram's horns unendingly, while the rest of the men screamed and banged their swords, one against the other, creating a frightful noise. Suddenly, the earth began to tremble and a sordid uproar broke the walls of the city, and they crumbled to the ground. Thus were the Israelites able to enter Jericho.

"YHWH has joined us in this moment of truth!" Zakai exulted, his heart beating as if about to explode. "Everything is true. Moses' promise was true, and so was the visit of the angel to my father."

Zakai the Levite had marched around Jericho, blowing the shofar that Gabriel the angel gave to Hanan, his father. He did so with all the strength and passion he was capable of. His purpose in life was now fulfilled, and the meaning of Gabriel's gift, foretelling the conquest of the land, achieved new clarity in his mind. Falling on his knees, a deep sob erupted from his chest. Zakai had come full circle by also accomplishing his father's mission.

That night Zakai died in his sleep. He was thirty-nine years old. Next to his body was the woolen sack with a precious jewel: the shofar that Gabriel gave to his father.

"The soul left his body," a Levite friend told Abital when he brought Zakai's corpse across the river back to the camp. "Zakai died at peace," he said. "Of that I am sure. The serenity upon his face as he lay on his deathbed showed that he was at peace with God and with life."

And on the day of the conquest, Joshua upheld the promise given to Rahab. The Israelites spared the hostel marked by a scarlet cord and all of its inhabitants.[5]

5. See Joshua 6:25.

CHAPTER 31

Shemaiahu

Moses Tells His Life Story—1386 BC

AT MOSES' COMMAND, TWO angels helped Shemaiahu to his feet. The Prophet seemed pleased to welcome him as a pupil. Shemaiahu had lived the life of a seeker, a life filled with purpose. He had shown great discipline and had chosen the right path of action. He had spoken truthfully, uttering the right words, and so, the angels—sempiternal guardians of heaven—were not tempted to judge him.

Moses ordered the vault of the heavens to be opened. It became Shemaiahu's privilege to watch all things unfold before his eyes in present time. All the stories of the past were happening right now in what was an endless present. Shemaiahu could see events unfolding in the world as no one had ever seen before. The ample cave of time became fully lit.

He noticed a wooden board in a corner with a piece of parchment and some writing instruments on top of it. The parchment was spread wide open, a clear invitation for him to record what would be forthcoming. Shemaiahu sat on the floor and placed the wooden board in his lap. Joseph sat down beside him.

"I am ready," Shemaiahu whispered.

Joseph said with appreciation, "You have accomplished much, son of Levi. Now follow the scribal tradition of your tribe and write down everything that you see and hear. When the time is right, Moses will give you the answers you seek. But first, you must know some things about him that no man has ever heard. Things that set Moses apart from all other humans, including me." Joseph extended his arm toward the wall and opened a window in time.

There before them was the Nile River. Its beautiful blue-green waters and the surrounding lush vegetation made Shemaiahu feel the freshness of the moment. A basket of reeds carrying a little child inside floated down the river. The baby's arms and legs flailed with discomfort, and he began to cry.

"You have been granted the honor of watching the unfolding of events from a special vantage point," said Joseph. "This is the backstage of human history. Observe carefully!"

A new window opened. It revealed a parallel world, a dimension not manifested in the world below. In this new window, Shemaiahu saw an angel hovering over the child. This was Lailah, the Angel of the Night, whose duty was to watch over Moses from the moment of his conception.[1] Shemaiahu learned that Moses' soul had received all the knowledge that would be available to humanity. Right before his birth he received all the wisdom that the world would acquire and knew well the story of his life as a man. Unlike all other living beings, Lailah did not strike a finger against Moses' mouth. She did not circumcise the child's lips, and so, Moses never forgot all he knew at the moment of his birth. He alone held in his mind a comprehensive knowledge of the past, the present, and the future.

Joseph's silhouette started to fade, and a deep, booming voice startled Shemaiahu at the same time as a bright beam of light pierced the darkness in the cave. It was Moses. As if answering a question that loomed in the space between them, he said, "I know that you, along with many others, believe that God punished me and took me away to my death. Many believe that I left without a warning. But you are wrong. My time of departure had come and I was ready to go. I crossed the portal willingly." The booming voice lowered to a whisper as Moses added, "My time on earth had come to an end. I did not enter the Promised Land with the children of Israel because my path was different than theirs." His voice gained a depth of profundity, as if it were coming from a distant impersonal source.

Shemaiahu had increased the skills required to receive telepathic communications directly with his mind. He could read deeply beyond what was said. Effortlessly, his mind understood that many of the precepts commanded to Israel could only be fulfilled in the Promised Land. Moses had wished to enter into the Promised Land to ensure that all the precepts would be met and that the path of final redemption of all of humanity would be achieved. But God had planned otherwise and did not accept Moses' plea. God told him, "Moses, I will endorse all those precepts to you as if thou performed them in life. You merit them, because you gave your soul to Me risking death. You bore the sins of many and made intercession for the

---

1. *Midrash Tanchuma*, Pekudei §3, in Sefaria, "Midrash Tanchuma, Pekudei 3:4-7."

sinners. You secured atonement for the making of the golden calf, begging for mercy on behalf of the sinners in Israel. Because of you, they turned to Me in repentance. Those precepts I will accredit to you.[2] But people must continue treading their path and fulfill what is theirs to fulfill. Your time on earth is done."

Moses repeated in a whisper, "My time on earth was done."

Shemaiahu tried to imagine what Moses was feeling at that moment. Was it sadness or disappointment? But he knew all too well that his human ruminations did not belong here.

As if confirming Shemaiahu's guess, Moses shifted his gaze and his focus changed. Then he looked straight into Shemaiahu's eyes. "Shemaiahu, you have mastered the human wish to accumulate vain power. You have taken a path that not many would dare to travel. You have refined your nature and senses, which is what brought you to me. Your desire to know who I am and what sets me apart, come from the pureness of your mind and heart as they work together in unison. I will now answer your questions."

This was the moment Shemaiahu had been waiting for.

The transmission of Moses' words as they traveled through the dense, watery substance between them heightened the tonalities of the voice. This confirmed what the angel Raziel had said: "*All that you receive and learn is like a ripple crossing the deep, boundless waters within the Universal Mind that sustains all. They will remain engraved forever and will be available to all who wish to learn.*"

With intensified trust and renewed fervor, Shemaiahu gave himself to receiving Moses' wisdom. His soul thirsted for all the knowledge he could gain. Right on cue, Moses exclaimed, "Look!" and a new window in time opened up before them.

Shemaiahu watched a man walking in the far distance. Even wearing the worn robes of a shepherd, the man looked princely. With a start, Shemaiahu realized that the man was none other than Moses.

"Yes," said Moses. "I was a royal prince in the line of succession to the throne of Egypt. But some royals rose against me. They wanted me dead, so I fled Egypt. No, I didn't fly away because of fear of death. I left Egypt to escape a cycle of hostilities that would make me prey to the most basic human instincts and it was time to prepare for what a Higher Will would bring my way.

"In my human form, I spent long years in the desert fields pasturing the flock. I lived in utter solitude long enough that mysterious emanations, both celestial and demonic, would come to me and fill me with awe or fear.

2. Babylonian Talmud, *Sotah* 14a.

"I was endowed with a hot and willful temper that needed to be tamed in the name of my soul's evolution. My insides were a battlefield where strong emotions ignited and led the charge against each other. To my dismay, anger would flare up, mostly when I remembered what I was forced to leave behind. But I understood it was essential that I overcome these powerful, vicious foes that would take me from my true path."

Moses was speaking frankly; the strain of those years reflected in his voice.

"In the desert, life was harsh. Very difficult. But as the years went by my mind and my heart grew calm. I was able to attain moments of peace. I delved deeper into myself to enter into a place where there are neither longings nor belongings. I learned to quiet my body. I learned to soften the eyes of my mind. The gates of my soul were opened in ways that only the stillness of life in the desert could allow. All of this prepared me for the role I was intended to play in the history of humankind."

A striking scene developed in front of Shemaiahu's eyes as he watched through the open window. He saw Moses pasturing the family's flock in the Desert of Midian, not far from Mount Sinai. Then a most implausible sight captured Shemaiahu's full attention: a burning shrub that was never consumed by the flames.

Referencing the burning bush, Moses said, "At the moment when I turned around and saw that awe-inspiring view, I heard the voice of an angel of God. It called my name and said, 'Take off the shoes from your feet; the place upon which you stand is holy.' Indeed, I removed my sandals and then I fell to the ground and covered my face in total awe. I was afraid to lift my gaze. Then YHWH, not His angel, spoke to me. You, Shemaiahu, must remember that it was because of my attitude of openness and my total attentiveness to what was happening that this Superior Force spoke to me! YHWH then commanded me to go to Egypt, free the Israelites, and lead them to the land that He had promised to their ancestors. That was my mission."

A very long silence followed. There was no mistaking the struggle Moses was feeling inside as he relived the conflict.

He continued, "I bargained with God. I asked in earnest, 'Why have you chosen me?' I pleaded and begged, 'I'm not perfect! In my many years of solitude I have become heavy of mouth and heavy of tongue. No one will understand nor believe what I say.'"

Moses stopped for a minute, weighing what he was about to disclose. Was his listener prepared to receive such information? He gave a little nod, as if to himself, and said, "I saw it beforehand and knew that it was not in God's plan to make me the final redeemer of his people. So I questioned

God. What purpose would I serve? I refused this assignment.[3] I was adamant that I would not participate in His plan. But God's will is unyielding. And as if He had not even heard my refusal, His final words to me were, 'So shall you say to the children of Israel: The Lord God of your forefathers has sent me to you. I Will Be That I Will Be has sent me to you. This is My name forever. This is how I should be called in every generation.'"[4]

When Moses uttered the Holy Name a strange, soft vibration filled the room and invaded Shemaiahu's entire body. He felt a pounding in the center of his forehead, between the eyebrows, and also in his heart. Listening to the Prophet's testimony sparked great compassion in him. Shemaiahu could not imagine that anyone but Moses could have endured the intensity of those moments.

Moses continued with his description of the struggle. "I cried out to God and said, 'I beseech You, oh YHWH, send now the message with him whom You have chosen to do the work.[5] Send the message with him whom You call the Messiah. He has been properly endowed to bring an end to our years on earth.' So it was that I expressed my thoughts to God with a fearful heart."

Moses concluded softly, "I had not been chosen to bring the Israelites into the Promised Land. Thus, I pleaded before Him to bring the true final liberator at once and put an end to the human affliction. But God's fury rose. My defiance stoked His wrath. At that moment, I knew I had to surrender." In the deep voice Shemaiahu now knew so well, Moses concluded again: "My time on earth had come to an end. I did not enter the Promised Land with the children of Israel because my path and theirs were different."

3. See Exodus 3:11.
4. See Exodus 3:14-15.
5. Exodus 4:13, in Silberman, *Chumash with Rashi's Commentary*.

CHAPTER 32

Moses' Encounter with God—1386 BC

IN A WEARY VOICE, Moses continued opening up to Shemaiahu.

"Surrendering to a Higher Force was the challenge that steered my life. Since the moment of my birth, I was led by this powerful, hidden source. It was an authority in my life which I experienced daily but could not always understand. Not having much in common with earthly beings as well, the sentient side of me acknowledged our differences with pain. I cried already in the crib, upset with the sounds of human voices that spoke behind closed doors. I recognized the often-dark intentions hidden in their voices and feelings of isolation took over me, making me want to escape. But, in time, I grew to accept my fate. I had to learn the ways of the world as I was destined to play a part in God's plan. I developed a relationship with this portentous hidden force that ruled every life, and I adapted to the world so that I could share my understanding of Him with humanity." Moses pointed towards the open space and exclaimed, "Look now! Be witness of what I mean."

Shemaiahu followed the pointing finger and saw that a new window had opened. This window revealed a scene in which Moses was preparing to leave the house of Jethro, his father-in-law and priest of Midian. YHWH had reassured Moses that those who sought to kill him were dead. After receiving Jethro's blessing, Moses gathered his wife Zipporah and his two sons Gershom and Eliezer and, riding on donkeys, they started the journey toward the land of Egypt, with Moses holding fast to the staff of God on every step of the way.

They made slow, steady progress, traveling through sandy hills and valleys until they reached a small hostel on the side of the road. When they dismounted and prepared to get some rest something unexpected happened. An angel of God appeared before them in the guise of a giant serpent. The serpent turned its full attention on Moses. Striking quickly, the snake swallowed him from the head to the hip all the way to the mark of his circumcision.

Shemaiahu's heart was thrumming at the sight of this. It was unbelievable what he just saw happening, right before his eyes! Why would God send an angel to ambush Moses and put him to death? It was incomprehensible. Moses had spoken face-to-face with God. Furthermore, he had been chosen to unshackle God's children, to free them from slavery. And now God wanted to kill him? What type of entity was He, this God? Who was this Being that was capable of such bizarre, unpredictable, unfathomable deeds?

A new window opened so that Shemaiahu could witness a previous event, the time when Jethro gave Zipporah to Moses in marriage. Jethro had demanded of his new son-in-law not to circumcise their firstborn son. But this demand was in direct conflict with the agreement God had made with Abraham. God had decreed, "This is my covenant, which you shall keep, between Me and you and thy seed after thee. Every man-child among you shall be circumcised."[1] In return, God promised to reside amongst them and grant them a land for their descendants.

Given his abilities, Moses could foresee that a time would come when Jethro would recognize the unicity of YHWH and give himself willingly to His service. Not wanting to anger Jethro and in anticipation of such a reassuring future event, Moses decided to not circumcise the child after his birth. Knowingly, he broke the covenant between Abraham and God, and according to the law of God a corrective consequence was now in order. The serpent was precisely that, an instrument of divine justice.

Zipporah was a strong woman, bright and practical. With one look she recognized the underpinnings of the gruesome event. Without wasting a moment, Zipporah circumcised their son and tossed the bloody foreskin onto Moses' feet. She knew that her action would transform darkness into light as well as tether even more securely the soul of Moses to his body and to his physical life on earth. With grand ceremony, she shouted, "For you, Moses, are a bridegroom of blood to me,"[2] thereby affirming her unshakeable connection to Moses. And so, at the moment the blood touched Moses' skin, his soul was anchored in his body. Shemaiahu stared transfixed as the serpent coughed up its prey. Moses had been released from the grip of Samael, the Angel of Death.

When the window closed Shemaiahu asked, "Tell me, Master, because it is very difficult to understand: Why did God want to kill you, precisely when you were fulfilling His stated will?"

---

1. See Genesis 17:10–11.
2. See Exodus 4:24–26.

Moses answered with words of caution. "There is much you have to learn about the world behind the veil and how that world reverberates in the world below. The world from the beyond is a complex dimension, governed by extraordinarily strong and oscillating forces which turn with ease into their opposites.[3] Because of that, much of what happened in my life on earth may seem merciless, fruitless, random, and without a purpose. But no, it is not so. At the end, balance is always restored, opening the way for something new. Secretly, in the depths of my heart, I held the temptation of exiting the world, but God's blow and Zipporah's quick thinking rendered me unable to do so. I could leave the world only when my task was completed, and that is what eventually happened. Yes, Shemaiahu, it is difficult to recognize at that very moment the valuable, but at the same time contradictory, ways in which God makes Himself present."

Shemaiahu remained silent as a remarkable episode of his own life flashed through his mind. He remembered the time while alone in the fields he experienced the two contrasting forces that Moses just described. First it was the angel Gabriel who visited and prompted him to continue on the journey to find Moses. That was a peaceful and joyous moment—so beautiful! But right away, a very dark shadow, darker than any abyss, engulfed him and made him fear that he might die. Just as Moses described, so, too, in his own life had the forces been manifested and turned into their opposites!

"God spoke his name, letting me know that *I Will Be* was His name forever," said Moses. "But be clear about this point, Shemaiahu: even though His name is known, God will always be concealed in numerous layers of reality."

Moses fell silent. It was true: it was nearly impossible to comprehend the fullness and vastness of this magnificent Being and of the world He had created. In spite of His complexity, God had promised to be omnipresent. Even so, He remained incorporeal.

"Throughout my earthly life," Moses continued, "I had to learn how to deal with and fathom that intangible reality. And I did learn to deal with it— by opening up to listen and then waiting for the guidance that comes from the silence within. That is where He speaks—in the silence of the heart.[4] My understanding of God, dear Shemaiahu, evolved and changed through time, and so will yours.

"Life in the desert prepared me for my first encounter with the angel of God in the burning bush. I disciplined my mind, tamed my emotions,

3. This phenomenon is called "enantiodromia." Jung defines "enantiodromia" as "the play of opposites in the course of events. The emergence of the unconscious opposite in the course of time." Jung, *Psychological Types* 6:426.

4. Teresa, Mother. "In the Silence."

refined my instincts, and controlled my desires in such solitude. I trained myself to go beyond the curtain that separates the angelic realm from the human. Then, when I came to meet YHWH in Sinai, I was pulled even higher.[5] I entered spaces that only the prophet Enoch had visited before being taken by Him—a radiant chamber of fire and crystal where the Great Glory of God sat upon His throne.[6] This time, it was God, not His angel, who pulled me higher. I was permitted to enter the sphere of His throne, the Throne of Glory. There, I was allowed to touch the holy throne before returning to the world in my flesh. This was a thing that had never happened before. Not even Enoch, the greatest amongst the angels of God, was permitted to return to the flesh. But I was sent back so that I might fulfill my destiny and complete my mission."

Shemaiahu needed time to ponder and process the vital information he was receiving. Aware of that, Moses paused the narrative and then, when Shemaiahu seemed to have regained focus, he resumed his story.

"I met God face-to-face. I, Moses, the son of a living woman, met God one on one. In His presence my human capacities were rendered totally unsuitable. My mind found it difficult to think, and my body, suddenly unresponsive, couldn't move. My will was weakened to the point of near paralysis. Though my voice faltered, I tried to remain calm and clear, safeguarding the likeness of the man I knew myself to be, while I faced this intimidating Presence. Apparently, I was meant to be a mediator between the people and God. And so, I remained true to my duty by trying to sustain myself with a measure of dignity while I dialogued with the Almighty."

It was time to unveil a new window. Through this one, Shemaiahu witnessed the enthusiasm of Aaron, the Prophet's oldest brother, who went to the desert to meet with Moses. The two brothers kissed and spoke at length. Moses taught Aaron everything that God instructed him to do, and Aaron agreed to be his spokesman. Moses then showed him the signs of His grandeur that God commanded to be performed in front of Pharaoh and the people.[7] Moses added, "My brother and I would pave the way so that this mixed multitude, a conglomerate of people named the Israelites, could leave the land of Egypt."

Every step in the journey was an opportunity for the people to develop spiritually by conquering a lower nature that is impulsive and passionate, in commonality with all living species on earth. This is a nature firmly attached to the world of survival and materiality.

5. See Exodus 33:17–23.
6. 1 Enoch 14:18–21, in Charles, *Book of Enoch*.
7. See Exodus 4:27–28.

"In Egypt, where they had lived for generations, people experienced the riches of matter which kept their lower nature satisfied. Now, they were being asked to trust an unseen, Transcendent Reality that exists beyond the physical world. They were asked to recognize that there is unity behind the multiplicity of appearances in the external world, and they should appreciate what is eternal and immutable, both of which rest beyond the temporal and variable. Not an easy task!" Moses gestured a soft smile, then continued. "The Israelites were supposed to follow the call that the One made to their souls. This was their journey toward redemption, the homecoming to their Source. Their souls were to be refined, become subtler, and be raised ever higher as they neared the promised land. This had been the pact that YHWH made with their forefather, Abraham."

Shemaiahu tried to keep his mind as focused and steady as he could. It was not easy. At times, his emotions would feel muddled and his thoughts disorganized. Moses had managed to do just that: steady his emotions and thought, thereby mastering the art of translating the information he received from the beyond into terms the inhabitants of the world could understand. Shemaiahu feared that in some distant era, people might be inclined to dismiss Moses' role as an intermediary between YHWH and humans; therefore, he was careful to extoll Moses in his note-taking.

Moses had primed his soul to become a vehicle able to capture the purest universal truths. His brain was attuned to the frequencies of the multiple layers in the universe at the same time as, being open to receive the most profound emanations from the beyond, it vibrated harmoniously with the active intellect of God.

"Men like this," Shemaiahu registered with a throbbing sense of respect, "are prophets. The process of cleaving to God is what is called prophecy."[8]

Shemaiahu praised Moses for his willingness to stay committed to the earthly realm, as weighty and challenging as this commitment could be. Approvingly, then, he recorded, "The Prophet strived to serve his fellow men as they struggled to rise in their earthly path and return to their spiritual Source."

8. Blumenfeld, "#7: Prophecy of Moses."

CHAPTER 33

The Laws of God

MOSES POINTED TOWARD A new open window. A dizzying multitude of Israelites were all making their way across the Sea of Reeds. Shemaiahu squinted trying to make sense of the millions of tiny figures and caught his breath in wonder when he realized what he was seeing. These were people from every generation in the past, the present, and the future.

He watched Moses with his arms raised high guiding the people into the receding waters, all the while loudly proclaiming the secret names of God. The waters receded as if in fear, and the seabed transformed into dry land for the safe crossing of the multitude. An assembly of angels gathered above in the heavens to bear witness to such a wondrous event. Moses' sister, Miriam, was there, walking among the people and joining in songs of praise to the Almighty. Some of the women played flutes and tambourines while others sang, "*Sing to the Lord, for He is highly exalted.*"[1] Before long, all of the people joined together in this joyous and happy celebration of freedom.

When the last Israelite had set foot upon the other side, the waters came crashing back into the channel with a mighty, thunderous roar. The Egyptian army, in hot pursuit of the Israelites, did not realize until it was too late that the sea would not stay parted for their own crossing. The waters enveloped them, and men and horses, every single one of them, perished.

Shemaiahu's body contracted in terror. A vast multitude, drowning. Whether guilty or not, all of these people were drowned. Moses picked up on Shemaiahu's distress. He knew it would take some time for him to grasp the nature of God's intervention on earthly matters such as this. Speaking slowly, he explained. "In this process of spiritual evolution, the Egyptians constituted a blind, unreflecting counterpart to the conscious, mindful

1. See Exodus 15:20.

individuals God sought the Israelites to become, and thus, they were to be blotted from God's book. The Egyptians remained stubbornly attached to the gifts and material possessions of the world. They failed to appreciate the nonphysical, transcendental sources of wellbeing. They felt invincible and used their unlimited power to govern ruthlessly over the lives of their fellow humans.

"But the priests of Egypt were knowledgeable. They were versed in the laws that ruled the universe that the one God created. Nevertheless, they erred by choosing to honor as equal to God their numberless lower spiritual powers. They even honored as equal to God their pharaohs and the stars in heaven. They failed to realize that all of these were intermediaries created by Him. None were independent in their authority. By disavowing the true power that stands behind the universe and its laws, the Egyptians injured their ability to participate in the greater plan of evolution. They and all of their generations to come were doomed." Solemnly, Moses declared, "Shemaiahu, hear and understand this: it is the law of God that there is a consequence for every thought, every project, and every action fostered by a human entity. If something disrupts the greater purpose of creation, it must be rectified. If there is no reflection, or if the course of action, whether royal or plebeian, is not amended, it is destined to perish and disappear. This is how it was, this is how it is, and this is how it always will be."

And so Shemaiahu came to understand with great clarity that the laws proclaimed by God to govern human existence were an essential component of all that exists. These laws were firmly cemented in the substance of life, and not even God overruled them. Since the beginning of time, God had measured every action with a consequence—including those shaped by His own deeds. When He saw that His deed was good, a new day and a new undertaking followed.[2] This is the nature of creation and this is how it continues to flow.

***

Shemaiahu recorded on parchment all of these powerful truths. The laws of God were a corrective dynamism, and this awareness remained registered as well in the canvas of his soul for eternal safekeeping. It was essential that these laws would be understood and acted upon by every person, knowingly and willingly, in service of the higher goal of development that YHWH had set, since the beginnings of time, for all humanity.

2. See Genesis 1:3–5.

Moses fell silent. His task was neither easy nor comfortable. It never was. His job was to be interpreter, translator, and mediator between YHWH and His people. He gathered his thoughts as he watched Shemaiahu work. Having decided what still needed to be said, he began again with precision of purpose. "God cares for all of His creations, even the wrongdoers. He is not gladdened by the downfall of the wicked. When the Egyptians were drowning in the waters, the angels rose to sing a hymn of praise but He silenced them, saying, 'Do not sing praises today. How can I listen to your singing when the works of my hands are drowning in the sea?'"[3] Humbled again by this awareness, Moses lowered his voice and delivered a concise and essential message: "God is not a blind force that stands fiercely behind the execution of His laws. He hears the cries of His people."[4]

As Moses spoke, the curtains of the heavens opened up completely.

It was the first day of the month of Sivan, the third month since the day the Israelites exited Egypt en masse. Now they were approaching Mount Sinai. They had grown in the realization of YHWH, of God's presence in their lives as they traversed the desert under divine protection, guided by a pillar of cloud by day and a pillar of fire by night.

The people had witnessed miracles all along the way: the opening of the sea; the food sent from heaven; the sweetening of their water; and the defeat of their enemies. Now as they stood unshackled from the chains of slavery, it was clear that their freedom was the greatest miracle of all, and the time had come to meet with Him. The Israelites had achieved a state of holiness and union and solidarity never before attained by people of such diverse and disparate origins.

It was on the first day of the month of Sivan that God descended upon Mount Sinai. Shemaiahu watched as a violent quaking shook the land and a dense shroud of smoke veiled the mountain. Moses gazed at the images, his eyes fixed and distant as he recalled the events.

"As the divine Presence rested upon it, the hillside of the mountain where the people encamped reached a new level of sanctity. The air became thicker and the sun stood still. Time had come to a standstill. From within a dense cloud, the Ten Commandments were delivered by YHWH in one single, all-encompassing expression. His voice boomed from the midst of the fire, the cloud, and the opaque darkness loud enough to be heard throughout the entire assembly.[5] The people were impressed by the events but they did not understand the message, nor did they grasp the significance of what

---

3. *Talmud Megillah* 10b.
4. See Exodus 2:23–24.
5. See Deuteronomy 5:22–24.

they were witnessing. They only perceived the outward manifestations of thunder and lightning and heard the sound of a trumpet whose clarion call thundered from the skies. They were afraid to witness the dramatic showing of YHWH's might. In fact, they recoiled from the sheer power of the display. It rendered them unable to process or understand the message being revealed to them."

Moses anticipated that the display of power might be overpowering for Shemaiahu as well and so, in deference to his disciple, he paused to give Shemaiahu enough time to take in the immensity of the scene.

At last, Moses broke the prolonged silence. "The people begged me not to let God speak directly to them. They were too afraid to hear, let alone comprehend what God was saying. It was especially difficult to process the message since all of the commandments were uttered in one single expression. At that moment I drew near the opaque darkness where God was and He and I merged. We became one. God proclaimed the commandments and the law, and I became His translator and His spokesman.[6] I used words, signs, and symbols that I knew the people could understand. The people heard my voice as I articulated clearly the Ten Commandments.[7] But I tell you with certainty, Shemaiahu: the messages came straight from God. My human self was only the intermediary that delivered them in all their essence."

Shemaiahu drew in a deep, shuddering breath. He and Moses took a moment to pause in reverence at the recounting of this seminal moment in time.

At last, Moses pointed his finger, and Shemaiahu followed it, knowing that he would be shown another historically transformative event through yet another window in time. Shemaiahu was shown images of Moses ascending Mount Sinai.

Moses said, "Since YHWH's will was to speak directly to His people, I went up to the mountaintop so that He could deliver again His words, except that this time they were engraved by His own finger onto two tablets of stone[8]—two ethereal blocks of sapphire taken from underneath the Throne of Glory. The wondrous letters, having been etched in fire, were clearly visible in black. A spiritual white fire surrounded the letters, the purpose of which was to make them pregnant with limitless meanings. Then again, the letters had been sealed with fire upon the two blocks of sapphire.[9] This mag-

6. See Exodus 20:18–19.

7. See Exodus 20:1–17

8. See Exodus 32:16.

9. *Talmud Yerushalmi Shekamim* 6:1, 49d; *Midrash Tanchuma, Bereshit* §1, in

nificent writing could be seen shining with majestic radiance from every angle. A myriad of heavenly angels gathered around me because they, too, wanted to witness the delivery of the sacred sapphire tablets. The Ten Commandments would serve as an eternal guide for all of God's people through every step of their development."

Both Moses and Shemaiahu stared through the window at the tablets. It was a formidable sight to behold, even for a nonphysical being like Moses.

However, at the very moment that Moses was receiving the tablets, disturbing events were bubbling up among the people waiting at the foot of the mountain. Something ominous was brewing. Shemaiahu watched in horror as a group of Levites surrounded Aaron forming a protective barrier with their bodies while the voice of a man cried out from within the crowd, "Moses has been away for too long! I saw him floating in the air.[10] What if he died?" The man pointed at Aaron and demanded, "You! Make us a god that will protect us on the journey!"

An old image of the ghastly scene where an angel of God in the guise of a serpent ambushed Moses flashed through Shemaiahu's mind. He remembered Moses cautioning him about the strong and oscillating dichotomy of the world beyond, in other existing dimensions. Shemaiahu realized that this was happening. In fact, the crowd's rebellion was indeed the making of God's chosen adversary, Satan.[11]

Satan often would appear during a crisis or a time of great distress and uncertainty. The goal was to confuse the people by showing them fierce, frightening images of darkness and gloom that were not easy to dispel, handle, or control.[12] Shemaiahu watched the frightened people shouting as they pushed and shoved one another. An increasingly angry crowd raised ugly voices to echo the man who had demanded a new god. The crowd surged up against the Levites who, wisely, had formed a defensive circle around Aaron.

Shemaiahu's heart was flooded with compassion as he contemplated the ordeal that Aaron was forced to navigate. Aaron faced a horrible conundrum. If he went along with the crowd, he would anger YHWH, which no one with a sound mind would risk doing. Nevertheless, after some time, Aaron realized that the unruly crowd was not to be reasoned with. Fearing for his life, he succumbed to their demands. He instructed the mob to bring

Sefaria.

10. Shemot 32:1, in Silberman, *Chumash with Rashi's Commentary*.

11. See Job 2:1–2.

12. Shemot 32:1, in Silberman, *Chumash with Rashi's Commentary*.

all the gold they possessed, throw it onto the fire, and from the molten gold an idol could be molded.

When the fire was high, a man named Micah emerged from the crowd gathered around it and ran straight toward the blaze. When he got close, he threw into the fire a splinter of stone that was engraved with an obscure injunction, "Raise, ox, raise." This was the same splinter Moses used to haul out their ancestor Joseph's coffin from the depths of the Nile River.

As soon as the stone fell into the fire, a golden calf was formed right in front of the eyes of those gathered around the fire. The calf seemed to be alive, and the people were shaken. Micah shouted, "The spirit of Joseph lives in it!"

The crowd answered in a roar, "*This* is your god, oh Israel; this is the god who brought you up out of the land of Egypt!" And they worshiped this golden calf by burning peace offerings in its name.

Shemaiahu was appalled. His body shook in consternation, for he knew there would be serious repercussions. In fact, he feared for the people's lives. From behind him Shemaiahu heard the voice of Moses explaining in grave tones, "I, too, followed what was happening with concern. I knew the laws of YHWH. The golden calf was a blemish in His plan for the world, and a corrective reckoning, some kind of retribution, would follow. Indeed, at that moment, God spoke to me in anger. His voice was no longer close—it came from afar. He made it clear that His judgment of the people would be harsh. He said, 'The ox knows its owner, and the donkey its master's crib, but Israel does not know; my people do not understand.'[13] Then He commanded, 'These are stiff-necked people. Now, therefore, let me alone, that my wrath may burn hot against them and I may consume them so they'll disappear. Then I may make a great nation of you.'[14] With this thunderous roar, God's sentence was sealed." Moses shook his head. "There I stood, Shemaiahu, facing this portentous, ominous, uncompromising force but yet I bargained and pleaded for the sake of Israel. I begged of Him, 'Why should Your anger be kindled against Your people whom You have brought up from the land of Egypt? Please, retreat from the heat of Your anger. Please, reconsider the evil intended against Your people. Remember Abraham, Isaac, and Israel, your servants to whom You promised, 'I will multiply your seed like the stars of the heavens. And the land they shall keep as their possession forever.'[15] These words of mine brought before Him a recollection of the righteous deeds of previous generations.

13. See Isaiah 1:3.
14. See Exodus 32:7–10.
15. See Exodus 32:11–13.

"Memories and thoughts have as much power as a deed, and so it was that the remembering of our ancestors eased God's rage against the Israelites. He lessened the severity of his decree, at least in that moment, saying, 'For the sake of My name I defer My anger. My praise is that I restrain My wrath for the children of Israel, not to cut them off.'[16] YHWH yielded. He did not level upon His people the calamities He had threatened."

Shemaiahu looked at Moses with fresh admiration. The Prophet's commitment to the children of Israel had been boundless. But despite his intercession, the Israelites were unable to leave behind the mindset of enslavement, resistant to advance into deeper regions of awareness, unwilling to move forward. Shemaiahu could not help but wonder why Moses had wanted to continue protecting such reckless and ungrateful people. Why would he risk standing before God on their behalf?

Moses answered Shemaiahu's thoughts. "In His anger," he said, "God had wanted to eradicate the Israelites with a plague, after which He would bring another group of souls into the world. He told me He would make a new nation out of me and my descendants. But I did not want to start anew. My soul had been brought into the world for one purpose: to deliver from slavery this particular group of people. *These* people and not *others*. I, in my free will, wanted to complete that task.

"God and I did not seem to agree, and, at this point, I felt weary. I decided I would face God one more time with the intention of making an appeal for forgiveness of His people, which is to say *my* people. I knew it would be difficult to change His decision. But I had to try. I said in a firm voice, 'But if You don't forgive their sin, blot me out of the book You have written.'[17] I said this in earnest. I preferred to let go of my life and get out of the world than to start all over. The idea of God's reprisal had scared me. It weakened my strength, my resolve. The world had become a place that offered mostly conflict, suffering, and death. The light was gone and all I could see was darkness."

Shemaiahu was dumbfounded by Moses' honesty and by the courage he had shown. He had risked his life by daring to challenge God. Why?

Once again discerning Shemaiahu's thoughts, Moses explained, "For most people the physical life feels very real, but it is not the whole reality. Their physical senses are attuned to the world they can perceive, but what they perceive is a small fraction of the information that is available to them. Write it down, Shemaiahu! Tell the people that we cannot rely on just our physical senses to inform us of the complexities of what we experience! Even

16. See Isaiah 48:9.
17. See Exodus 32:32.

more so is this true when we encounter or confront otherworldly forces as vast as the almighty, all-encompassing YHWH. He is an impersonal force. For Him, life and death have exactly the same value.

"When each gate is opened, be it life or be it death, it will lead to a different outcome—a significant one. Aware of this, I spoke to God and told Him that I wished he would change directions. And YHWH listened to my words. He chose restraint and lessened the weight of His judgment on these idolatrous people. Even so, He did not annul the sentence. The threat of a future calamity still remained hanging in the air. He admonished me, saying, 'I descended to rescue them from the hands of the Egyptians, to bring them up from that land to a good and spacious land; to a land flowing with milk and honey.[18] I will not go up in their midst but send an angel before them, lest I destroy them on the way. For they are stiff-necked people.'[19] After God finished speaking, a chorus of soft voices affirmed, 'Better is the few of the righteous than the abundance of many wicked men.'[20]

"Within my mind," said Moses, "God's words continued flowing in an unwavering stream of crystal-clear thoughts. I was made to understand that the threat of destruction for all humans persisted. He had created the world and wanted it to function faultlessly so that it moved toward the completion of His project. God made it clear that He would not twist the universal laws to satisfy a personal wish such as mine.

"Know, Shemaiahu, that our human nature and the nature of the divine are different in kind. We have different perspectives from which we consider our options and make decisions upon our actions. My wish to protect the people was grounded on condescending sentimentality. On a shortsighted apprehensiveness. Those notions are transient and therefore alien to the deep spheres of existence inhabited by the Supreme Being."

After these words an absolute silence followed. Shemaiahu was shaken. He sat in a state of deep contemplation for what felt like a very long time. Time had ceased to exist on its normal continuum. Then again, Moses indicated that he was not yet finished with his story, so Shemaiahu wrested his faculties back to his note-taking.

"Appeasing God's anger was a grueling, strenuous effort, but I continued my intercession on behalf of the people. With all my might I kept trying to reach a truce that would favor them. But when I saw them prostrating themselves to a golden calf, I was crushed. The children of Israel were

18. See Exodus 3:8.

19. See Exodus 33:2–3.

20. See Psalm 37:16.

cluelessly worshiping a statue built by their own hands! They were hailing this golden figure as if it were *Him!*"

Shemaiahu heard in his every word all the hurt, outrage, and disbelief that Moses had suffered. Moved by compassion for his pain, but yet still in search of knowledge and truth, Shemaiahu mustered his courage to risk muttering a few words on an obviously sensitive issue. Cautiously, then, he dared to speak.

"Yes," he said, "the people acted wrongly in giving free rein to their impulses. They forgot it was YHWH who took them out of Egypt and they worshiped a golden figure. They stoked God's fury. But you, their visionary leader, could not contain your impulses either, a difficult thing to do, I know. At that moment and in a fit of rage, you threw the holy tablets to the ground and they were smashed. In your fury you seized the golden calf, threw it into the fire, ground it to powder, and scattered it over the water. Then, you made the people drink from those waters."[21]

Moses did not rebuke Shemaiahu's argument but responded calmly, "It was not I in my anger who destroyed the tablets. It was God. Think about it—how could I have destroyed them? They contained the Ten Commandments and the holy laws, the book of God. They contained the entire blueprint for creation. It was not possible for me to destroy that which He established as the basis for His creation.

"However, there was no question that the ground upon which I stood had been defiled. The sacred letters could not stay in that desecrated place. There was nothing else for them to do but take flight. When this happened, the tablets became heavy—too heavy, heavier than a corpse—and so they slipped from my arms, fell to the ground, and were smashed to pieces.[22] It was not anger that filled my heart. It was disappointment. I had given to these people all I could give.

"In their journey out of Egypt, the children of Israel initiated what was also a spiritual journey. They emerged from slavery in every sense and at all levels of their being. With every step they took they seemed to be acquiring a deeper understanding and a truer connection with the unseen forces that guided them along their way. They witnessed God's display of His devastating powers as they lived through the plagues that hit Egypt. They saw how Pharaoh's arrogant personality was degraded before the Almighty. They experienced the wonder of crossing the Sea of Reeds and the miracle of the food sent from heaven. After participating in all of these transformative events, they should have grown in wisdom! They should have attained the

---

21. See Exodus 32:19–20.
22. See *Midrash Exodus Rabbah* 46:1.

queenly wisdom awaiting to be crowned on Mount Sinai in the time when YHWH descended with the express purpose of meeting with them! But this mixed multitude dragged each other down. They disregarded everything. With a single spectacularly idolatrous deed they disavowed the transcendence of the One God, thereby proving that slavery had not been left behind but was thriving inside them. The children of Israel were unprepared to receive the message awaiting delivery in Sinai. The work of the refinement of their souls remained unfinished."

CHAPTER 34

Human Nature and Its Connection with the Divine Presence

SHEMAIAHU, SENSING THE PROFOUND depths from which Moses was delivering his message, stood as if paralyzed. He hoped the Master would continue talking, but Moses seemed to be sinking even deeper into himself. The two of them remained shrouded in an extended silence.

A terrifying uneasiness began to build inside Shemaiahu. He felt as helpless as an abandoned child. He wondered whether the Prophet was gone from him forever and felt apprehensive. What if this wondrous sage, this source of security, wisdom, and comfort he had only just found, was indeed already lost to him?

With a flash of insight, he realized that these were the same kind of insecurities that lured the children of Israel into idolatrous ways as they waited at the foot of Mount Sinai for Moses to descend the mountain. They must have also felt as if the Prophet had left them behind. He had been gone for forty days and forty nights, and they knew he had carried with him no food or water. The people believed he had died. Shemaiahu felt an immense surge of compassion toward his kinfolk back home. They must have felt abandoned by him in exactly this same way.

A voice wrenched him from his thoughts. It was Moses. Shemaiahu's heart quickened. The Prophet had waited purposefully for this softening in his pupil's heart before reaching out to Shemaiahu with the gift of a new insight. "Growing in the capacity to feel compassion toward the other becomes an essential tool once we enter the physical world. Our challenge is to subdue the little arrogant self with all of its self-serving impulses at the same time that we open up space in our hearts for others. This is the work that we in the spirit realm are called to teach."

Moses fell silent so as to allow Shemaiahu to complete his notes. When Shemaiahu finished writing he continued.

"In God's project, spirit lodged into matter as far as it could reach. It is the work of all humans inhabiting the ground of matter to recognize that spirit is in them. Remember what happened in Mount Sinai, when people forgot their spiritual nature. Now, today and always, people must try again to link up with spirit.

"When spirit becomes part of life, it guides their humanity into new frontiers of development. Listen to this, Shemaiahu, and understand: even the worst of the worst among humans are all spirit. They will also be guided and will, sooner or later and in their own time, reach the end of their personal spiritual journey. It will happen, I assure you. Furthermore, no path is better than any other because every person's quest serves a collective purpose. It provides a challenge that enriches us all."

A question that had been floating idly in the air entered the space between Shemaiahu and Moses. In acknowledgment of its presence, Moses said, "I know you wonder about my understanding of YHWH."

Shemaiahu was both pleased and surprised. "Yes, Master," he said with a smile. "That is the reason behind my pilgrimage to find you."

With a twinkle in his eyes and the hint of a smile on his lips, Moses nodded. It was time to describe the moment when he had met God. "In our first encounter in the burning bush, I was unaware of the indescribable wonder I was about to experience. YHWH came to me first as an angel and then drew me higher and higher into spiritual planes that were ever closer in proximity to Himself. There, I received a myriad of mental impressions—thoughts and images—that required deciphering and interpretation. I was given information that needed to be formulated into meaningful concepts and scaffolds of ideas. Then these concepts and ideas had to be translated into the spoken word in ways that could be understood by my fellow men.

"Spending so many years in solitude taught me how to keep my mind quietly receptive. This state of being allowed me to remain open to God's communications. It also helped me bestow the messages with the proper meanings. After the first encounter I became a mediator. This was my mission in life. I stood firmly at the fringes of the lower world, but my head was always peeking into the higher spheres of reality, while an exchange between these upper and lower realities was constantly being transacted. Sometimes I felt overwhelmed by the task. When that happened, I felt sadly alone, and that loneliness would cause feelings of irritation to flare."

Shemaiahu did not like this. Moses confessing a weakness? The Prophet noticed the frown sprouting across his pupil's brow. He decided to slow down. From now on he weighed his words more carefully in an attempt to not overburden his earthly companion. Shemaiahu watched him nod in a sign of encouragement to his pupil before resuming his tale.

"I felt afraid. First of all, I dreaded doing the task I had been assigned. I feared God but also feared the reception I would be given by the people of Israel. So I protested. I argued. I tried as hard as I could to refuse the task. But God's grip was strong and it never lessened. Finally, I surrendered. I accepted that this was not a choice. It was my destiny. I answered the call of YHWH." Allowing another moment of self-absorption, Moses delved deeper into himself and pondered what needed to be said next. "On Mount Sinai God showed me another level in my connection with Him. He created various spheres of manifestation in the world, from the intangible to the most concrete. There is a never-ending interconnection between the Creator and His creation. But strangely enough, He sometimes acts elusive, as if absent, as if hiding within a boundless infinite."

Moses was now speaking rapidly, causing Shemaiahu to make every effort to keep up. "On Mount Sinai, I saw three dividing partitions. First, there was darkness. Then there was a cloud. Finally, there was an opaque darkness that was deeper than the first.[1] God was behind the three partitions, but I was the only person able to see behind them. Aaron, the priests, and all the people were far off, and they were unable to see what was made plain to me. I was brought up alone into the opaque darkness, which was the space from which God dictated the Ten Commandments and a still-unknown book of laws. After I listened to the laws being laid down, I spoke to YHWH. I told Him that I knew the laws were intended to help dark matter bloom, to bring light from darkness. The laws were an instructive manual intended to offer structure and guide humans so that they would become creative partners in God's project of evolution. But the laws were multiple and complex. Perhaps too complex, as they encompassed every little aspect of life. I knew they would be hard for humans to keep.

"I told God that these laws needed to be adjusted to fit with the grosser nature of His creatures. Shemaiahu, I tried so hard to engage with that majestic consciousness—with the One who dwells behind the dark curtains! I wanted God to know that His creatures are fragile and that He should not sever His connection to them. 'Your creatures are unpolished,' I told Him, 'unrefined and unprepared to respond in the way You expect.' But then I foresaw God's dissatisfaction with His children, and I dreaded His reaction. I tried to alert the Almighty that an abrupt, violent response on His part

---

1. See Exodus 20:21; Deuteronomy 4:11; *Shemot Rabbah* 45:5, in Sefaria."Three partitions" simbolize progressive veils between human perception and divine reality.

would result in a hopeless demolition of all that He had created in the physical world."

Pausing, Moses looked at Shemaiahu and said, "You surely know by now that the world from above and the world below are different. They are unrelated in the way they function. The supernatural world is eternal and unlimited, while the human world is, of course, limited and must function within the constraints of space and time. But these constraints are necessary, even vital. Without them, the human mind would not be able to think or articulate logical processes of any sort. Without them, there would be no capacity for reflection, for understanding, nor any possibility to plan a course of action. People would not be able to learn and adapt, to mend their wrongdoings, to correct their actions."

Shemaiahu realized that Moses had striven very hard to make the infinite, unlimited Presence consider his earnest arguments. Each word he used had been carefully selected so as to have that specific effect.

"To my surprise, my words had an effect. At that moment, I watched this limitless Presence react. I watched Him change His overpowering will and act mercifully. God had heard what I said in there, in this transitional space where humans and the divine can communicate. My work had been accomplished."

Shemaiahu recorded that it was Moses' task while he was embodied in a physical form to interact with and influence this all-powerful Reality. YHWH received what Moses presented in what was a very challenging interchange of qualities of consciousnesses. It was the ebb and flow of evolution. It was a necessary interplay between two opposite qualities: judgment and kindness.

Moses directed Shemaiahu's attention toward a new window. This window revealed a familiar scene where people walked in the bright light of a sunny day—men, women, and children and all of their animals tagging along behind them as they toted their belongings across a stony, barren plain. The pillar of cloud led the way, standing proud and tall so that even the most distant journeyman could see it.

A group of people bunched up all of a sudden, and Shemaiahu watched as two men ran from this group chasing after a third with a stick.

Moses narrated what Shemaiahu was seeing. "During the night, while they were sleeping under a cart, this man stole the remnants of food their family had brought out of Egypt. The thief was hungry and he didn't consider the pain he would cause. Food and water were scarce, and people were shaken to the core by the theft. Even being within sight of the pillar of cloud—which they knew was an angel of God—they still lacked the trust and understanding of the greatness that was implied, and their lesser preservation instincts prevailed.

"And this is what you should know about the nature of those beings called humans, Shemaiahu. Their nature is ruled by two very powerful emotions that allow them to survive: anger and fear. These emotions trigger and mobilize people to either fight to defend and protect themselves and their kin or break away into flight when they are in danger. This is how they believe they will preserve their lives.

"People have built lifestyles around trying to ensure that they will be protected. Some remain armored beyond what is necessary in a perpetual state of alertness, one that overvalues and misuses strategies like confrontation and fight. Furthermore, experiencing the material world can be overwhelmingly intense, and it may make them distort what it means to be human and make them forget that they are also spirit. That happened in the desert. The people forgot they were also spirit. They overlooked the help provided to them in the form of a guiding cloud, and an immense fear settled into their minds."

A scene opened before Shemaiahu's eyes so that he could witness for himself the events Moses had just described. He watched a moment unfold when the children of Israel came near the Sea of Reeds. The Egyptian army in their chariots were drawing near, and the Israelites cried out to God even after having cursed Moses.

"The people that you see were so afraid of the immediate danger looming before them they could not grasp the totality of what they were experiencing. They limited their understanding only to the first external layer of the event. And this is my teaching for you today: people must develop finer tools of perception and discernment in order to remain calm. In order to be able to perceive the multiple, deeper layers of reality involved in any given event, in any situation, no matter how frightful it may be.

"The people of Israel witnessed God's wondrous workings, but in spite of this they failed to trust and remember what they had seen. Their powers of perception were as yet gross and undeveloped. They failed to understand that He was by their side and that there was nothing to fear. That lesson had to be learned. Yes, humans must learn to remain still and, knowing that God abides behind it all, search for strength within."[2] Shemaiahu understood that the work of refinement of the senses and the work of refinement of the mind and emotions were the two most significant tasks a person can accomplish in life. Not much would be attained if a person remained restrained, knotted up in an elementary survival mode. This inner work of refinement was vital

2. See Psalm 46:11.

and needed to be carried on by each person at their own pace and in their own time.

"By cultivating these subtle instruments of perception, people would soften their obstinate, fearful, and belligerent minds. Then they would gain a broader and truer perspective of what they call reality. Gaining access to the subtle world dissolves fear. People must also understand that living life entails harmony and a commonality of purpose for all existing beings. Understand this, Shemaiahu, for *this* is the sure path to the Promised Land."

CHAPTER 35

The Work of Creation

SHEMAIAHU WANTED TO HEAR more about what was Moses' understanding of God. In what way could humans better relate to such an intangible reality? Moses answered Shemaiahu's appeal by opening up and sharing more of what he had experienced.

"There was a time when I, much like you now, wanted to know God. I requested to be shown who He was. I said to the Almighty, 'If I have indeed found favor in Your eyes, I pray to Thee: let me know Your ways so that I may know You. So that I may find favor in Your eyes.'[1] I begged God to show me His glory, and God answered me by saying, 'I will let all My goodness pass before you; I will proclaim the name of YHWH before you.'[2] But then He gave me a warning: 'You will not be able to see My face, for man shall not see Me and live. Behold, there is a place by Me where you shall stand on the rock, and while My glory passes by, I will put you in a cleft of the rock, and I will cover you with My hand until I have passed by. Then I will take away My hand, and you shall see My back, but My face shall not be seen.'"[3] Looking straight into Shemaiahu's eyes, Moses affirmed, "Understand this: not even I, having been assigned a holy mission, was permitted to grasp God's unbounded totality, of which 'YHWH' is just one name. I was not allowed to see His face but only catch a glimpse of the trail He left behind when He crossed before me. He covered my eyes so I would only see what I was allowed to see: the traces of His back, expressed as they were in the world He created.

1. See Exodus 33:13.
2. See Exodus 33:18–19.
3. See Exodus 33:20–23.

"The Endless Incommensurable Infinite, my dear one, speaks from within a whirlwind, and is something too strong to behold. One is only allowed to infer His attributes by the trail He leaves behind and by the countless manifestations and numerous testimonials of His deeds on earth. Look around, Shemaiahu, and observe the wondrous diversity of wildlife. See a world filled with God's fascinating creatures on the earth, in the sky and the seas. And above them all is humanity, which was intended to carry on a mysterious and vibrant partnership with God as cocreators in the world. Each element is important and so this should be conveyed.

"Write, Shemaiahu! Write it all! Let people know that every single creature, large or small, is important. Let people know that every life should be respected. Write, Shemaiahu, that whomever saves even a single life, saves the world."[4]

Shemaiahu was aghast to hear these remarks because it struck him in an almost palpable way how often they were overlooked.

Moses continued, "When the whirlwind passed before me, loud voices proclaimed from on high, 'YHWH, YHWH, a benevolent God! Compassionate and gracious; slow to anger and abundant in lovingkindness and truth; preserving lovingkindness for thousands; forgiving iniquity and rebellion and sin. Yet God does not clear the wrongdoings entirely. He visits the iniquity of parents on children and children's children to the third and fourth generations.'[5] As the voices were proclaiming YHWH's virtues, I realized that He was both a storm and also a rainbow. This insight would guide my life.

"And this is my message to you: all darkness is transitory. Allow yourself to be guided from within by the greater intelligence that lives inside, because this is God within you. And about what you call God, know that God is boundless and incomprehensible but yet He is experienceable. There is always a way to come closer to Him. The mind may not know how but the heart does. The heart sees and hears.[6] Sit still within your heart. Rest secure and be satisfied while there."

Moses encouraged Shemaiahu to continue opening up his mind and refining his senses, for these are the soul's instrument of connection to the Divine. "The process of coming together, of merging into the One," he said, "is complex and full of ambiguities. Still, it can come to happen as it is

4. Babylonian Talmud, *Sanhedrin* 37a; Jerusalem Talmud, *Sanhedrin* 4:1 (Venice 22a).

5. See Exodus 34:6–7.

6. Kohelet Rabbah 1:16, Midrash Rabbah on Ecclesiastes, in Sefaria.

definitely true." Then he restated, as if for emphasis, "We are all together in this great work of creation."

Thinking they were finished, Shemaiahu heaved a huge exhale and set aside his recording instruments. But Moses gestured toward another window of time. This one looked out upon the Israelite community as it directed an endless succession of complaints toward Moses and Aaron.

"If only we were left to die by the hand of God, there in the land of Egypt where we sat by pots of meat and ate bread to our fill," the people wailed. "For you have brought us out into this desert where this entire congregation will starve to death."[7]

Their rancor was so great, so violent, Shemaiahu feared for Moses' safety. He needn't have. Moses maintained his serenity and conducted himself with dignity. He commanded Aaron to call the community outside the Tent for a meeting. Then God appeared as a cloud and, speaking through Moses, said, "In the afternoon, you shall eat meat, and in the morning, you shall be sated with bread."[8] Shemaiahu watched as the people ate bread, white like coriander seeds, which they named manna. And whatever a person desired, the manna tasted to him as if it was that food.

When this window closed, Shemaiahu sat in silence and reflected upon how grateful he was that he had been spared bearing witness to the further suffering of his people in the desert. In contrast, Moses seemed detached, as if the pain and commotion had no relevance. Seeing his indifference shook Shemaiahu's sense of shared humanity and sparked an internal conflict. He voiced his discord, saying, "Dear Master, it is hard to understand who you are. Sometimes you speak from a place that seems impenetrable. I'm afraid of coming near you. I'm fearful of not being able to sustain my ground."

After what seemed a very long silence, Moses spoke in a voice noticeably deeper than usual. "I stand in the last frontier between the limited world of matter and the vast expanse in which God resides. I watch the world events evenly, knowing that they are guided by a script that has been written in the infinite spheres. As I see how these events are interpreted by your human understanding, limited and fixed as it sometimes is, it is my role and that of others like me to remain open so that I can act as an intermediary. I am a connector between the upper and lower. Both of these realities participate in the work of creation. Each offers a particular point of view. Even though they complement each other, they are different in every way conceivable. The infinite must constrict while the finite must expand—and this is how they come together. The laws were established to help in this

7. See Exodus 16:3.
8. See Exodus 16:10–12.

process. At times they may seem ruthless, but they are the rules by which the whole dynamism proceeds, and so they have no favorites."

Shemaiahu had resumed his work. He wrote that every person's behavior will be judged and that the judgment when pronounced will be suited to the abilities of the soul and the mind to understand what has happened as well as to understand the process, to reflect upon it, and then to enact change.

He registered that there were three types of people. First are those who are conscious enough to recognize and atone for misdeeds. These are the people who will learn from their mistakes and, motivated by their awareness of the effects caused by their actions, will avoid repeating them. These are the wise ones. These are the ones who can reflect and differentiate between the wanted and the unwanted, the desirable and undesirable, and act accordingly. These ones will move forward.

A second group of people modify their actions based on fear—fear of God and fear of punishment. For these people, carefulness born of fear is not transformative because it does not involve a reflection by which they learn. Reparation for the wrongness of a deed without thoughtfulness will not be effective and sustained. And if the event recurs, this will provide a renewed opportunity to act, learn, and grow.

The third set of people will never learn. These ones will not differentiate good from bad, truth from falsehood. They will remain fearlessly unaware of the consequences of their actions and will not be sustained.

In the end, everyone experiences the weight of God's laws in strict accordance with their level of awareness, which is to say their capacity to understand, as well as the actions they choose to make. Some people will see an increase in their lot. Others will see a decline. However, all will know that there is a consequence for every choice made.

***

Looking again through the window of time, Shemaiahu watched Moses coming down from Mount Sinai carrying two tablets of testimony in his arms. After having broken the first tablets, he had ascended the mountain a second time; these in his arms were the new set of commandments. As he trod down the mountain, Moses' face shone with a radiant brightness.[9]

Of course it shone, Shemaiahu thought. After all, hadn't he spoken to God? Hadn't they become one?

9. See Exodus 34:29.

The reaction of Aaron and the Israelites to this shining radiance was fear. They were afraid to come near him. Nevertheless, Moses called them to him so that he might instruct them on all that he had learned. And when the Prophet finished speaking with his people, he reached up to his head-covering and drew down over his face a veil. From then on, Moses removed the veil only when he was speaking with God or when he was instructing his people about God's laws.

He was a great teacher. He clarified the laws of YHWH with meticulous precision and care, word by word, one word at a time.

"Whenever I was deep within myself and in total betrothal with God," Moses explained, "at that moment I understood even more why He brought the laws to the people. I could fathom the structuring that this implied and the creative dynamism that had been set in motion. And so it is, Shemaiahu. No life nor consciousness could have emerged from this Unbounded Infinite without it also setting in place some constraining limitations and ruling principles. These ordering laws were necessary to secure life into the world; otherwise that life would be sucked back into the Infinite. These laws are needed at every level and at every moment."

Shemaiahu felt the urge to bow down until his head touched the ground. He prostrated himself not before a master but before YHWH. He honored the majestic glory of God's creation that was always in movement, continually building up and developing. He wished to be given the wisdom to discern how to conduct himself, how to contribute to what must be corrected, and to do this every waking moment. With deep reverence and awe, Shemaiahu prayed that he would find favor in God's eyes. That he would be able to offer himself to His service and His creation.

CHAPTER 36

The Human Soul

SHEMAIAHU FELT THE RESTLESSNESS of an unanswered question piercing his mind. He could stand it no more and said, "Please, tell me about the two stones of sapphire that Gabriel placed in my care. Is there some important truth hidden in them?"

Moses' face lit up. "The two stones of sapphire are broken fragments of the first set of tablets. They contain information that was not inscribed in the second set and must now be unveiled to the world. In fact, the time has come to convey this to the people."

Shemaiahu felt butterflies in his belly; his heart was beating fast. He did not want to miss any detail of what was about to be unveiled. To his surprise, Moses' revelation was direct and simple.

"People must overcome the fear of death," he said. "Yes—give up all fear of death! Listen with care." Moses went deep within himself, then reemerged speaking oddly of himself in the third person: "When Moses ascended up high . . ." He then broke off and a long silence followed. Moses seemed disoriented, as if he had lost all sense of himself—of who he was as well as where he was. He closed his eyes as if to come back to himself, then began again. "If the first tablets had survived, every sorrow on earth would have disappeared. The world would have been freed from that massive illusion regarding the shackles of death. Yes, Shemaiahu, an essential wisdom was lost when those first tablets broke. A wisdom that would have made the purpose of the unending cycle of death and rebirth unnecessary. Human consciousness would have soared instantly into a new dimension."

He explained that a Greater Intelligence had inscribed the first set of tablets with the codes and meanings that were organic to its supernatural nature. Later, Moses decoded and engraved them onto a second set of tablets, thereby preparing them in a language that the people could understand.

Shemaiahu recorded as Moses spoke, "The people proved they were not ready to be ruled by the first set of laws of YHWH, which were designed to guide them on becoming active partners in God's creation. Their senses were gross and unrefined for the task at hand. The people chose to remain trapped in fear, profoundly attached to the density of their physical matter, worshiping a golden calf. They did not understand that they had other choices and their minds remained limited by a raw attachment to the things of the world."

Moses concluded with sorrow, "People will remain mortal until they understand that they have choices as cocreators of the world. Only then will the Angel of Death cease in its function."

Not all of Shemaiahu's questions about the stones of sapphire had been answered. He wanted to hear more about them, but because he was unsure of exactly what the questions were he sat quietly while he wrestled with how he should phrase them.

As if his thoughts had been spoken aloud, Moses said, "The two stones of sapphire hold the secret of immortality. The angel Gabriel held them in custody but when the time came for the message to be unveiled, he brought them to you, dear human messenger. Humans should know that the world of unrefined matter houses a precious jewel that is more exquisite than anything known. It is even more exquisite than the mind. This jewel is equipped to understand and act upon the awareness that death does not exist. That wonderful jewel stands just above the human body. It is the seat of the human soul, where our dualistic nature morphs into one. Into the Universal Consciousness."

Moses and Shemaiahu now entered into a dialogue about the nature and purpose of the human soul. "The soul's nature is subtle and ethereal, a bright spiritual sparkle created so that it can strive and flourish on earth's material denseness. It is wonderful to watch how the soul cuts through the darkness of human instincts, rising above impulses to self-gratification. It is the soul that integrates matter and spirit and joins them together into fullness. The soul opens up a space of awareness, of self and other, kindling the light of consciousness." Moses remained quiet for some time. A throng of words wanted to come out, but he needed to choose carefully how to continue and not overwhelm his pupil. "The universe was created with wisdom. I said it before and I'll say it again: it is a great design provided with a set of rules that bring order, proportion, and beauty into it."

Shemaiahu had been listening quietly with his head bent, gazing down. "But Master," he said, evoking an ancient human complaint, "the rules are too many, too strict, too difficult to foresee or even recognize that one may be breaking them."

Moses agreed, saying, "I know, but these rules are inevitable; they are compulsory. A much-needed component of God's great plan. They provide stability while at the same time propel dynamism, with a great potential for development. Such is our world: complex, huge, and expansive."

A long silence followed. Shemaiahu then heard his name being called and prepared to register carefully. What now would follow was surely very important.

"The human soul has been invested with a unique power, the power to end all wars. The human soul is able to recognize and hold within itself every set of conflicting opposites that collide in the world. It is capable of harmonizing them into a new, compassionate solution, a new whole. This courageous work is carried in the individual soul as it stays connected with the divine Universal Consciousness.

"Light and dark, life and death, love and fear, folly and reason. These sets of opposites are essential to the life of matter in the world. They are an initial step in the development of conscious thought. Being able to distinguish opposing factors is at the basis of human thinking. It provides the basis for rational thought.

"Human life is immersed in irreconcilable strife as all of these opposites collide against each other. People struggle. They label their neighbors as enemies. They try to overpower one another. But as humanity matures and consciousness develops, conflict between opposing factors will come to an end. Conflict will become unnecessary. It will be replaced by people seeing things with a comprehensive and universal way of thinking.

"As hard as it may be to accept this, dark factors such as war and evil are also part of the plan of God. All things, good and bad, are part of God's plan. Seekers like you will come to recognize this truth. When you do understand this, you will no longer be led astray and you will choose and act accordingly. Only then will you know the true face of YHWH."

Moses added words of encouragement. "Although the prospect of integrating the opposites seems both intimidating and even impossible, do not worry, because a Higher Intelligence rules everything. This Supreme Intelligence guides the human project and the merging of good and bad toward fulfillment. God is the Universal Mind, and He does not abandon nor does He forsake the human realm. You will learn to recognize this the more you continue on the path you are treading now."

The message had become more personal and Moses paused to allow Shemaiahu time to delve into it and maybe ask some questions. But Shemaiahu remained pensive, absorbed into himself.

Moses continued, "When the soul of a human has developed to rise high enough, it may reach the Sea of Wisdom. This is where all kinds of emanations coming from the heavenly realm have fallen. It is from this place that the wise may draw out the power to discern and understand both orders: the upper and lower worlds. For nothing is now withheld from them."[1] Moses paused, then said, "With a stilled mind, enter the Sea of Wisdom. It is a portal to Higher Consciousness; it is a portal to God. There, you will find what is needed to thrive." He cryptically added, "At the right time."

With these words, Moses faded away until he disappeared altogether from sight. Instinctively, Shemaiahu reached out to grab his arm but there was nothing to hold on to. Moses had vanished. Feeling utterly shattered, Shemaiahu fell on the ground, burying his face between his legs.

But then again, what right did he have to complain? The Prophet had come to him and had participated openly, wholeheartedly. He, Shemaiahu, a mortal man, had spoken with Moses and had been gifted with a road map of life! Certainly, he was thankful for the mystical gifts that had been lavished upon him, but now his human side could only think that he wanted Moses back. His departure had left Shemaiahu conscious of a crushing void. Split in an inner discord, a part of him was thankful for all he had been given while another part sought to extend, to stretch the experience so that he could receive even more.

He heard a loud, deep voice. "Enough!" the voice roared. "It is a condition in the long path of spiritual ascent that you accept what you receive and are happy with what you have harvested!"

Shemaiahu, recognizing the truth in the rebuke, quickly regained his composure. These bursts of conflicting emotions were a natural component of the human condition. He now knew that any unbridled emotion could become an adversary when, uncontrolled, it ran amok.

"There is no forever. Experiences are meant to come and go," he reminded himself. "Let it go!"

For a moment his mind stood still. Then it went back to work, trying to offer an alternate path. Maybe the time had come to return to his family? To the life he left behind in the world below? As he pondered these questions, he heard the voice of Shuah in his mind. *"Pray thou with a loving heart, and He will do what thou needest. He will hear what thou sayest, and He will accept thy offering."*

And Shemaiahu prayed with all his heart the prayers of a humble servant and asked whether Moses would ever come again.

The barely audible voice of Moses spoke in his mind. "Shemaiahu, I am here."

A shudder coursed through Shemaiahu's body.

1. Gikatilla, *Gates of Light*, 20.

"There is no such thing as death. Nothing is ever lost. Everything remains in wait amid the numerous layers of reality existing in the universe. This great expanse that God has created is eternal . . . and everything, all of it, remains for your enjoyment. You will always be able to find me because I am always here."

CHAPTER 37

Up and Away

THE HEAVENS NOW OPENED completely, and Shemaiahu was allowed to look farther up, into a dimension that existed far beyond time and space. He glimpsed an immense garden, as bright and radiant as crystal, shining in the distance. His body rose softly from the floor and then, floating, he was transported into that garden. When he arrived he was overtaken by immense joy. Could this be the garden of Eden?

He looked around with amazement and saw that the moon shone brightly like the sun, and the sun's light was seven times brighter, like the light of seven full days. Together, their combined light radiated across tiny little crystals in the air, which deflected the rays in a multiplicity of beautiful colors. Like a kaleidoscope, one color lay upon another in countless combinations and possibilities. Shemaiahu sensed that in this place, every bruise and wound ever inflicted on him would be healed.[1]

As Shemaiahu strolled through the garden, he saw a tall wall made of light that surrounded the garden like a veil. Magnificent crystals and stones of all colors lay all around. Amethysts and quartz, green jaspers, lapis lazuli, and sapphires shone in splendor. Incorporeal entities ambled about. They shone with a bright divine light achieved with spiritual awareness. They moved with an equanimity that was in keeping with their surroundings. One of these entities shone brighter than the others and was moving toward him. As it came closer, Shemaiahu recognized the countenance of Moses. A soft, graceful glow hovered over him. It was Shechinah, the holy presence of God that, although veiled, had always been by Moses' side.

The Shechinah exuded a fragrance so wondrous it seemed to enter not through his nostrils but through the pores of his skin. Lilies and lilacs would

1. See Isaiah 30:26.

be envious; hyacinths and gardenias were mere understudies; myrrh and the light savory sweetness of honeysuckle could not even compete. In this garden, the waters from below had joined with the waters from above; the split between them came to an end. Here, the Prophet had completed his soul's journey. Here, Moses and the Beloved had embraced. Here, they had merged into one.

"Welcome," Moses said. "You are granted the unique privilege of being able to glimpse that which awaits you at the end of the path. Even though this view will remain before your physical eyes for a very short time, it will persist as an eternal image, having been engraved in the density of the infinite fluid that exists within you."

Shemaiahu felt great expectation for what was to come. After all, he had requested that he might see Moses again, and his wish had been granted.

"Devote yourself to keeping your heart and your mind open and free of all intrusive, gross desires, and I will always bring to you what your soul needs to know and remember. There is no separation, no true conflict nor opposition between the things in the material world; such a belief is deceptive. Everything you know, everything, whether you like it or abhor it, is interconnected and is part of an all-encompassing one. Even more, every single thing accomplishes a task for the One. Humanity will eventually come to understand this."

Moses showed Shemaiahu the four rivers of clear waters running through the garden and then flowing out into the world in all four directions, north and south, east and west, to nurture the diversity of life below. Shemaiahu heard the sound of the crystalline waters flowing and smelled the fresh fragrance of the verdant plant life thriving in abundance all around, and it seemed to him that everything was bright and inviting. This was the exact place where he wanted to be.

"A larger river flows in from beyond these walls to water this garden and its rivers," Moses explained. "You cannot see it but it is there. This is the process. The water flows into this source and then out into the world. It is the ultimate goal to be nurtured and merge with the One Consciousness. And humanity has all the resources necessary to get here. To accomplish this goal. To unite with the One.

"Creation exists simultaneously, always expanding, in multiple levels. Humanity sits at the pinnacle of this wondrous work because of a unique capability that God awarded to humans. Humans can make choices and, steered from within by free will, they can choose their own direction. No other entities—no other being on earth nor angels or seraphs—share this privilege of being able to choose freely."

Moses' form began to recede and so, too, did his voice begin to fade. Then Shemaiahu heard the last of his words that made him feel at ease. "Shemaiahu, the goal of being human has been made clear to you. I'm here waiting. I'm always with you. Now go and do the work." As Moses faded into a pale background so too did the vision of Eden disappear. Had it all been real?

Yes! Shemaiahu affirmed this had not been an illusion! It was not a mere dream! The encounter with Moses and all that he was given to experience had actually happened—but it had happened in a supernatural dimension. His time in the realm of the beyond must come to an end. And just as a puff gently blows out the flame of a candle, the crystalline lights went off.

CHAPTER 38

Shemaiahu Returns to the World

SHEMAIAHU OPENED HIS EYES to find himself lying on his blanket which was spread over the hard floor of a cave. His back felt stiff and his neck and shoulders were painfully sore.

"I must have been in this position for a very long time," he said to himself.

He had been entirely free of his body, and now, the familiar sensations and spasms in his arms and legs were slowly bringing back an awareness of his physicality, his earthly self. He began to recognize the place as his eyes scanned the walls of the cave where he had sought shelter. He had a vague sensation that his climb up Mount Nebo must have happened a long time ago, but he was unable to say when. He was too weak to even raise his body from the ground. Too weak to do anything but ruminate. Why? Had he forgotten to eat?

With some agitation he felt around for the staff and his knife and was relieved to locate them right by his side, exactly where he had placed them. With great effort he raised himself on his elbows and looked around. He felt confused and disoriented.

It began to come back to him. He had been talking with Moses! Stricken, he whispered, "But where is he now?"

It took him a while to recall everything. He remembered that they had conducted a profound conversation that had lasted a long, long time. A vague memory of descending the steps of the heavenly ladder filtered into his mind. It was the same ladder he had climbed up on his way to enter the site where he met first Joseph and then Moses. The memory of the angels that had escorted him came to mind. Shemaiahu lowered himself back onto the blanket.

"I traveled to the world of the beyond," he mumbled, "but now I'm back."

Indeed, Shemaiahu's soul had entered deep into the upper realms, absolutely freed from his corporeal identity. But now, as he had returned to the earthly plane, the subtle body lodged itself again, firmly, in the denseness of his physicality. Slowly, he was returning to his human perceptions. Back to the ordinary forms of cognition. A cutting fear, cold as an icy wave, stabbed his chest. What if he had already forgotten what he had experienced?

Immediately, the voice of Moses echoed from the beyond, "All that you have received and learned will persist, engraved in the eternal waters that flow inside your mind. There they will remain engraved forever, available to you and to all who wish to learn from you."

Shemaiahu felt relieved. He recalled how he had traveled far to reach Mount Nebo in his search for Moses. He remembered the angelical beings that crossed his way. Some came to help him in his endeavor. Others came to impede his journey, as when he struggled with the Angel of Death. He remembered the care with which Joseph, the son of Jacob, came to prepare him for his encounter with the Prophet.

The angel Raziel had given him a new name. But who was he really? Who was he now? Shemaiah? Or Shemaiahu? By which name should he now be called?

"I am a new man with a new name," he answered himself, "I am Shemaiahu, the man who met Moses."

Tears filled his eyes. He felt sorely tired, but could it be that he also felt sad? That these were tears of sadness? He brushed away the thought and noticed some fruits and a few stems of cacti just out of reach, near a wall of the cave. Strange. Weak as he was, he did not feel hungry. In fact, he absolutely would not eat! A bitter irritation was overriding his attitude. He felt immense sadness. All he wanted now was to rid himself of the heaviness of this body. He wanted to depart from this physical vessel so much like a prison cell. He wanted one thing only: he wanted to return to the higher realms.

There is no death, he thought, uncertain of how he should feel about that idea. His mind was at war with itself. He struggled with the strong desire to return to the subtle realities he had glimpsed, that world of living waters—the Sea of Wisdom—where he had felt safe and nurtured. He closed his eyes. Futile though he knew it would be, he could not help but hope that maybe he would never wake. Maybe it was now in God's hands to decide that he was ready to go home.

He remained lost in thought deep within himself, and did not hear the movement around him until he was jolted awake by the touch of something cold and moist on his face. His eyes flew open. A midsized dog with thick, golden-brown hair with a white ruff around its neck and white socks on its legs was leaning over him and sniffing him with curiosity. Where had the dog come from? Suddenly it came to him that this was Epher's dog.

He distinguished the backlit figure of a person standing in the threshold of the cave. The man was dressed in a black cloak. His face was framed by a long, curly beard. Epher! What was he doing here? Too weak to say anything, Shemaiahu gave up the struggle. He closed his eyes and everything went black.

Hours passed during which Shemaiahu faded in and out of consciousness. Epher never left his side. The Midianite tried to keep Shemaiahu awake by squeezing the liquid of fruits onto his lips. Shemaiahu's eyes fluttered open when he tasted the sour fruit on his tongue, and heard Epher's encouragement. "That's right. Keep it in your mouth. It will do you good."

In a constant effort to help Shemaiahu sustain consciousness, Epher placed a cup of goat milk to his lips and directed him to drink up. It was a struggle, but Shemaiahu did as he was told because it would have taken even more energy to object.

At last he was able to sit upright.

Epher sat by his side, ready to catch him should his muscles give way.

"I was worried about you," he said in a soft voice.

"Why?"

"Your mother, very agitated and upset, came to me in a dream. Even though we have never met something inside of me knew that she was your mother." A soft smile curved his lips. "I then decided to take a journey to the mountain, not really expecting to find you, just to look around and explore the area, as I sometimes like to do."

Shemaiahu felt no desire to answer nor share what he had experienced, and so he remained locked within himself.

Epher said courteously, "I think you should come with me. I'll take you to my place. Then you may decide what you want to do."

Time passed. Having regained some strength, Shemaiahu finally stood up. With machinelike movements he folded his blanket and gathered his canteen, knife, and staff. Then, sluggishly, he followed Epher and the dog down the hill.

Along the way, Epher asked respectfully, "Did you find Moses?"

"Yes, I did," was the answer, and they continued walking in silence.

It would take them five days to reach Epher's dwelling. That Shemaiahu remembered well. They moved slowly, walking for some time and resting or stopping to spend the night under the shadow of a large stone or a cluster of trees. Close to the end of the fifth day, Shemaiahu caught sight in the distance of the tall boulders that covered Epher's encampment. He recognized the thick forest that stood in front of the entrance and shielded the vital pond of water encircled by lush vegetation. As they came closer, Shemaiahu felt a freshness that enlivened him. Scanning the place with his eyes, he appreciated anew the beauty of the surroundings. His ability to experience the pleasures of life on earth was slowly coming back to him.

That night, he sat next to Epher and ate what was offered. Epher the Midianite was a truly kind and caring friend, and Shemaiahu felt able to open up and share some of what he had seen. He talked about the Angel of Death and how he overcame its onslaught. He described the encounter with Raziel, when he was given a new name by which he would henceforth be known.

"I was born into a new stage of being, Epher," he said with a sigh. "And now I must be ready to share these things that I experienced with such intensity." As he spoke those words, Shemaiahu fixated his gaze upon the floor. Then he looked up at Epher and asked, "How many days was I away?"

"It has been about two months since the day you left."

Shemaiahu remained in silence. It seemed much longer.

"What do you want to do now?" Epher asked.

Shemaiahu shook his head.

Playfully, with a smile, Epher teased, "You may spend as much time as you desire here with me—but you may not stay forever!"

It was a gentle reminder that Epher valued and protected his privacy highly. Shemaiahu thanked him for his kindness and confessed that he did not know what to say. He still felt unable to think rationally enough to know what he should do.

That night as he lay on his blanket, Shemaiahu thought that in some indefinable way he had been completed, made whole. As he examined the thought, a familiar but almost imperceptible presence filled the room. It was the same incorporeal being he had met a long time ago but now, with all he had experienced, his understanding had been enlarged. He now knew that this invisible being was a twin side of himself that inhabited the higher realms of reality. And that in spite of the peacefulness, equanimity, and wisdom it inspired, this being was not to be called God. It had taken a great effort to reach this ineffable being, and then only to discover that he had always been within reach. By connecting with him, Shemaiahu restored a lost but essential wholeness.

Shemaiahu felt a pull to enter into the inner sanctuary, as it was a quiet and relaxed state of mind where questions were answered with clarity and precision. Taking a few deep breaths, he mentally drifted into that space where his thoughts were not rushed. Giving free rein to his feelings, he spoke of his sadness at being separated from Moses. He admitted to the crushing disappointment at having to return to a world that he would forevermore see as sorely lacking. From now on, everything would be measured against the tantalizing taste of the higher dimensions he had been allowed to experience.

"I was in a place of no struggle or need. I felt comforted and secure. Why did I have to leave?" Patiently, he waited for an answer. He had learned how to listen.

The being replied without haste or judgment. The answer made Shemaiahu feel both heard and accepted. "Shemaiah, your request was granted. You asked to find Moses so he would provide answers to your questions."

Shemaiahu recognized this to be so, but something inside rebelled nevertheless. He asked with a note of defiance, "Why did you call me Shemaiah?"

"Because Shemaiah is still alive within you. That side of you needs to digest more of what was received in the beyond. But the dense matter of the body in which this new understanding is nested remains attached to history, to memories of the past, to a world of lack. Shemaiah in you still evokes and ruminates on that which you were before you initiated your journey. These memories must be relegated since you are no longer who you were. You have become much more than the son of Zakai and Abital. More than a Levite, more than a scribe. More than the husband of Dinah and father of your children. You are much more than the memories of your past life experiences and also much more than the desires and fears of days gone by. It will take some time for your body to readjust to who you truly are now. When that happens, you will again be Shemaiahu. So be patient."

The being vanished and Shemaiahu fell asleep.

✳✳✳

He woke the next morning with a clear sense of purpose and walked toward the brown tent. There he found Epher cleaning edible pods, methodically unsheathing the green seeds lodged inside the plants.

Epher looked up, smiled at his guest, and gestured that Shemaiahu should sit beside him.

"Look," he exclaimed with delight. "These are new kernels! I let them dry up in the sun, then I plant them. I discovered that if I dry them first, the plant sprouts faster and stronger. And they provide plenty of food!"

Being in Epher's company always felt good. They shared a meal. Afterward, they walked among the bushes in companionable silence. At the fringes of the green land, when a view of the vast dry desert opened before them, Shemaiahu realized that he was ready to leave.

"Dear one," he said, "I soon will be going. It will be hard for me to go but I must continue onward. I will be on my way in two days."

Epher had lived in seclusion long enough to understand how hard it was to return to the village where everyone led active lives. He nodded. He was thankful that his friend had recovered his health and felt ready to move on. His wish was that he would live a long life, and was pleased that he had played a part in keeping him alive.

That night Shemaiahu had a dream. In it, his mother was standing among a group of people. Everyone was happy, as if they were celebrating. She seemed young, younger than she looked when he had last seen her. She told him, "My son, don't feel sorry for what you left behind because nothing is ever lost." Pointing toward a golden dome that was built with the wings of angels and was suspended high in the heavens, she added, "We are always in the company of winged beings from the higher realms. Look! To your right stands Michael, to your left stands Gabriel, before you stands Uriel, behind you Raphael. Over all of these is the subtle presence of God.[1] Trust and seek and you'll always find what you need in the all-inclusive web of existence He created."

The next two days Epher helped Shemaiahu prepare food and water for his return to Kiryataim. Epher offered to accompany him part of the way, and Shemaiahu accepted his help. When the two of them approached a hill overlooking the land of Reuben, it was time for Epher to bid him farewell and turn back toward his home.

Shemaiahu squinted to better see the outline of Kiryataim far in the distance. He took a deep breath, and with some hesitancy, started walking toward the village. His legs felt heavy; they were resisting to move forward. But he did anyhow. The time had come to return to his family and his kindred. *Besides*, he reasoned, *that is my task now. Teaching them what I know.*

---

1. Scherman and Zlotowitz, *Complete ArtScroll Siddur*, 324.

CHAPTER 39

Return to Kiryataim—1385 BC

SHEMAIAHU WAS NOW A new man with a new name. The road had been long and eventful, but he had achieved his goal of finding Moses. He had been led to a spiritual encounter with his innermost essence as well as other distinct forces that existed beyond the veil. He had been forced to confront himself—his certainties and insecurities.

But overall, the hardest part had been facing the Angel of Death. At that moment his old personality crumbled down and a new challenge came about: embracing a new budding self. For some time, he felt as if he were a child in need of protection, too fragile to affirm himself in the world. But then, in the beyond, he was offered all the help that was needed.

Struggling to overcome an inner resistance, Shemaiahu pushed himself to continue walking toward the center of the village. Thoughts galloped through his mind. Who would he meet first? How would the encounter be? He was not ready for any of this. He shook his head, trying to dismiss any worry. The experiences in the mountain had been intense. It was impossible to explain to anyone what he had been through. How was he to describe that his soul had left his physical body and then came back? That he had met celestial beings and, above all, that he met Moses? All he experienced was not to be kept only to himself, but he needed the quietness he left behind to further digest it and present it to the world. This was his mission! Shemaiahu felt gloomy and overburdened when suddenly he remembered the invisible being always by his side. With a hint of a smile on his lips, he continued walking.

Kiryataim could be glimpsed in the distance, and the first thing Shemaiahu saw from afar was the sanctuary he had built for YHWH. It stood proudly on the hill overlooking the town; it seemed to be waiting for him. His eyes now ran down the slopes of the mountain where he saw a few young men leading their flocks, probably seeking greener pastures. He squinted trying to distinguish if his son was among them. He felt excited and realized that he had missed him.

The young men in the distance walked with staffs in their hands, a sign of the pride of being a shepherd. That familiar feeling of identity and purpose came back to him in a rush. In this moment he realized that even though it felt as if he had been gone an eternity, he had not been away too long. Even so, a lot had changed inside of himself and he felt unsure of how to handle the new stage of life that he was entering into.

It was early in the morning when he walked into the common court-yard of a group of houses. From there he spotted his house. The house that belonged to his precious family. A few women were working in the com-munal kitchen, preparing meals for the day. There were too many people; the noise they made hurt his ears. Shemaiahu felt an impulse to turn around and run back to Epher's house and become a hermit, just like his friend was.

One of the women happened to glance up from her work and rec-ognized Shemaiah. "Dinah! Dinah!" she shrieked. "Where are you? Look who is here!" Dinah answered the call and came running from the grove of acacia trees where she was churning milk in the shade. Their daughter Zehava, trailed by a few friends, hustled to keep up with her mother. Mean-while, a group of people, mostly women, gathered in a noisy cluster. Dinah's steps slowed as she came closer, as if she were afraid that by approaching the figure at the center of all the excitement she would dispel an apparition. The crowd fell back to a respectful distance. No one should stand between a man and his wife.

Dinah came to a halt at a short distance from where Shemaiah stood, burying her hands in her apron; she felt unsure if she should reach out and touch him. She was happy to see him, of course, but with so many wild emotions surging through her, she dared not speak. What would she even say? And then there was the way he looked—so different! She surveyed him with curiosity. He was slimmer, the angles of his face more pronounced. His dark hair had grown long, and his face was framed by a thick, heavy beard. He seemed older. Looked different. Little did she know the ways in which he had changed, not only in his looks but mostly inside. She soon would discover that Shemaiah was no more a man of this world. As they came closer and their eyes met, Dinah thanked God wholeheartedly for keeping Shemaiah alive. But he hadn't made a gesture of reaching to her, so she lowered her gaze to the floor, unable to stand the awkwardness of the moment. Then she muttered, "I will let Father know that you are back," and left hurriedly to get Ohad. Shemaiah would need to get Ohad's approval as head of the tribe to enter into town and into their house.

Ohad came rushing into the courtyard and, with much deference, embraced his son-in-law. Unaware of the uncomfortable emotions floating in the environment, he yelled vivaciously, "You have much to say, I can tell. Has no one offered you something to drink, some food to eat?" He was happy to see Shemaiah and relieved to know that he was alive. This was a fine day—a great day! Shemaiah was alive!

Ohad slung his arm around Shemaiah's shoulders and they headed toward his house. They walked up a long winding ramp that led to an enclosed space up on the roof, where they could talk privately. Ohad gathered all the best pillows and arranged them artfully against the wall. He gestured that Shemaiah should sit on a cushion in front of the pillows so he could lean back and be comfortably supported.

They wasted no time on small talk. Right away, Shemaiah spoke about the issues that pressed him. It would not be easy, but he hoped Ohad would understand. After all, he was a sensible man that cleaved to God.

"I know this will sound strange after being gone, alone for so long," he said, "but I must have a place of my own, a secluded place where I can sit in prayer and be with God." As he said that, Shemaiah's confidence broke, his voice faltered, and his body trembled. "I have returned to complete an assignment that supersedes every other task and responsibility. I have been instructed that I must write all that I was taught and everything that was revealed to me during my time away." As if he were waking up from a deep slumber, with his mind and emotions sunken in a strange torpor, he suddenly realized the enormous toll this would take on his family and on himself. "This has to be so, despite my love for you and for my family."

Ohad nodded thoughtfully. He knew his son-in-law well enough to understand that this must be an essential commission for Shemaiah to be taking it so seriously. Although he understood, something had been left hanging in the air. Ohad simply waited.

Finally, Shemaiah spoke up. "There is more." He looked up and met Ohad's gaze, then dropped his eyes and looked away. "During my journey, I was given a new name by which I must now be called. My new name is Shemaiahu."

And suddenly it came to Ohad. *So—this is what it is*, he thought. *This explains Shemaiah's distance. His detachment. He is in fact detaching himself from us. From his family. From the village. Maybe even from life.*

Ohad went out of his way to communicate respect as he posed the most obvious question. "But Shemaiahu," he said, careful to pronounce the new name with deference, "what about your wife and your children? And will you stay here with us? Here with our people? Will you teach us the things that you have learned?"

Ohad was a good and well-disposed man that had cared for their tribe with kindness and wisdom. Shemaiahu knew him to be a man who honored YHWH. He trusted that Ohad would understand enough with the briefest of explanations.

"At this time," he said, "there is much that I must process and work through. What I must do first is sit by myself and be with God. This is my only task right now."

Ohad did not raise an objection. He chose to be reconciled with Shem-aiahu's needs. He would allow his son-in-law to manage his homecoming as he desired. But his heart ached with disappointment.

One day, he told himself, *he will come to his senses. He just needs some time to recover.* The two men descended the ramp in silence, the silence between them more clamoring than the bells of a hundred ewes.

Shemaiahu's daughter Zehava and son Aviel had been waiting in a room on the first floor of Ohad's house to speak with their father. Their reunion was warm but also strained. Shemaiahu listened attentively as they described what was new in their lives. But he felt awkward. It was as if he had forgotten how to talk to them. The man who had been such an intuitive, natural father suddenly did not know how to relate to them. Granted, much had happened in the months he had been gone. Then again, he truly didn't know precisely what his path would entail, and so he didn't want to overburden his children unnecessarily with things that would only cause uncertainty and fear. Shemaiahu felt vaguely unsettled by the unsaid things.

As the evening fell, Dinah brought food to her father's house and they ate together as a family. Then the youngsters left to go to sleep in their own beds at home. At last, Dinah and Shemaiahu could face one another alone. Ohad had warned Dinah of some of the changes she could expect. He alerted her that her husband was a very different person, more so than she could ever imagine. Even so, she was not prepared for what Shemaiahu told her. From now on, he said, they would live in separate dwellings.

Later, Ohad observed that Shemaiahu had gone deeply into himself "to follow the call of God," he explained to Dinah. And Dinah, ever the perceptive wife, answered, "Shemaiahu was already gone. Since the time he built the sanctuary on the hill, he has been gone." And so it was that on the first night of his return to Kiryataim, Shemaiahu slept not in his own home with his wife and children but in the room on the rooftop of his father-in-law's house.

CHAPTER 40

Shemaiahu's Last Days—1384–1382 BC

THE NEXT MORNING, OHAD announced to the family that Shemaiahu would be able to make use of a small stone house that had been erected not far from the sanctuary. The roof of the house consisted of wooden beams covered with layers of branches smoothed down with clay. Shemaiahu was happy to accept the offer. He placed a screen in front of the door that, when lowered, served as a sign to all that he wished not to be disturbed. The house had a wooden door but no windows, so no one could peek inside. Each day, Zehava brought her father his food. Sometimes, when the sun shone brightly and the birds sang, Shemaiahu would invite her inside where his daughter was contented to remain near her father in companionable silence while he worked on his book.

Other than these special hours shared with Zehava, Shemaiahu avoided every possible distraction. In the house he had very little, in fact only what was essential to stay active and do his work. His most precious possessions were his blanket and staff. A small cushion made of calfskin served as a sitting stool and a wooden bench was his desk. His writing tools and a supply of parchment were the only other things he needed. All of this, given to him with Ohad's blessings.

Sometimes he left the house to take walks, avoiding small talk with well-meaning neighbors, but allowing himself the pleasure of speaking with his son Aviel, who sometimes brought the flock to graze in nearby pastures. Father and son would sit side by side and play their flutes.

Shemaiahu prayed concentratedly many times throughout the day. On Friday afternoons he would walk into the fields until he reached a little brook. Here, he would bathe in the waters and prepare for the Sabbath. But most days were spent in his little house, where he sat beneath a stream of sunlight that entered through a large hole he had punched open in the roof.

In this one-room abode, he worked diligently to write down what had transpired between Moses and himself. The words of Moses came back to him as if the Prophet dwelled inside of his mind, in a stream of thoughts and sounds that continued to flow until the book was finished. This was a book written by Shemaiahu the scribe as dictated to him by Moses, and it was destined to be circulated amongst all the people of the world.

A small white turtledove came to visit him every day. She fluttered into the room, coming through the roof with the first rays of the morning sun. She liked to perch on his right shoulder, where she twisted her head this way and that as she watched him at his work. Shemaiahu wasn't bothered in the least by her presence. Every day, he offered her crumbs of his daily bread. Every day, she declined. In this way she, like Zehava, gave him quiet companionship as he worked.

Spring was near; he could smell it in the air. The blossoms on the trees had started to appear in the land, and the cooing of doves filled the air. The time of singing had arrived.[1] "The turtledove is here to take you with her," a clear voice said from within himself, and Shemaiahu answered silently, "If only I had wings like a dove, I would fly away and be at rest."[2] But the time to go had not yet come, and so he continued his work.

One morning Zehava came to the house. She called out, "Father, it is I. I have brought your food. Will you eat?" But there was no answer. She repeated her greeting and her question, then bent her ear toward the cottage door. Hearing nothing, she sighed in disappointment, understanding that it was not a day when she would be invited in to sit beside him as he worked. She set down the bowl with bread, olives, a stew of grains, and a flask of goat milk next to the door. She would return at sundown to retrieve the empty bowl and would be relieved to find this evidence that her father had not forgotten to eat.

But that particular day was different. When in the evening Zehava came to the door, she found that the bowl was exactly as she had left it. She called out to her father but again there was no answer.

Never again would she hear her father's voice.

Shemaiahu had died when the last rays of light that signaled the beginning of the Sabbath faded. Those who found him said that he had prepared carefully for his death. He was dressed in a clean white robe to honor the Sabbath, and was lying on his blanket which was spread on the floor. His wooden staff was leaning against a wall in the corner of the room. His book, with each piece of parchment in its proper order, was by his side. He had

1. See Song of Songs 2:12.
2. See Psalm 55:6.

made all these preparations in anticipation of his departure, and when his time came, Shemaiahu simply left.

Ohad gave orders to prepare for the burial. Shemaiahu would be buried in the family's plot inside a cave on the hills outside of Kiryataim. He would be buried the next morning, after the end of the Sabbath, when the air was fresh.

Ohad, Aviel, and two other men carried the body from the cabin, with Dinah and Zehava walking behind them. The body was placed on one of the benches that lined the inner walls of the cave. Outside, a lamb was sacrificed in his name. There was no wailing or lamenting, as Ohad had admonished his family that Shemaiahu would not have approved.

Then they all went into the room where Shemaiahu had spent his last days. Aviel gathered the parchments. The handwriting was meticulous and graceful. It was clear that this work had been left behind so that many could read and appreciate it. He then lighted the ritual incense and made sure that the smoke reached every corner of the room, a practice that was followed to help the soul leave this world and move beyond to its new life.

Shemaiahu the scribe was dead—or so the people believed.

A sensible eye could see that he was perched at the top of the ceiling in the sanctuary he had built to honor YHWH. Shemaiahu himself watched as his body was carried ceremoniously to the cave. Throughout the ceremony he smiled and directed blessings and gratitude toward his loved ones. Forty years he lived amongst them, but then a transformation occurred that led him to emerge into a new state of being.

Shemaiahu looked up to the sky and saw that a portal had opened, as he knew would happen. Several beings stood in wait for him, so he rose, strolled toward them, and crossed through the open doors into the other side of the veil.

EPILOGUE

The Legacy

AVIEL WALKED INTO THE room to find his mother in deep concentration. He paused a moment to smile at the sight, then greeted her cheerfully. "May God give you peace, Mother."[1] Dinah glanced up. Seeing him, she smiled.

She had taken upon herself the task of sewing together, in their proper sequence, the many pieces of parchment on which Shemaiahu had written. When finished, Shemaiahu's work would unfurl in a continuous scroll. The parchments were long and the meticulous penmanship was presented in well-spaced columns the width of the palm of a hand. Dinah believed that her husband's manuscript would become a book that would be treasured by generations to come.

As Aviel stood at his mother's side, observing her hands as they danced the needle over the parchments, Zehava entered the room. She was holding a parchment in her hand. Aviel took in the sight of this parchment with one glance before exclaiming with excitement, "Peace be with you! I have been looking everywhere for this very parchment! I thought it was lost! Mother! Zehava!"—he called for their attention—"This is the parchment that my father had intended as his last offering. Zehava, tell me, where did you find it?"

Dinah, surprised by her son's outburst, stopped what she was doing. What was all of this commotion about? Zehava handed the parchment to her mother, who recognized in an instant the undulating characters that were so distinctively Shemaiahu's workmanship. But this parchment was different. All around the written letters were artful renditions of white doves, vines, buds, and flowers sketched in all the many manifestations of bloom. The ink drawings were colored with sensitivity in delicate pastel

---

1. See Numbers 6:26.

shades. These painted shapes were features that appeared on none of the other parchments.

Dinah looked at her daughter with a question in her eyes.

"I helped father with his paintings," Zehava hastened to explain. "We did this together."

Aviel took the parchment in his hands. His eyes devoured the words. Tears of pride and happiness sprang to his eyes. Then he explained what this parchment was all about.

"For our father," he said with a nod of appreciation, "the connection with the Almighty was indispensable. One day as we were pasturing, we sat together and played our flutes. He explained that music elevates one; it creates a special space for introspection." Aviel remained silent for some time, as if trying to understand all this even more. "Father was very aware of the subtle levels of existence. He encouraged me to always speak about them to others, so people would learn that the world is more than what we are able to see with our eyes. 'Teach them about the transcendent realm,' he said, 'the realm of the one substance, of the One God. Make sure that you speak clearly, stating your words in a way that even the simplest commoner will understand.'

"Father offered me his ideas about God. He said that the Almighty is the essence of all there is in this world. It is a force to reckon with—within and without—every day of our lives. He assured me that God bestows Himself in unexpected ways, but we must remain attentive or we may not recognize His influence in our lives. In fact, Father said that God cannot be compared to anything we understand. We lack understanding and we also lack the right words to speak of Him, unable to grasp His presence. Even so, he insisted, we should never stop trying to stay in connection with Him.

"And so this parchment, which is unique among all the others, is intended to be used as a book of nightly prayers that will help guide people in their personal interaction with God. Father wanted us to know that God is an incommensurable, impersonal Force who does not share our feelings, worries, or concerns. Because of this, we may, at times, feel forsaken. 'YHWH is not a man like us that we should invite to debate,'[2] he said. 'God is neither a father nor a friend. He is impersonal. He is detached in His limitlessness.'" Aviel look at them intently. "Believe me, Mother, Sister; I listened to him carefully. I held inside me many unanswered questions. 'But Father,' I said, 'I'm confused. Let me ask you a simple question: when we pray, is someone listening?'"

---

2. See Job 9:32.

Softly, Dinah put an arm around her daughter's shoulder as if seeking support. She had pondered some of these very same questions. She bowed her head and said, "Yes, my son, it is difficult to know to whom we are sending our pleas. But, tell me: did your father give you an answer?"

"Father wanted us—wanted all the people—to know that we can make a direct appeal to God without the need of animal offerings as sacrifices, and without the intercession of a priest. Father believed in the power of people speaking directly to God. He believed in the power of prayer. When we pray by addressing God directly, with our hearts and minds lined up, we rise above ourselves and are filled with an extraordinary power."

Dinah looked at the lovely illustrated parchment and started to read it out loud. From the first words it was clear that this was an appeal to God, an inspired compilation of timeless wisdom and ageless compassion.

> *"May the words of my mouth and the meditation of my heart be acceptable to you, Oh God.*[3]
> *Hear Israel, the Lord is our God, the Lord is One.*[4]
> *In you, Lord my God, I put my trust."*[5]
> *(Silently say the petition that is in your heart.)*
>
> > *I now forgive whoever has hurt me,*
> > *And whoever has done me any wrong;*
> > *Whether it was deliberately or by accident,*
> > *Whether it was done by word or by deed,*
> > *In this incarnation or in previous ones.*
> > *May no one be punished on my account.*
>
> *My God, the soul which You have placed within me is pure. You have created it; You have formed it; You have breathed it into me. You preserve it within me; You will take it from me, and restore it to me in the hereafter. So long as the soul is within me, I offer thanks before You, my God and God of my fathers, Master of all creatures, Lord of all souls. Blessed are You, God, who restores souls to the dead.*[6]
> *Hallelu-Yah!*

Shemaiahu may have left the world to join his ancestors but, even so, people always remembered and spoke of him warmly. He had been a sensitive, wise advisor who taught them ways to get closer to God. And so he is praised until this very day.

3. See Psalm 19:14.
4. See Deuteronomy 6:4.
5. See Psalm 25:1.
6. "Morning Blessing," in Scherman and Zlotowitz, *Complete ArtScroll Siddur*, 20.

THE END

Bibliography

Blumenfeld, Rabbi Mordechai. "Maimonides #7—Prophecy of Moses." Aish. https://www.aish.com/sp/ph/48925042.html.

Borowski, Oded. *Daily Life in Biblical Times*. Atlanta, GA: Society of Biblical Literature, 2003.

Chabad.org. "What Is Shechita"? https://www.chabad.org/library/article_cdo/aid/222240/jewish/What-Is-Shechita.htm.

Charles, R. H., trans. *The Book of Enoch, or 1 Enoch*. Oxford: Clarendon, 1912.

Chassinat, Émile. *Le Temple d'Edfou*. Le Caire: Institut Français d'Archéologie Orientale, 1928. http://www.sofiatopia.org/maat/peret_em_heru.htm.

Cruz-Uribe, Eugene. "A New Look at the Adoption Papyrus." *Journal of Egyptian Archaeology* 74 (1988) 220–23. https://doi.org/10.1177/030751338807400123.

Eyre, Christopher. "The Adoption Papyrus in Social Context." *Journal of Egyptian Archaeology* 78 (1992) 207–21.

Faulkner, Raymond O., trans. *The Ancient Egyptian Book of the Dead: The Book of Going Forth by Day*. San Francisco: Chronicle, 1994.

Gikatilla, Rabbi Joseph. *Gates of Light*. New York: HarperCollins, 1994.

Herzog, Chaim, and Mordechai Gichon. *Battles of the Bible*. New York: Fall River, 2006.

Josephus, Flavius. *Antiquities of the Jews*. Translated by William Whiston. Repr., Peabody, MA: Hendrickson, 1987.

Jung, Carl G. *Nietzsche's Zarathustra: Notes of the Seminar Given in 1934–1939* 1. Princeton, NJ: Princeton University Press, 1988.

———. *Psychological Types*. Vol. 6 of *Collected Works of C. G. Jung*. Translated by H. G. Baynes. Princeton, NJ: Princeton University Press, 1990.

Kanawati, Naguib, and Ali Hassan. *The Teti Cemetery at Saqqara, Volume 2: The Tomb of Ankhmahor*. Warminster: Australian Centre for Egyptology, 1997.

Kaplan, Aryeh. *Meditation and the Bible*. New York: Samuel Weiser, 1978.

Luban, Marianne. *The Exodus Chronicles*. Encino, CA: Pacific Moon, 2003.

Luzzatto, Moshe Ḥayim. *Derekh HaShem*. Translated by Aryeh Kaplan. Jerusalem: Feldheim, n.d.

Maimonides, Moses. *The Guide for the Perplexed*. Translated by Michael Friedländer. Mineola, NY: Dover, 2000.

Nachman. *Likutey Moharan*. Translated by Moshe Mykoff and Simcha Bergman. Notes by Chaim Kramer. Jerusalem: Breslov Research Institute, 1993–2004.

Papyrus Ashmolean Museum 1945.96. Ashmolean Museum, Oxford.

Pritchard, James B., ed. *Ancient Near Eastern Texts Relating to the Old Testament*. Princeton: Princeton University Press, 1950.

Purrington, Mr. "Carl Jung on the 'Subtle Body.'" Carl Jung Depth Psychology, August 8, 2020. https://carljungdepthpsychologysite.blog/2020/08/08/carl-jung-on-the-subtle-body/.

Scherman, Nosson, and Meir Zlotowitz, eds. *The Complete Artscroll Siddur: Weekday, Sabbath, Festival (Nusach Sefard)*. Brooklyn, NY: Mesorah, 2018.

Sefaria. "Midrash Tanchuma, Pekudei 3:4-7." https://www.sefaria.org/Midrash_Tanchuma%2C_Pekudei.3?lang=bi.

———. "Pirḳe Rabbi Eliezer 13." https://www.sefaria.org/Pirkei_DeRabbi_Eliezer.13?lang=bi.

Silberman, A. M., ed. *Chumash with Rashi's Commentary (Includes Bereishith, Shemoth, Vayikra, Bemidbar, and Devarim)*.Translated and annotated by Rabbi A. M. Silberman. 5 vols. Jerusalem: Feldheim, 1985.

Simpson, William Kelly, ed. *The Literature of Ancient Egypt*. New Haven, CT: Yale University Press, 1973.

Steinsaltz, Adin Even-Israel, trans. *The William Davidson Talmud: Babylonian Talmud with English Translation*. Digital ed. Jerusalem: Sefaria, 2017. https://www.sefaria.org/william-davidson-talmud.

Teresa, Mother. "In the Silence of the Heart God Speaks with You." Goodreads. https://www.goodreads.com/quotes/252954-in-the-silence-of-the-heart-god-speaks-with-you.

www.ingramcontent.com/pod-product-compliance
Lightning Source LLC
Chambersburg PA
CBHW071836020726

47502CB00004B/1390